W9-ABG-506

WITHDRAWN
NDSU

MRS. PALMER'S HONEY

NOVELS BY

FANNIE COOK

The Hill Grows Steeper
Boot-Heel Doctor
Mrs. Palmer's Honey

Mrs. Palmer's Honey

by Fannie Cook

DOUBLEDAY & COMPANY, INC.

Garden City, New York

1946

N. D. S. U. LIBRARY
FARGO, N. D.

PS
3505
O5483
M5

COPYRIGHT, 1946
BY FANNIE COOK
ALL RIGHTS RESERVED

PRINTED IN THE UNITED STATES
AT
THE COUNTRY LIFE PRESS, GARDEN CITY, N. Y.

To
ROBERT JEROME
and
HOWARD

76717

*This story and all its characters are fictional,
but the Ville exists, a real place
within a real city*

MRS. PALMER'S HONEY

PROLOGUE

THAT MORNING DAWN SMILED TIMIDLY ACROSS THE VAST gray fabric of roofs spread from the river to a distant crescent of hills. The river was the Mississippi, a mile wide and muddy. It held the city within a giant bend ribbed by bridges. Near the crook of the bend were skyscrapers, but mostly the city was an immense hive of home neighborhoods where two-storied school buildings seemed tall.

One of these neighborhoods was the Ville. It lay a little north of the exact center. Once it had been Elleardsville, a suburb, but the metropolis had grown around the region as a tree will in time encompass a foreign body, and now no one living there ever thought of it as anything but the Ville, part of the fabric, part of the city.

Few white people ever thought of it at all. Few knew it was there. Though several miles long and several wide, the Ville remained obscure and lived secretly. Streetcars and busses ran along its boundaries as if afraid or too incurious to enter.

Prospering white people lived miles west, where the fabric began to fray into large estates, small farms, emerald golf courses. Vaguely they believed St. Louis had but one colored district, the be-taverned crisscross of shabby streets near Union Station. Observing that region's slatternly ways, they would at times consider sending their dark-skinned cooks to a clinic for tests and treatment.

Prospering colored people lived in the Ville and let the people

1

from the pretty fringe of the fabric believe what they pleased. It was only among themselves that they called it the Ville, and only to one another that they spoke of its ways. To them the black folks near Union Station were "immigrants," newly come north from Mississippi or Louisiana. A few were Ville folks fallen from grace, but more were sharecroppers with the dust of cabin floors still beneath their toenails, dreams of northern freedom still in their eyes, snuff still in the mouths of the women as well as the men. Their ways slowed the climb for other Negroes. Because of that, the Ville bore them a grudge.

Houses in the Ville were low—cottages with slanted attics. Suburban trees were still to be seen, and suburban fences around the small front lawns. Here and there a door was painted a brilliant blue or a porch of happy yellow was trimmed in scarlet, but by and large the Ville lived sedately in imitation of the white folks' way of living.

Unlike a white folks' neighborhood, however, the Ville did not pivot around a central shopping district. Instead there was a campus worn bare by the great American game of baseball. Flanking the campus were handsome modern brick buildings which the Ville would have regarded with pride had it been able to take pride in a handsome insult.

The buildings were for black folks set aside to live separately. They housed a Negro high school, a Negro grade school, a school for doubly handicapped children—both Negro and blind or deaf or lame—a Negro teachers' college, a Negro city hospital. Indoors were jobs and learning and cures, fine gifts ungraciously given and ungraciously received.

At either end of the campus stood splendid structures erected by a brown woman grown fabulously rich from marketing a fluid which straightened Negroid hair. One was an orphanage; the other a hotel, primly run, a model of Christian respectability.

The Ville was a city within a city.

I

A VAGRANT RAY FROM THE TIMID DAWN TAPPED HONEY'S eyelids. Sleep became a tossing mist. At first she knew only that another day had come, then that the ache along her legs was from all that crazy dancing with Snake. Turning, her brown body relished the smoothness of the new sheets.

The first thing the Hoop girls had done with their defense-factory pay was to fill a chest of drawers with neat stacks of new sheets and pillowslips and towels. Honey had made pink ribbon tie-arounds for them like the Palmer tie-arounds while Eulatha, laughing, tore up the old linens. Eulatha liked to tear up.

Eulatha woke now with the suddenness of a pistol shot. An elbow caught Honey in the ribs. The telephone rang, and Eulatha was after it, a man hunt in her eyes.

"Better you forget that Jo-Jo," Honey mumbled.

Eulatha came back yawning.

" 'Mis Palmer for Honey,' " she mimicked, soprano. Then, in a surly contralto, she added, "Tell her you got you a job now—with holidays!"

"Hush your face!" Honey scolded.

At the telephone in the next room her voice was smooth and sweet.

Mrs. Palmer said she was in a terrible fix. Mr. Palmer was to be awarded the First Citizen's medal——

3

Honey said she felt right proud of that, all the Hoops had, as soon as they read it last night. It was in the Ville newspapers——

—and it was to be given to him, Mrs. Palmer continued, at a ceremony at the Auditorium late this afternoon. Mr. Palmer —"You know how he is, Honey!"—and Mrs. Palmer giggled in fond adoration of all Mr. Palmer's ways—had forgotten about ration points and Honey's not being there any more, not for months now; in short he had invited one after another for dinner just as he always had before the war. This time he had invited those who were going to sit on the platform with him at the services, men Mrs. Palmer didn't know, and their wives, whom she didn't know either. Fortunately the mayor hadn't accepted. Bruce was home on leave with a sweet soldier boy from Maine, and Dorothy Jane had invited one of her beaux and—in a whisper—there'd been no word from Junior in Africa for forty-eight days now, though Mr. Palmer had scarcely mentioned it, and of course, this being his big day, Mrs. Palmer wasn't saying a word, not a word!—and anyhow Mrs. Palmer was at her wit's end and would Honey save her life?

"What time must I save it? I reckon Mr. Junior ain't wrote no letter—like he done us that time at college."

"As fast as you can get out here, Honey. . . . I hope you're right!" There was a whistling sigh.

"I'll make tracks," Honey answered and went back to bed to warm her feet.

"You're a fool!" Eulatha observed. "You done cooked Palmer turkeys for twelve Thanksgivings. Now the war freed you and you're going back to cook more. What-for you earning eighteen hundred a year?"

"What-for Mrs. Palmer lend me money during the depression? What-for Mrs. Palmer help me to keep all you Hoops rolling?"

4

"Rolling downhill. . . . Ain't she took it off a dollar a week? Poof! Every penny of it!"

Honey studied the ceiling dreamily. "I ain't never minded much about any of the depression, onliest thing I hated so was going on the streetcar with all them runs down my stockings!"

Laughing, Eulatha imitated Honey's voice. " 'Someday when I gets me lots of cash money, I'm going to buy me two pairs of silk stockings every Saturday. Two pairs!' Now you got lots of cash money and the white folks' war fixed it so you can't buy no silk stockings a-tall!"

While Honey was putting on her clothes she paused occasionally to button or tie something for one of the little children who came because they found her hands gentler than Big Mama's. Some were her own brothers and sisters; others were the children of sisters who had married disastrously or not at all. Two called Eulatha Mama. All gave Big Mama their first obedience.

Idly Eulatha watched Honey and wondered what her sister thought about her own body. It was the color of bottled bourbon, lean like a young girl's, though Honey was past thirty. The breasts were firm and the waist small. The legs tapered smoothly.

It was a sleek body. Eulatha thought it wasted on Honey, who had sought so little pleasure from it. Last night was the first time in years Honey had danced, the only time she had ever really danced.

Carmen, in the far bed with two of the baby girls, stirred and stretched. Carmen had been created a schoolteacher out of Honey's dimes and dollars fetched from the Palmer kitchen. A Spanish course at the high school had changed her from Carrie to Carmen, a transformation Honey discovered on the night she attended a school play to inspect the costume which cost her a week's wages. She saw on the program it was worn by

5

Carmen Hoop. She saw too that Carrie had a preference for *dicktee* folks, so Honey came home and told Mama to let the kid go to teachers' college. Mama said it would break up the family, but Honey, who had mothered Carrie more than any of Mama's children except Lamb, answered that she'd break up Carrie if it did, break up her head with a chair.

Dressing, Honey became in rapid succession two people. First she was a pretty, demure, big-eyed woman in a maid's uniform. Then she slipped above the uniform a street dress so similar to her own bourbon tones that it seemed to return her to nudity. With quick movements she put on a pair of ivory earrings, a turban to match her dress, crowded her feet into high-heeled slippers, clutched a brown patent-leather purse beneath her elbow, tossed a plaid heather tweed coat over her arm, and in a swirl of graceful motion turned to leave the room, a modishly dressed brown girl, dashing but no longer demure.

Eulatha closed her eyes. Chuckling, she delivered a compliment and a taunt. "Some folks is maids and looks like teachers, and some folks is teachers and looks like maids."

The covers of Carmen's bed heaved. A hard voice answered, "Certainly—Honey is the Hoop beauty. No doubt about that. None whatever."

Briefly the thrust silenced Eulatha. Then she rose angrily on her elbow.

Honey interrupted their talk. "Eulatha, you keep your mouth shut! You got Jo-Jo, and someday Carmen'll get her a *dicktee* man. So hush your fighting. You're going to wake up Lamb. Lamb worked the night shift. He dead asleep down there."

Carmen spoke from the depths of her covers. "Lamb isn't the only one asleep in the basement. Snake is down there too."

Honey came back to the center of the room. "What's that evil doing in our basement again?"

Both beds were silent.

"He's your evil," Eulatha answered at last.

6

"Talk fast!" Honey commanded. "What's he doing in our basement?"

Eulatha yawned. "Mama, she done it. Told him he could come back."

"Snake?"

"Yes, Snake!"

Carmen sat up. "Ben Boston's worth forty Snakes. Why you don't marry Ben while you have the chance is more than I can understand."

Eulatha laughed. "Teachers, they can't understand lots. That's why-for they're teachers."

Honey wasn't listening to their talk. Thudding sounds came from the stairway. Big Mama was limping a step at a time down from her attic bedroom.

Midway, Big Mama stopped. She saw Honey dressed in her best, looking both pretty and ladylike, more than most white women could do.

"Is you going to church with Ben?"

"Mama, why-for you let Snake sleep with our Lamb?"

Mama resumed the downward thudding, her big knobby hand rubbing the rheumatism in her left thigh. "You ain't answered."

"I'm helping Mrs. Palmer with her Thanksgiving dinner."

When Honey earned extra, Mama got extra. "Honey, you my bestest child. Lawd Gawd, this misery at your poor old ma this morning!"

"Snake, he's evil, Mama. He ain't going to do Lamb no good."

"Snake, he ain't evil. He just down on white folks. Poor fellow, he needs a place to sleep."

"He's been sleeping. You let him go back yonder to sleep where-at he been sleeping ever since we run him out."

They moved into the kitchen. Mama's nightgown showed

7

from beneath a green calico dress. She was a big-boned woman, tall, lilac-black, and nearly toothless. Her crinkled lips had a trick of creasing into a swift and surly grin.

She lighted a fire under a pot and said to Honey, "Eat some grits."

"Mama, you got to answer me about Snake. He don't belong down there with Lamb."

"Snake, he's going to pay right good for that there bed."

"We Hoops got more money now then we ever had! We don't need Snake's money none."

Mama's lips folded upon each other. "That's right. Hoops got war money now. Ain't no sense sleeping crowded up no more. We going to move. Then Lamb, he'll have a room to himself, and Big Mama, she gets Snake's cash money just the same."

Honey saw that Mama was in one of her moods. "Where-to we going to move?"

The big hands fumbled in a pocket. They gave Honey a patch of torn newspaper, marked with a red checkmark from Carmen's pencil. It was an advertisement of a house "to rent for colored."

"You come home early, Honey. We'll look at it, just you and me. You're the onliest one I got to count on."

"Mama, this here ain't in the Ville. Mount Vernon Street's white!"

"It says 'for colored.' "

"It ought to say 'for trouble.' Mama, this ain't got no sense to it. Carmen, she's crazy!"

"What-for we Hoops got war money 'less'n we spend it! Tell me that!" Mama leaned her face toward Honey's angrily. "You come home early like I said."

"Mrs. Palmer's going to need me. Reckon I can't come home early." Honey shook her head. "This here's white, Mama. I know."

8

"Ain't going to be lily-white no more when the Hoops move in!" Mama, dishing out grits to the grandchildren and children crowding around her, rose to ecstasy. "The Hoops, they been down long enough. The Hoops going to roll to glory. That there house, it's got ten rooms!"

"The Hoops ain't got no call to go to moving out of the Ville. First you take in Snake, then you want more rooms. It don't make sense."

The little children were standing in a row eating from bowls Big Mama placed upon a long board supported at each end by a raw-wood horse. Her own cup of coffee stood untasted. Her grin came and went in sudden clicks. Her eyes were far back in her head like china-doll eyes come loose, about to fall inside.

"Honey sweet," she whimpered, "seems like I been crowded down all my life. They've been times when I never thought about it none, but I was feeling it just the same. Now come this here war. The Hoops got luck for once. Money, money, money, coming in fast. Defense jobs and Lamb not fitten for the Army. So now we on Easy Street. I want to see my children living good——"

"We living all right, Mama."

"You living all right, Honey, 'cause you don't want nothing. You got your pretty face and good clothes and a *dicktee* beau. Ben Boston, he's right nice. You got a chance at Snake too, I reckon, come you want to pleasure yourself with trouble. But Carmen, she ain't got no man. She needs a teacher man or a preacher man or the likes of that——"

"Carmen got to get her a man with her own flesh like everybody else do. Carmen will. Someday Carmen'll get her a good man."

"How she gonna get her a good man with her home overrun with Hoops like as if they was ants?" Mama asked, waving to the row of children.

"You don't see our neighbors carrying on the way the Hoops

9

do! Mostly the Ville's better'n we is. We ain't good enough for the Ville. We got to wait."

"Your papa, he can't stand this crowding up no more. Working like he do out at that there swell country club, he can't come home to this here dicebox and listen to the rattling. He don't hardly come home no more at all. Onliest time he come back is to fetch him clean clothes or the likes of that. He sleeping out there most the time." Big Mama's eyes were glazed with tears.

"Reckon I'll try to come home early, Mama."

"You got to come, Honey! Ain't no other one of my children I can count on."

"Take Carmen with you."

"Carmen ain't proud of her mama no more. 'Sides, Carmen ain't got none of the kind of sense a body can use."

Honey spoke slowly. "Ben, he likely will come around this morning, Mama. Tell him to fetch me at Mrs. Palmer's along about the middle of the afternoon. You be in the back seat, Mama."

Snake, lounging against a tree, saw as soon as the door opened that Honey-this-morning was not at all Honey-last-night. Same dress. Same hat. Same earrings. Same head held high. The walk still had panther in it, but the panther drowsed.

He remembered the first time he ever saw Honey. Under his breath he mumbled, "Hot stuff!" A fellow he didn't know laughed at him and said, "She's got a nickname. The men call her the Virgin of the Ville." Snake answered hopefully, "Because she's not?" The other said, "Because she is," and sauntered off, chuckling.

Snake fell in step with her now. "Your panther," he teased, "must have joined the Y.W.C.A."

Her proud head tilted higher. "Snake, I don't want you teaching Lamb no bad."

10

"Ain't Lamb slave, black, and twenty-one?"

"That's what I mean, Snake. That kind of talk——"

"Talk never hurt nobody."

"Ain't nothing but talk ever did hurt nobody. Bad talk. Then fighting begins."

He took her elbow. "You kind of a mother to Lamb, ain't you, sweet?"

"Lamb's a good boy. Honey's got a lot of faith rolled up in Lamb. You lay off of him!"

"What-for you think I hurt Lamb? Lamb and me are friends. Friends ever since last August. The day I begun to work on the line. The day I met the prettiest girl in the Ville."

"All I know is, Lamb, he's kind of young in the head and you old in the head. You got hate in your heart and Lamb got love. Mama ain't got no call to let you two go to sharing a bed."

"Last night you thought Snake good enough to dance with." He was leaning over, smiling into her eyes, teasing her. "To drink with too."

"I like you, Snake, but you ain't no good."

"Good! Good! Good! What is all this here good? How you know Honey's so damned good?"

"Honey's good," she said quietly.

"How you know?"

" 'Cause I don't wish nobody evil and I don't do no evil."

"You don't wish white folks evil?"

"No."

He laughed falsetto. "Me neither. Onliest thing I wish that there Hitler would come right on in this here town, ride right up Olive Street on a white horse and shout that this here war's over and the black man, he's the big winner!"

"This ain't no war between white folks and black folks——"

"That's all you know about it! This here war's to see if Snake Williams got him the right to join a white union. Not the

11

damned auxiliary union where he can't vote. Not the one that makes him work in a separate building because he's not good enough to use a white man's toilet."

"Hush your talk! That ain't this war, and you knows it!"

Again he laughed falsetto. He ran his hand up her arm. He chanted, "Dear little white man fixing for a fall."

"Snake, that's the kind of talk I don't want Lamb to hear none. You got to keep still with such talk." She shook her arm free of his hand.

Snake seized it again and squeezed. He whistled softly into her ear. Briefly his lips brushed the edge. He saw lightning race through Honey's body.

"Please, Snake," she said.

"O.K. I ain't going to teach Lamb nothing he don't already know. That boy black, but he ain't crazy. He sure sees what this war's for. This here's MY war. It's a war about me. Wherever I live. Africa. India. Deep South. It's a war to find out whether the ball and chain is going to come off my leg. Snake ain't one to stand by idle, taking no sides."

He whistled a soft dance tune between his teeth. He smiled at Honey. His smile was malefic.

Honey wanted to answer, but she didn't know the answer. There was always so much sense and so much crazy in what Snake said. Those eyes with their long lashes making haloes around them were the devil's eyes.

"You got you a union out at the plant," she said at last.

"Sure, we got us a union! White man's union. Union to keep us out of their toilets. Keep us from voting when anything real come up. One of these fool-yourself unions. I got me a button." He touched it.

He didn't return his hand to Honey's arm or look into her face again. His freckled tan cheeks sagged. His eyebrows scowled low over his eyes. As he walked, he held his elbows rigidly against his body, twisting like a dancer.

12

"Don't take on so, Snake. Ain't nothing you can do about it. You just make yourself sick."

"Ain't nothing nobody can do about it," he grumbled. His mood changed. He leaned over and looked into her eyes. "You is a good girl, Honey. You ain't got no hate in you. That's right for a woman. I reckon a woman, she ain't got the nature for hate. Only for love. . . . Go dancing tonight with Snake?"

"I got a date."

"I slice that black man's neck! You got a date with Snake. Snake's going to buy Honey an orchid and take her prancing mighty fine, prancing high!"

"I is got a date. Snake . . . I'll go dancing . . . come you promise to move out of our house."

They watched the earth-colored plant bus rock toward the corner. Lamb was across the street, ready to get in, waiting for Snake. He was black and thin of body, but chubby-faced. He looked like a good boy on his way to school.

The bus was filling rapidly. Snake gave Honey's arm a final fond, insinuating squeeze. "Got to hurry." For a moment he looked as he had last night, then as he turned to Honey in farewell, his face wore a scowl. "Could be some of them high-riding white men fixing for a fall!" In another instant he was loping toward the bus, a tall, lean, shambly body with big feet and big, dangling hands on swinging arms.

Honey's heart was pounding. Snake was the only man who had ever made her heart pound like that. If only he were all evil, she thought; but he's good too. He's like a kid who's been hurt and gets mad to keep from crying. Likely if somebody took him in her arms to cry it out, then maybe he'd be good.

Reckon Honey's arms might go to getting her into a heap of trouble.

Honey didn't look to see whether she knew any of the other women on their way to prepare Thanksgiving turkeys for white families. She scorned them for baldly displaying bundles of shoes or uniforms or folded, empty reticules in happy anticipation of gifts or even of gifts self-given. They were older women, the age of Big Mama, and as stiff of joint. They wore their work and their troubles showily, as badges to be seen. In their own homes they were Big Mamas, slapping and loving and ruling. At work they were yes-ma'am women. At church they were ladies and benefactresses. Between places they were strangers to themselves and to one another. Their daughters had become workers in defense plants and this morning were enjoying their holiday in bed, wearing gowns which matched their robes. Some had bed jackets of maribou.

Honey wondered whether all this new and easy money was good for the Ville. Its pulse had quickened. Its heart, like Mama's, throbbed for more. It had a little new furniture and some good clothes and hungered for things not to be bought while guns had to be made. Most important of all, the Ville had taken out its anger, looked at it carefully, and concluded that it was good.

Before the war the Ville's resentment had mated with laughter. Honey could remember parties Mama gave for the neighbors, cocoanut-cake parties where the talk would be of the ways of white folks and the laughter loud and scornful and sure. Most Ville parties had been like that. Someone would tell about going to a white folks' store to buy a dress and how a lady buttoned it up for her, but later when the brown woman wanted to buy a pair of gloves she wasn't allowed to try them on even by herself. Wha-wha-wha-wha-a-a-a-a-a! They would throw back their heads and laugh at the white folks. They would have a good time.

Now people were working too hard for parties. Talking on the busses and streetcars, in church and at the market, they no longer laughed. Boys carried knives. Girls carried sassy tongues and swift elbows.

14

Honey's heart kept hovering around Snake. Through all his evil, she could see a man she might have loved with her whole heart. He would have stood taller, looked straighter, laughed sweeter. He would not have been a man in love with Honey and with the devil too.

Don't you go to mothering Snake, she admonished herself. You done mothering enough with Mama's babies. Mothering ain't nothing only a sweet feeling made up mostly of hurt and fear and hope and the kind of love what is hurt and fear and hope. You got to learn to let it alone. It's sure your poison. When you pick you a man, Honey Hoop, you pick a man who's going to take care of you!

Then she saw Ben coming toward her and saw that he was such a man and that she didn't want him.

Ben Boston approached bowing and smiling. He was an undertaker and made good money. He was neatly dressed in a dark blue business suit, a brown overcoat, and brown hat set level on his brow. When he removed his hat to greet Honey, his eyeglasses twinkled as if amused by their repetition of the round of his head, of his cheeks, of his mouth, of his nostrils, of his ears.

The eyes back of the glasses were gentle. Ben's skin was black satin, smooth and gleaming.

In a way he loved Honey as unwillingly as she loved Snake, if what she felt was love. Ben Boston knew he ought to marry an educated girl, a girl who talked as up-to-date as Honey looked, a girl light enough to make the ticket seller at the white folks' theaters hesitate. Only such a wife could help him up the ladder his mother had held steady for his climbing all these years.

But his heart clung to Honey. It loved her beauty, her gentle voice, the modest way she was folding one gloved hand upon the other even now. He saw no panther in her walk, only a grace which made him think of nymphs in floating draperies, a biblical urn on the shoulder, flowers in the hair. He admired her chin held high, her head back-tilted and a trifle on the side. He waited for the arch smile which would lift one of those even, widely curving eyebrows in sweet and modest coquetry.

The wide space between Honey's eyes, her drowsy lids gave to the upper half of her face a look of deep serenity. The lower half was handsomely formed and spirited.

"How are you doing?" Ben asked in his good-morning voice.

"Nicely, thank you," Honey replied.

"Miss Carmen said over the phone I'd likely find you along about here. I planned to carry you to work in my car, but a tire wearied out on me just now. If I have your permission, I'll ride with you a ways on the streetcar."

"You're right welcome," Honey answered.

"Your mother told me about the house on Mount Vernon." Ben was tactful. Knowing the whites said "Mount Vernon Avenue" and the Ville "Mount Vernon Street," he said neither.

"I'm not for moving out of the Ville, Ben. Can't figure what's come over Mama. Too much money, I reckon. The Ville's the onliest place to live come you're colored and ain't in search of trouble."

"I've got a sister hasn't ever been out of the Ville," Ben said.

"You mean never?"

"Never. Loraine went clear through grade school, high school, and teachers' college. Finished Sunday school. Had appendicitis the week our hospital moved in."

"Ain't she never been downtown or to Union Station or to the movies or——"

"Only to this little old movie in the Ville."

"Why-for is that, Ben?"

"My mother's been against it. Loraine's her only girl. Seems like she must have had so much trouble bringing up us boys that she got to being afraid of bringing up a girl. Figured she'd be safer staying right in the Ville."

16

"Maybe she figured Loraine would be happier not going places she wasn't wanted."

Ben thought about this. "My mother isn't one to take much stock in happiness."

"Seems kind of funny teaching her to be smart in school and not letting her find out what she's going to be up against."

Ben laughed. "When Loraine was a little kid she used to hide when she saw the white man who delivered for the dairy. She figured he looked white because he was sick. She still stares too much."

Honey's mind was considering the value of happiness. "Bringing up our babies at home, I always figured, after teaching them to be good, the next thing a body should do was let them be happy. Their noise runs you nearly crazy that way, but always seemed to me that was right."

"You'd be a sweet mother, Honey. Any baby'd be lucky to find himself yours."

Honey laughed softly. "I ain't hankering for babies, Ben. Reckon I had enough with Mama's fifteen and all them others at the house. Reckon that ain't no way to talk except that it's the truth."

Ben was silent. . . . "I reckon you couldn't help loving a baby."

"I loved all Mama's once they was born, but I cried every time I knew another was coming."

"You cried? . . . What made you cry?"

"Mama, she got times when seems like she just gets fed up. Them's the times everything falls right smack in Honey's lap. Reckon I done washed more diapers than most girls ever seen in they whole lives. Washed diapers and babies and looked to Mama's temper besides. Not that Mama ain't good. She's mighty good. Reckon I loves my mama more'n anybody in the world except Lamb. But I loves her like as if she was my sister.

17

Mama was only fifteen when I come. We closer in years than I is to my baby sister."

Ben whistled. "Your mama looks old enough to be your grandmother."

"I ain't had no fifteen children. And I don't seem to be hankering for none, Ben."

To herself Honey commented that she had refused Ben right polite. Just to look at Ben a body could see he was fixing to be a papa in a nice house with a nice automobile and a nice wife, only I ain't going to be that wife. If I going to break down for any man, I going to want to.

She puzzled a little over how she had suddenly made her decision. It was a right funny time to make it just after her and Ben had the only real talk they ever spoke. Most of the time talking to Ben was like playing hopscotch back and forth over the same squares, what he thought about the weather, what his mother thought about it, how pretty Honey looked, how pretty his last funeral was, and how pretty the minister prayed. Honey never seemed to be able to make herself care about any of it.

At the intersection there were a dozen or more fat brown women waiting for the car. Their talk stopped as Honey and Ben approached. A great chocolate bonbon of a woman dried her eyes in deferential memory of other occasions when she had seen Ben Boston. Several greeted him.

One inquired about Honey's mother. She answered softly, "Nicely, thank you." Her manner was polite but cool.

After that everyone stood in silence looking for the streetcar or facing the great scarlet ball which was the sun dulled by the smoke of the city.

As they got into the car, the women held up their passes without glancing at the motorman. They seated themselves in little groups where they could find spaces. Honey and Ben stood. Snatches of the talk floated up to them.

18

The car was crossing Enright Avenue where the *dicktee* folks lived. Boastfulness came into the colored women's voices. The street was broad and heavily treed. There was little traffic, and the houses stood far back, as if withdrawing from the little there was. These were ample houses with generous porches and side yards of an age less crowded and less hurried.

Ben said, "See the third house, the one with the bay window? I got that house rented out. I bought it two years back. It's where I'm going to live someday. . . . I hope I am."

Honey's forehead pressed against the window. Chills ran in waves down her back as she saw Honey Hoop living in that house. She walked through the first floor, empty of sleeping beds, spread the china-closet shelves with gleaming white paper, edged them with fancy scallops just like Mrs. Palmer's. The doorbell rang. It was *dicktee* folk, friends of Ben's, light-skinned women in furs with rich, dark-skinned husbands. She could hear his mother, who didn't take much stock in happiness, hurrying down the steps. Honey knew she wouldn't like being mistress of that great house.

A second later Lamb-back-yonder-waiting-at-the-corner plunged a dagger through her heart. "Ben," she gasped, "why-for was Lamb waiting for the bus?" Her terrified fingers dug into Ben's arm. "He worked the night shift, Lamb did. Why-for——"

"Honey girl, what's come over you?" Ben whispered. "Maybe Lamb's shift was changed."

Honey breathed in deep, swift snatches. The tune Snake had whistled pounded against her throbbing ears. "White man fixing for a fall. . . ."

"I reckon I ought to see about Lamb. He been acting funny."

Ben laughed a round, carefree laugh. "How old's Lamb?" he teased. Then he whispered a thousand meanings, "Reckon some folks want babies more than they know they do."

19

She wasn't listening. She was trying to force her memory to toss up what had been said at home about Lamb's working hours.

Their car stood at the transfer point. Nearly everyone was getting off. Ben and Honey got off too. They crossed the street to wait for the car running toward the fine houses near the farm-land fringe. They were now in the white part of town.

Echoing Honey's change of mood, the women stood untalking as if preparing for entry into foreign territory where combat would be solitary. Some heads twisted obsequiously, some defiantly.

They were no longer neighbors to one another, yet Honey, aloof from them in the Ville, now felt herself a daughter of their family.

In the westbound car, sleek with shiny chromium rods to hold to, handsome with fine green plush seats, the sociability did not return. The car was nearly empty. The colored women sat singly, each next to a window.

Ben and Honey sat together. Back of them were a pair of shriveled, elderly women. They too carried folded reticules hopefully; they too were going out to cook turkeys not their own. They stared at the colored women.

One mumbled, "They always sit strung out."

"For meanness," the other answered.

"Yesterday I had to stand all the way out to my job."

"And the seats next to them empty, I bet."

"Ten empty seats, all next to niggers."

"They oughtn't be allowed to string out."

Ben sought his handkerchief and mopped his brow.

Honey spoke in low tones. "Reckon when you gets your tire fixed, Ben, you mightn't mind going around to my house and asking about Lamb. You could phone me. At Palmers'. I'd be mighty obliged."

Ben's black satin cheeks folded back. "You still worrying

about Lamb!" Then the folds became wrinkles. "It's the talk in this car that bothers me."

Honey's hand dropped to his forearm in comfort. She whispered in his ear.

"Hush your nonsense, listening to that, Ben Boston! These folks ain't nothing but what the Palmers call poor white trash." Ben was nice, right nice.

For a moment Ben's feelings snuggled within the comfort of that phrase. Then he shook his head. "It isn't friendly of them."

"Nobody ain't friendly, Ben, only your own. I don't take up none with the girls at the plant, and they is colored girls. I just do my work and speak a polite good evening and go back home."

The car was filling now with white people. Ben noticed that several whose eyes passed Honey by chance returned them to stare at her beauty.

She wasn't talking to Ben any more. He saw that she wasn't going to talk. She had her mind fixed on Lamb.

When Ben got up to leave she said, "It's right nice of you, Ben. I thanks you." Her smile was sweet.

"I'll call for you at Mrs. Palmer's," he answered, smiling back.

2

BEN WALKED BACK, THOUGH FOR HIM THERE WAS NO
pleasure in being outside the Ville. He walked so that he might
think.

He must win Honey soon or lose her forever to Snake.
Either would very likely rank only second to Lamb. Ben
thought he might get used to that, but a world without Honey
would be only time and more time, gray, silent years dragging
by painfully, without joy, without hope.

Honey hadn't said anything about Snake and the dancing,
but Ville gossip traveled fast, and Ben knew.

He walked gravely through the white men's streets, passing
white women who stared at him as if wondering what lush
secret within the body of a black man made their own men
so fearful. It was a tawdry neighborhood. Families in house-
keeping rooms. Curtains, but no iceboxes.

Ben felt the stares. When he passed white men, there were
none. They looked beyond him, certain that a black face would
not be that of an acquaintance requiring a bow. They were
poor men, and by their standards Ben was rich, a circumstance
they didn't surmise. He was just a coon, a darky, a smoke, a
black clown, a nigger—at best, a janitor to serve them.

That he was walking in a land where men were determined
to keep him a stranger was in the air just as winter was in
the air. A thousand signs, each invisible, the total clearly

22

visible. Once he stopped and studied the curbs and streets, the houses and the cottonwoods, the lampposts and the shabby lawns, the dirty papers whipped by the wind. A fact like that ought to show. He put out his hand. The air ought to feel different here.

He sighed. He had no complaints. He hadn't starved. He hadn't gone cold. Life had been pretty good to him. But he was lonely.

Forty times a day his mother said Honey wasn't the only girl in the world. No, she wasn't, he would answer, knowing she was.

Ben didn't look lonely. People were always at his heels, seeking help in their trouble, bringing him their money with a "God bless you, Brother Ben" on their wide, trembling lips. All day long he was surrounded. Yet he was lonely. A man in a crowded room, his own room, lonely.

His undertaking parlor was the most elegant in the Ville: Venetian blinds, deep carpets, a fine organ, stained-glass windows; outside, brass railings highly polished, a wide doorway, a yearly coat of paint.

He gave the prettiest funeral in town, and he didn't hurry folks in sorrow. If they wanted to wait a week, it was all right with him. All day and most of the night, every night and every day, the parlors were filled with people. Ville folks might get married anywhere and everywhere, but they were buried, most of them, from the Resurrection Room of the Boston Deceasement Home.

He couldn't be an unpleasant man, he argued to himself— furtively wondering how unpleasant he might seem to Honey— because one by one the mourners walking about the Deceasement Home would tiptoe up to him and whisper, "I knows you was gentle with Jim," or "All I hates so bad is that Lovie didn't see how pretty you laid her out. Maybe she didn't have much alive, but dead she got the best!"

23

It began because he pitied the lifeless bodies which had been forced to live out their lives, their only lives, as black folks, their skin the wrong color for dignity. So he tried to give it to them in death—dignity and beauty and love.

His mother, fearing he would make no money, told him all that was ridiculous and the white folks would laugh.

"The white folks won't come," he had answered. "Maybe it is ridiculous. Maybe life is ridiculous. Maybe what white folks do at funerals is ridiculous too."

He went on giving comfort to the living by ceremony for the dead. His funerals lasted four days. They began with the Sad Hour at 1 A.M. That was for the sobbing which must be done when death strikes at life; hurts less for being done with others. On the second day friends came, and flowers; the face of the dead was admired; shoulders were patted; Ben was everywhere telling them when to come for prayers, that night and the next noon and night, and the next. The Ville had to come after work or before. On the last day there were services at a church, and then the body came back to the Home for the Grand Review.

It was the Grand Review that showed Ben how to make money out of his pity. A school principal died, and Ben printed a black-edged program. OBSEQUIES, it read, FOR LAVERNE ROMEO WASHINGTON, A.B. The services which had already been held were listed in small print, but in larger letters, the order of the final program was announced, the choral songs to be sung, the solos, the prayers said and by whom, the Scriptures read, the name of the minister to speak the Obituary, the lesser minister who would give the Benediction, and the important man of God who would orate the Eulogy, the woman who would read out the telegrams, the one who would read out the letters, the one who would announce the flowers, lightly touching sprays and baskets as she spoke of the love for the deceased in the hearts of the senders.

24

In blackest ink stood the name of a man who would speak for the school, the one who would speak for the Board of Education, the deacon who would speak for the Baptist Church where Laverne Romeo Washington, A.B., began life, and the elder who would speak for the Episcopal Church which the school principal had accepted as a necessary concomitant of his success. Farther down were the names of the Pallbearers, the names of the Flower Bearers, the name of the man who would speak for the Alphas. The program was something to save. Ben divided around the grief and the honors as far as they would reach. After that every wife wanted him to do as much for her husband.

He made a little from the printing. He made a little from the cards of thanks. He made a little from the fees for the singers, from the candles burned for four days, a little from everything.

But it was from the procession that he got rich. At first he rented cabs for the mourners. He didn't like JOLLY JAUNT CABS written on the sides. So he bought his own cabs, one by one, black cabs with extra doors. At night when the cabs weren't needed for funerals, the plain black doors were lifted off, replaced by red doors with yellow letters reading BOSTON CABS. It took the Ville a long while to catch on, and in the end no one seemed to care. They liked Ben Boston. Liking and loving seemed to be different things.

Ben had long assumed that, to be loved, a person had to be good. He had always wanted to be good. He had tried. Really tried. Looking back, he couldn't see much to be ashamed of. But Snake Williams, whom he hadn't met, must be better than good. People said harsh things about him; yet Ben believed his goodness must be clear to Honey's eyes.

Or could it be something else? Surely good women the world over wanted good husbands. By white standards there

25

weren't many good husbands in the Ville, though in the Ville there was lots of love for husbands.

He was still turning it over when a Negro lieutenant got off the streetcar, briskly consulted a notebook, and came toward Ben.

"Can you direct me?" he asked. Then he read out the Hoop address.

"It's in the Ville," Ben answered, nodding in the general direction.

"The Ville? I'm a stranger here."

But he acted as much at home as Ben felt preparing a funeral.

"What's the name you want?" Ben asked, shrewdly.

The lieutenant looked at the notebook again.

"Williams."

"I'm walking that way."

Ben kept glancing at the man in olive drab as if the reasons for Snake's success with Honey might be on his visitor's body, a mark to be seen, a way of walking, a virtue which curved out the chest, or a grace which curved it in.

The stranger's eyes were here, there, everywhere, sizing up the Ville, looking back over his shoulder toward the white blocks farther west.

"Starts all of a sudden."

"The Ville ought to have gates," Ben answered. "It's got a fence—only it don't show."

"What are you doing to break it down?"

Ben wriggled his coat in place across his shoulders. "No reason to break it down. Not until our people are made welcome out there."

"Never will be welcome as long as there's segregation."

"Chicken and the egg."

"Living side by side, colored and white will learn to like each other. Can't get to know a neighbor you haven't got."

"We're pretty far south here," Ben replied. His tone sought to end the discussion. Why was it Negroes could talk of nothing else? Meet a man and he was talking about the same thing the last man talked about. Seems like we can't settle down to living, we're so full of the way we're treated.

The stranger—a tall, tan man with dark eyes and long black lashes, a lean, erect body, and a quick, jerky walk—went on asking questions.

"What's the N.A.A.C.P. done? What's the Urban League done? What's the March-on-Washington done?"

It was too fast for Ben. "Urban League does a whole lot teaching our people to keep their places nice. PICK UP, PAINT UP, FIX UP. They have a slogan about it."

"What's it doing about getting rid of segregation?"

"Complain about it a good deal. . . . I'm not sure anything can be done. Believe they did fix it so we could play golf in the big park and have picnics." Ben wanted to tell about the tall trees and fine lawns in the city's park, as nice as in the finest white cemeteries, but the stranger didn't seem the sort who would want to talk about trees and lawns. Clearing his throat, Ben added, "Like I said, to me it doesn't look friendly out yonder. I don't go where I'm not wanted."

They walked in silence for a while.

"Your occupation?"

"I'm an undertaker."

"Professional Negro. That's why the fence doesn't worry you."

"How's that?"

"You profit from segregation."

"I give a pretty funeral. They'd come to me no matter where they lived."

The stranger stood still, his heels together, his tall, flat body erect, a pasteboard soldier. He was a quick walker and a quick talker, but now he stood unmoving. Then his body

27

relented, his rumbling voice thickened as if he cared very much about the Ville he'd never seen before.

"Let's get this straight," he said, "because there are lots of Villes in the U.S.A. Thousands of professional Negroes. Segregation packs too many apples in the barrel. Rotten up against good. The rot's bound to spread. Let's not talk about your business. Let's talk about Negro teachers in a segregated school. Take away segregation and they go up against stiffer competition. Some of them couldn't make the grade." He paused. His attention strayed for a moment. They were near Honey's house now. He was looking at some automobiles parked across the street.

"Would you count that good or bad?" Ben asked.

"Good."

"I'd count it bad."

Perhaps all this had something to do with his marrying Honey —or maybe not getting the chance, since it had to do with the net entangling them.

The stranger said that the men who would lose their jobs didn't count, only the children counted, the ones who would have better teaching and grow up to be really good doctors and good lawyers and good teachers. "Stop feeding off our own ignorance," was the way he put it.

When Ben began to argue, the stranger shot back, "You're thinking of the individuals. I'm thinking of the masses."

Ben smiled a slow, gleaming smile. "I bury them one at a time, sir," he said.

The stranger laughed and patted Ben on the shoulder as if he hadn't found him unpleasant at all, as if he found him a man to like. Then Ben was saying things he hadn't expected to say.

"In the Ville the home's everything. That's what we hold to all the years we're coming up. In nearly every home around here,"—he waved toward the rows within sight—"in nearly every one it's the mother who's everything. Women stay. Men come and go. The mother brings up her babies, and when they begin to have babies and no home for them, she gets to be Big Mama. She's boss. Big Boss. Why? The times men can't get jobs she can always get a few days' washing or a job cooking. She's the earner. Some husbands can't take it. They wander away. 'Desert their families,' the white folks say. It's just that they crawl away in shame. . . ." He thought he saw Lamb in one of the cars.

The stranger asked, "Then what? So this is a matriarchy. O.K. A matriarchy imbedded within a patriarchy. What are you driving at?"

"It's jobs that keep a man's head high. Only good job a Ville man can get is a separate job. Lawyer for Negroes. Doctor for Negroes. Teacher for Negroes. Social worker for Negroes——"

"When they get it, what do they do with it?" The stranger didn't want an answer. "Where do they live? Around here?"

Proudly Ben began to tell about Enright Avenue.

The stranger twisted it. "They put on airs. Swell clothes and big automobiles and fancy weddings. They ape the white folks and look down on their own."

"They give every Negro something Negro to believe in. To aim for."

The stranger thought this over. "That counts," he yielded at last. "Even if they have them hoping the wrong things. The men of the matriarchy and the women too must learn new ambitions. . . . I've got a brother around here I'm looking for."

Ben held him. "Why would a man have to look up his brother's name?"

"Know my brother?"

"No."

"He uses different names," the other said and frowned. As

29

if all that was less important than what they'd been talking about, he put his hand on Ben's shoulder and looked steadily into his eyes. Ben had the strange feeling that the lieutenant liked him better than he liked his own brother.

"There's a big river of life in this country. Negroes can't go on swimming in a little creek of their own. That way they'll never reach the sea."

"The river doesn't want us——"

"Right now the river's in two parts. One's flowing toward democracy. The other away from it."

"The second's about the only one I've ever seen."

"It's showy. Cascades and waterfalls and such. The other's better for traffic. Boats and barges. It's a stream widening out. We've got to make it engulf the other."

"Seems to me it's up to the white man."

"Is. It's his problem. Mostly they know it. Some in their heads. Some in their hearts. They don't like knowing it. But it's our problem too. Where we've got the chance to widen the river . . ."

Ben was suffering. The stranger had destroyed his pride in the house on Enright Avenue. And cast aspersions on the best folks of the Ville. "Lots of teachers and doctors still live around here. Across over there's a teacher; never made as much as a principal, but he's proud to say he's brought up five children, every one college educated, and all the years he's never let go of his subscription to the *Atlantic Monthly*."

"Um-mm."

"Lots of Ville folks get ahead and stay right here. They've got nice manners. Dress their children clean and pretty. Do without to educate them all the way through college." He was pleading for the lieutenant's approval.

"What do they do with their spare cash?"

"Give it to this organization or that——"

"To get the Negro ahead——"

30

"Somebody's got to look to us!"

"Right. But it's not enough. Creek stuff."

"The river——"

The lieutenant poked a long forefinger against Ben's chest. "As goes labor, so goes democracy."

"They keep us out of their unions!"

"I'm not claiming Negroes haven't a tough problem. I'm not claiming we can have it easy and win too. But without democracy, we'll be done for. Done in and done for."

They stood looking at each other, silent, thinking.

The tan face lighted up. The lieutenant saw someone he knew. He rushed forward to meet a white man rushing forward too. They shook hands and slapped each other's shoulders and talked like friends who had once seen each other every day. The lieutenant said he was here between trains. The white man—a chunky fellow with a huge wart on a huge nose—held out his brief case and said he was still at it, here from New York for three days straightening out some organizational problems.

Then he turned and introduced Lamb, calling him "Mr. Hoop." He called the stranger "Lieutenant Marshal." Not Lieutenant Williams. Lieutenant Marshal. Ben's bewilderment became an ache. They had come out of one of those parked cars. Other men were coming out. Bending their bodies and straightening up, white men and colored from the same car. He turned on his heel and walked away. Lamb's face had a glory smile on it. Honey could be told that he wasn't in any trouble. Trouble? What was trouble? Sometimes trouble and getting ahead looked like twins.

He heard the lieutenant calling good-by. Ben waved without looking back. Honey mustn't marry a man who used several names! All that about the big river and the creek doubtless had something to it. He slowed, thinking. Beyond the fence, the man's the earner. In the Ville, the woman. Only in that way

31

was Enright Avenue not in the creek. But that way he was ready to live out there. There wouldn't be any days out washing for Honey. No husband deserting.

He quickened his steps. He'd phone her about Lamb. And when he saw her, he'd tell about Snake Williams's names. She had the right to know. Likely there was a grand reason. The river or something. No one could meet the lieutenant, so sure of himself, so sweet around the eyes, so firm around the lips, so kind in that rumbling voice, without believing he came from a good family, and his brother——

Despair hollowed out Ben's heart with the jagged knife of self-doubt. Fear poured acid on the raw flesh. Honey! He was tired now, very tired.

The front room in Honey's home was a widened hallway used as a parlor by day, a bedroom by night. The beds folded. One stood in the corner. The other was a couch to sit on. Both wore pink cretonne. Except for the beds, the room was furnished with repaired and mended cast-offs from the Palmer home, a splotchy green rug, a wobbly wicker bench with cushions, some dining-room chairs. Defense money had added a blue lounge chair with wide soft arms.

Snake sat in that one, stretched out, his head nearly level with his feet. He looked across the room at his brother, the lieutenant, with hatred. Emery Marshal, bringing in chairs, acted as if he lived here. Snake's eyes narrowed with rage.

That was the way it had always been. Snake got hold of something of his own and it turned out to be Emery's. It began the day his father horsewhipped him. It was his own fight with his own father—Emery had a different father—a fight begun the week their mother died. Snake's father was a northern Negro come South. The South frightened him. Each year it became harder to go out among white men. It was easier to stay at home and drink, helping his wife wash for the towns-folk.

After their mother died, Snake's father said the boys would have to stop school and go to work in the sawmill earning liquor for their dad. It was Snake who sassed him; Snake who dug his toes in the dirt and wouldn't be dragged to the mill; Snake whose flesh was raw for days. But it was Emery who walked out and got himself a better home. Walked forty miles to Uncle Blake's, and got himself a good home and a six-months school instead of the two-months-winter-two-months-summer one Snake had fought for. After that Emery turned up now and again to "look after" Snake. Whee-ee-ee! Look after him! That was funny. Every time he came he took away the spoils Snake had been fighting for. After Uncle Blake died, Aunt Blake kept Emery, scrubbed him up every day fit for Sunday school. When Emery came to visit, Snake would spit on his fine clothes. Nothing anyone did against Emery ever seemed to count much. Emery cared only about Emery's opinion of Emery. He was only pleasing himself, he said, coming to see about Snake in the home he'd run off from. Once he'd taken Snake back with him, but Aunt Blake, before the month of trial was over, said Snake had to leave. After that there was sharecropping for Snake and high school for Emery, crap games and the numbers racket and jail for Snake and college for Emery.

This today was the meanest of all!

For months Snake had been talking under his breath to the men at the plant, jeering at them for not being fit for white folks' toilets, for thinking they had a union when they couldn't vote for wage and hour demands, the only demands that counted. He'd told Lamb when it was time to call them to a meeting and where it should be held—not near the plant grounds at all.

Lamb was chosen president. Being president turned a happy

boy into an angry orator. While Snake was dancing with Honey, Lamb went around to union halls and meetings. He came back set on the CIO. His anger subsided; his oratory flamed.

Not caring what letters they'd use to strike with, Snake let it ride. Then this morning the big shots from the union turned up. From Chicago, they said, but the fat guy had known Emery in New York. All but one knew Emery somehow, and that one said he'd heard of him and acted as if Emery were a god to pray to. They wanted his advice, they said. They called him Emery and he called them Bill and Guy and Pete, and the one he didn't know, Putney. Not Mr. Putney. Putney.

Earlier, talking to Snake and Lamb, the big shots acted as if they were teaching somebody dumb his ABC's. Talking to Emery it was all half sentences understood and answered and Emery doing the explaining. It was a damned funny business, that great college man Emery barging in on Snake's fun!

"Turns out after all these years," Snake said across the room, "me and you are sniffing round the same bitch."

The white men turned on him for that. Union wasn't a bitch.

"I done made it. I ought to know."

They told him, all talking at once, that he'd done a great thing for the wrong reason. The future of democracy was safe only if labor led the way. Everything good for labor was good for the Negro. Progress had to be marched shoulder to shoulder, white man, colored man. Division meant scabbing, and scabbing meant failure. That's what the union must do— keep peace between black and white.

Snake snickered at their nonsense. "Union's to make trouble between white and black. That's what it's for!"

Snake left the room to fetch his whisky bottle.

When he came back their eyes looked at him differently. They were talking about the war and democracy and how you had to fight for democracy even before you had it because that was your only chance of getting it. Fascism hates labor unions worse than it hates Negroes. Or Jews. It uses minority hate because it wants to kill the unions. Let fascism win anywhere in the world, and all mankind everywhere will lose.

"Fascism would be hell for everybody, but the hottest flames would burn the Negro. He's got to see that! Got to understand it!" It was Emery talking to Lamb.

The white man with the wart said, "Hell of a lot easier to make the Negro understand it if some of those southern congressmen would shut their traps."

"Won't help until the South gets a new heart."

"And that won't happen until the southern cracker learns something."

The talk was of the world and its welfare. Emery stopped them. "That's our job, isn't it, gentlemen? Let's have a look at those papers."

Then they settled down to work, except Snake, who slid even farther into the big chair, farther beneath the drink haze in his head, muttering "*Our* job! Whee-ee-ee! *Our* job!"

Even Lamb forgot about him.

3

AFTER BEN GOT OFF THE CAR, HONEY ENJOYED HER RIDE IN A different way. During the twelve years she had worked for the Palmers, this route had grooved itself deeper and deeper into her memory. Places to remember. Nothing to feel. Seeing Delmar Avenue again was like going to a moving-picture show. It did its stuff and you didn't have to do anything but watch. What it was meant something, but not to you. White folks' apartments, white folks' hospitals, white folks' home for the aged, white folks' pharmacies, white folks' tearooms, white folks' stores.

Makes it nice for me, she thought. Gets me away from all them rolling Hoops. Reckon for me it's like it was for the Palmers when they went to China that time. Mr. Palmer, he come home looking ten years' younger. Said he hadn't felt responsible for what went wrong.

Honey wondered how Mr. Palmer was getting along during this war. His money seemed to buy him nothing but worry about everybody else's troubles. Nice of him, right nice of him, but that way of living had no sense to it. A man that nice had to be looked to. Mrs. Palmer had tried and Honey had tried. But Honey knew the only person who could ever look after a body was the body himself. Maybe Mr. Palmer had learned something from this war. She thought of him sometimes when she saw newspaper pictures of a soldier making himself a foxhole. Time for Mr. Palmer to be making himself one. A man ought to be able to be as smart as a fox. Leastways a white man ought.

The wheels of the car hummed lightly. Once the hum swelled as it merged with a hum from the sky. Honey could see the plane, a gray line against a pale mist. It was one thing to put on slacks in the morning and shape a tiny piece of metal to go into a plane. It was something else to sit back and think about the whole plane. This way the nonsense of it showed. Going around up there was unnatural, and that was all there was to it, but it wasn't Honey's worry.

It was that way thinking about the Hoop family whole, not thinking about each one and his own particular troubles. Easier to think about the family and easier to watch the plane fly. Violently she put from her her concern about Lamb. That kind of feeling belonged to the Ville. She was away now. She might as well enjoy her trip to China.

At the end of the line she was the first out. Hurrying along the curving sidewalks was like walking through the park: big trees, space, and shrubs. The maples edging the street were bare, but the oaks back in the yards were bronzed and huge and handsome. The faces of the houses frowned as proudly as ever. Within doors pride was said to have changed into hurry and work and willingness to work. The country was at war, and the rich wanted to prove they thought themselves no better than the poor, as ready to die and to work.

Honey stooped to pick up the morning paper from the Palmer driveway. This was like coming home to a place where you knew everybody and where everything was and could speak up some, but where you worried and wept with only that part of yourself which liked to worry and weep. The tears made you feel better. In the Ville tears came from your guts and left you with a headache.

At the back door Honey tapped on the glass and heard

quick heels. Mrs. Palmer looked affectionately at Honey's costume, her smile, her dreamy eyes. Then she sighed and pointed to a turkey just unwrapped.

Honey pulled back the paper. "How many that got to feed?"

"Twelve, I think."

"It looks more like a mosquito every minute."

"Um-m-m-m."

"It *is* a mosquito. For twelve it is."

Mrs. Palmer sighed again. "I don't seem to know how to manage. I can't think what I ought to do." She drew her corduroy housecoat more snugly around her. It was green and matched the green of the kitchen. Mrs. Palmer always looked too small for her own house.

Honey moved toward the basement door. "I'll try to figure out something while I take my things off. Ain't that Mr. Junior wrote nothing for how long you say?"

"Forty-eight days. Nearly seven weeks. We ought to have heard."

"That Mr. Junior having too much fun with the girls like always. It was that way the other time."

"He flies one of the combat planes, Honey. . . . Don't you see the pictures in the paper?"

" 'Pears to me you better be putting your hair up come everybody going to be staring at you and Mr. Palmer all day long."

Mrs. Palmer's hand touched at her hair. "I know it looks terrible."

"How's Miss Dorothy Jane and her young man?"

"It's someone else——"

"After all them chocolate pies I made for Mr. Jim!"

Mrs. Palmer peered cautiously at the doors. She whispered, "It's an art-school student this time. A 4-F, Honey, from head to toe if you ask me. Mr. Jim went into the Air Corps when Junior did, and all of a sudden Jim got married, and Dorothy

Jane's had one beau after another ever since. Not one of them had any sense."

"Shame on that Mr. Jim. . . . This turkey, he sure a mosquito. . . . Mrs. Palmer, it don't seem fair, the way this here war done bore down on you. Taking both boys and upsetting Miss Dorothy Jane like that. And you having this big house to look to all by yourself. Don't seem right. Anyhow appears wrong about Mr. Junior. When I think how we used to look after him so careful-like and now he up in them clouds where all them guns——"

"How about your brother?" Mrs. Palmer asked and made herself smile.

"Lamb? He were called but he weren't wanted. It's his lungs. Lamb, he earning right fine. All but Carmen is in defense."

"Carmen's the teacher?"

Honey nodded. "Right odd, appears to me, the way this here war, it done bore down on the Palmers and poured gold on the Hoops."

They frowned into each other's eyes. Mrs. Palmer spoke first. She had been a pretty woman, but now only her deep eyes and neat mouth were pretty; her skin was colorless and her light hair dulled with gray. Once in a while a laugh would dissolve her frown, and then for a moment she would be pretty again. "The thing about this war is that it makes me feel so— so helpless, Honey; as if the whole thing's my responsibility and yet I can't do a thing about anything, not even help my children to be a little safe. . . ." Her lips trembled. Aimlessly her cupped hands pressed at her hair.

"That's like the depression treated us Hoops. Ain't no use worrying, Mrs. Palmer. It passes and we still going along. Everything always do pass, come a body can hold out with his waiting."

"Of course I wouldn't want my boys out of the Army. I

39

want them to be doing their share. I sometimes think I worry more about Dorothy Jane. Miss Dorothy Jane," she corrected herself. Having Honey back seemed like a return to the years of Dorothy Jane's little-girlhood. "I'm worried about Miss Dorothy Jane. I wish you'd kind of try to find out . . . what she's thinking. . . ."

"Likely she's thinking how she can get even with Mr. Jim. I never would have believed it none of Mr. Jim. Seemed so nice. This here turkey it *is* a mosquito. . . . You better be turning up your hair."

Honey went down into the basement. When she returned she was a maid in a white uniform.

Back in the kitchen Honey found a khaki-clad soldier with an apple in one hand, a thick sandwich in the other, chewing and leaning over a spread sheet of funnies.

"Lawd Gawd, Mr. Bruce!"

"Corporal Bruce, Honey!"

"Ain't you no colonel yet? I done told everybody you a colonel."

"In disguise, Honey, in disguise. What's the low-down on chow?"

"That's it. That mosquito to feed the lot of you."

"Quit your kidding!"

"Ain't even ready for the oven. Mr. Bruce, be a nice boy and open that bird for Honey. Open it up while I get at these dishes. Appears like your mama ain't washed a dish since I left."

Bruce chewed. "Don't know how to clean a turkey."

"Just cut off the head and open the stomick. I'll do the cleaning. I hates so bad to do that first part. Always seems kind of like a killing. Ain't that what you learning to do?"

"Me?"

"You a soldier, ain't you?"

40

"Honey, get this right. I'm a mail carrier. I'm a typist. I'm a bedmaker. I'm a potato peeler. I'm a fall guy. I'm an errand boy. I'm a——"

"Bruce-y, what's this about Junior? You think likely anything could have happened to Juney?"

"Mother said anything?"

"Her heart's kind of gnawing."

"Probably some damned-fool sergeant got the gripes. Held on to his mail."

"I reckon you making that up."

"There's no way in the world to tell! Junior'll be all right. He always did know how to get out of a tight place."

"Sure did, Mr. Junior. He the onliest one of the Palmers ever had that kind of sense in him."

"Junior's all right."

"You stay kind of close to your mama today——"

The telephone rang, and Bruce left to answer it. When he came back Honey had the turkey's head off. Her lips were pushed against each other, her nostrils rigid, her brows drawn down.

Bruce frowned. "I ought to do that for you."

"Get out of here, come you want to like that there sandwich——"

"Honest, Honey, I don't know how to open a turkey. I'd make a worse face than you're making."

"Fine no-'count soldier you are!"

"Honey, I'm a man of mercy—a litter bearer."

"What's going to be on them litters?"

"That's for Hitler to decide."

"He done made up his mind, Hitler has. Reckon that where he ahead of most white folks. They ain't right sure."

"We're sure. We——"

"You going to take that sandwich out yonder or you going to stay and not like it?"

Bruce hesitated. "I ought to do that for you."

"Palmers all time ought to do this and ought to do that! Mr. Bruce, honest, I never can figure out why Palmers don't just see how lucky they is and not go to bothering their heads about what they don't have to."

She twitched at the blade with her thumb. Then she brought the knife down firmly. Her teeth were together, her lips drawn back like Big Mama's. Disgust tightened the cords of her neck.

"This bird goes in soon or he ain't going to be no nourishment for nobody. Not today, he ain't. You want to help, you go out yonder and tell all them Palmers Honey got to know fast how many is going to be eating off this here mosquito."

After Bruce was out the door, Honey mumbled, "Reckon that fixes it up with all his ought-to's. Mr. Bruce, he too much like his papa."

Honey had the turkey stuffed by the time Bruce returned.

"Me and Corporal Evans of Maine and Mother and Father and Dorothy Jane and—pfui-i-i-i-i!—her Al and four of Father's friends and four he hardly knows——"

"Mr. Bruce, I ain't joking."

"I'm not either. That's the chow list. Honest."

Honey picked up the newspaper bundle of entrails and went outside to the garbage can. When she came back she washed her hands. And washed them again.

"Always seems like to me after that there job I ain't never going to have clean hands again. I sure hates to knife a bird."

"Will it be enough?"

"I reckon I got to talk to your papa. Where-at is he?"

"In the sunroom. Dad's writing out his speech."

"I got to see him anyways."

In deference to appearing before Mr. Palmer, Honey pulled aside her kitchen apron and tucked it under her left elbow.

42

She thought Mr. Palmer looked old and more in need of a foxhole than ever, but when he arose to shake hands with her she saw that he was happy.

"Nicely, thank you," Honey answered. "We Hoops is right proud. Our paper, it carried a long piece and your picture on the front page. . . . Mr. Palmer, about the company for dinner—I can get the table set and the vegetables ready from cans and my biscuits made and all that, but I hates so bad to say it, but that there turkey Mrs. Palmer bought, not expecting no company, it ain't going to do for all them people you done asked."

Mr. Palmer, seated again back of his desk, puffed for a moment, and then, holding the cigar in his loosely folded hands, let the smoke brush past his cheeks. He sat in the haze as if it were incense and he an oriental god, aware of the impartial approach and retreat of the centuries, unaware of shortages in his own kitchen.

"The restaurants have no reservations left," he said calmly. "I phoned last night. Stretch it a little, Honey, stretch it."

"You ain't asked the kind of company you can give no stretched bird to. I been thinking, Mr. Palmer, we could have cocktails here and I could make up the turkey into them little biscuit pies you eat in your fingers. I done found some olives in the icebox. I could fix a right nice cocktail party. Afterwards, maybe you could go to the country club for your real dinner——"

"The club's had its reservations filled since last Saturday."

Honey's eyes were rolling.

"Excuse me kindly," she said. She carried the phone on its long cord down the basement steps and closed the door as she always did when it was for her.

At first Papa spoke just the same words Mr. Palmer had: "Everything taken since last Saturday."

Honey answered, "Papa, this here table for fourteen for

43

the Palmers, they got to have it. I'm out there now, and we ain't got only a turkey size of a mosquito———"

He said it couldn't be done.

"Papa, sweet, listen to Honey. I worried about Lamb. That no-'count evil Snake, he going to lure Lamb to trouble. I want to get back yonder and tend to Lamb. See?"

"It's going to mean disappointing folks already got their reservations."

"You know how Mama is. She ain't going to look to him———"

"What time, Honey?"

"About one-thirty before I can get them out there. Papa, see that it's nice!"

4

FOUR MEN, SHORTLY TO BE ANDREW PALMER'S DINNER GUESTS, sat in Sterling DuPree's study. The yielding leather armchairs comforted their bodies; nothing comforted their minds.

Sam Smith, the florid-faced, short-armed, potbellied one, had come up from Texas ten years ago following an ugly quarrel. He brought with him an important industry and continued making hearty profits limited now by government regulations. This, or perhaps his native temperament, kept him chronically angry.

Furiously he smashed both fists upon the arms of his chair and shouted, "Palmer's got to be told!"

Sterling DuPree recrossed his legs. Gus Schneider relighted his pipe. Tom Rusk tore a paper to bits.

"We arranged this Auditorium meeting, didn't we?" Smith shouted. "We got the right to run it!"

Sterling DuPree, in his desk chair, swung around to face Smith. DuPree was a handsome, elderly man, a successful trial lawyer. The elegance of his ways reflected the elegance of this palatial house in which he had lived since birth.

"Let's hear from the gentlemen who called upon Andrew." DuPree looked above his spectacles at Tom Rusk and Gus Schneider.

Tom saw that this was tough for DuPree because DuPree preferred Palmer the man to Smith the man. They all did. But this wasn't a tea party.

Gus Schneider continued his habitual silence.

Tom spoke slowly. "Gus and I got in to see Andrew at four yesterday afternoon just after he got back to town. He's tickled with all this, of course; showed us his office library on Negro problems; talked a lot. He was mighty pleasant, only we couldn't make him catch the idea."

"Why the hell didn't you come out with it?" Smith demanded.

Tom frowned and ran his hand over his bushy pompadour. "Smith, this isn't a seller's market. Andrew got the award from the committee very likely for doing a lot of things we guys tried to keep him from doing. This business of crusading for the Negro wasn't our dish. Remember that!"

Mr. DuPree twirled his pencil. "Fact is, we edged in on this thing after the award was announced. We got the committee to agree to a public meeting in celebration of the award. We couldn't let our Negro citizenry get any erroneous ideas."

Smith pounded his fists. "Niggers got to realize there's a war on and this isn't the time to try to get white men's jobs!"

The DuPree pencil made a quick stop. "Fact is, industry needs some colored men——"

"What we need, we'll take," Smith snapped. "And we won't have the niggers telling us what we need! All this talk about rights makes me sick. They got no legal right! They got too much lip. First they had porter jobs at our plant. Then we opened a separate building for them. White foremen. Now they want upgrading. Palmer's got to make them pipe down!" Mr. Smith's anger coughed his face purple.

On Mr. DuPree's long forefinger the yellow pencil with its heavy eraser at last found the precise point of balance. Sterling DuPree sighed. Smith was always forgetting the President's order about jobs for Negroes. He fixed his glasses more firmly on his nose. "Sam," he said, "that executive order should never have been issued. But it *was* issued. We've got it to contend with. I've gone into this thing dozens of times with clients. Only way out is to have the Negroes give it up of their own accord. Convince them this is a bad time for change. It *is* a bad time for change. Riots and all that. Let them show the good sense not to go forcing their way into industry now." Above his glasses his eyes searched for the effect of his words.

Tom Rusk smiled. "It certainly won't do to let Palmer get the idea he's free to say what he pleases."

Sam Smith shouted, "The niggers got to stay out of the picture!"

Gus Schneider's silence spread across the room.

Smith continued, "If they want to stay out of trouble."

Mr. DuPree frowned. "I'm the last one to advocate marring the beauty of a dinner party with this sort of thing, but I believe with a little tact we may be able——"

Sam Smith couldn't stand Sterling DuPree's dawdling. "That's why we're here, isn't it?" he muttered. "To make a plan."

They fell silent. The DuPree pencil drew its favorite Grecian frieze pattern. The Schneider pipe puffed. Tom Rusk paced the floor.

There was a wall around them now other than the walnut one of Sterling DuPree's study. The bricks were made of the past in whose safety they had faith, but the mortar, apparently, was magically compounded. No one had seen it mixed. No one had heard the trowels smooth it on. No one had watched the wall rise. It was just there. It was always there when they thought of Negroes.

A Negro servant, yes; a Negro equal, no. A Negro nurse, yes; a Negro neighbor, no. A Negro workman, yes; a Negro foreman, no.

The yes and no tick-tocked painfully in their minds. They tried to justify the duality by a principle to be formulated and given to Andrew. If properly made, Andrew would accept it from them and change his ways.

Tom ceased pacing. He saw that the others had been try-ing to scramble up the wall. He laughed. Abruptly he became the Tom Rusk who laughed and joked and was charming. His charm had sold thousands of houses. He was a gentleman realtor, never in a hurry, never forgetful of little profits, yet a big-deal man. Tom believed in profits as DuPree believed in the past, yet Tom had divided loyalties, for he liked to be liked almost as much as he liked profits. The desire for approbation barked at his heels. It kept him trying to scale the wall, scratch-ing his knees as he scrambled, invariably giving himself a nasty fall, landing again and again at the very place where he had started. The disasters put wistful shadows in his eyes. Tom Rusk was an interesting-looking man. When he entered a restaurant, people would inquire his name.

Tom was saying what they all wanted to hear. "You guys will have to back me up. I'll drop a hint to Andrew, naturally, as if the thought just occurred to me. Then you fellows will come in strong! We'll make him see he owes it to the welfare of his city——"

Sterling DuPree interrupted, "Mistake came in having to get his consent by wire. If he'd been in town, we could have sounded him out before we ever arranged this meeting."

Tom resumed, "Might even be easier to put it across with the ladies present." The others smiled. In meetings the presence of ladies was always wine to Tom's tongue.

Mr. Schneider broke his silence. "Keep it simple."

Mr. Smith asked, "What are you going to say?"

Tom frowned. "A war's on. This isn't the time for them to be making trouble. Andy can concede if he wants to that the way the South has behaved to Negro soldiers has to stop——"

Sam Smith shouted, "You're not going to change the South! The South's got one hell of a problem. It's got the right to meet it in its own way without anybody butting in!"

Mr. DuPree raised a calming hand. "Gentlemen! Gentlemen!

48

No use to drag in a question which doesn't have to come into it at all. No earthly use in that. What we want to get across today is that the Negroes should behave themselves. It's production we're talking about. No striking for skilled jobs they've never before had. We'll use them where we can. They must wait. The man we're honoring today is their great ally and friend. That proves we're for a lot of things—not necessarily everything—a lot, everything within reason, that Andrew Palmer stands for. Things like better health and housing——"

Tom Rusk laughed, "Looks like I'm the only guy in the real estate business around here! That man in the White House! Those housing projects!" He was a clown mocking himself.

The others laughed. The joke was on Tom this time. Rusk was a good guy, a back slapper who made you like it. Sometimes he slapped too hard, as if purposely getting you ready for a fall.

Tom stopped laughing. "Palmer must say now is the time for patience. Later on *we*'ll do the house cleaning—do it *ourselves*."

"You've got something there," Mr. Smith conceded. "This is none of their business. That's good!"

Mr. DuPree made it better, putting it into long phrases and fancy sentences. He wove in the gallantry of the armed forces overseas, but he was talking, really, about the undesirability of change, and he identified the welfare of the city with the welfare of the men in this room.

Tom laughed. "The real trick of the year will be getting Andrew Palmer to say it!"

The DuPree pencil paused. "Seems kind of presumptuous, eh? Telling the First Citizen how to make his speech." Mr. DuPree chuckled.

"He has to be told!" Mr. Smith shouted.

"Palmer's a good fellow, finest in the world."

"Too up there in the clouds for me," Mr. Smith said.

"Andrew wants to give the Negroes a better chance," Sterling DuPree said. "Very commendable." After all Palmer was a gentleman and Smith a boor.

"I began life a poor boy," Mr. Smith stormed. "Who gave me a chance? I made my own chance! I don't believe in all this truckling to people. When I went to work a half century ago I was only eleven and I put in a twelve-hour day——"

They had heard it all before. When Sam Smith got angry, he always turned autobiographical. The others lit cigarettes and restlessly waited it out. Smith was a big money-maker, a success. You couldn't tell him to shut up. He ended, "I can't ask Mrs. Smith to sit next to niggers."

Mr. DuPree laid a pacific hand on Smith's shoulder. "Our wives will sit together. In the central box."

As they stood to say good-by, they felt good about once more having defended their city. They were always defending their city. Didn't they sit on boards and committees, they and Andrew? Together they constituted an interlocking directorate for the organizations which ran things, a directorate building the future. To that end it clung frantically to the past.

5

DOROTHY JANE SHOVED SOMETHING INTO HER CLOSET AS Honey came to the door. A long white dressing gown made her look like a little girl playing house in her mother's clothes.

"I got to get at this bed," Honey said. "My! My! That your new beau?" She studied a large photograph of a long-haired youth with dim eyes and a drooping mouth. The picture in a plastic frame stood on the cluttered surface of a lavender-and-scarlet dressing table.

Inside and out Dorothy Jane lived amid clutter. Inside, the clutter was of her father's making. Adoring him, she accepted all his principles. Adoring her, he sent her to exclusive clubs and schools where his principles were decried.

When she was forced to choose between her father's way and the Country Club's way, she would choose the Country Club way, blaming her mother for the decision: "Mother says I have to go!" . . . "I don't want to, but Mother says . . ."

"Miss Dorothy Jane, what's this about Mr. Junior?"

"Oh, nothing. Mother's an old scaredy cat."

"Like your Mr. Al who ain't in the fighting at all, not even in no factory?"

"Mr. Al's an artist. He's got other things to do."

Honey stood her mop in the corner. "That's the way some of the folks around our house talk—the no-'count ones."

"Al's a good artist. Ahead of his times."

51

"Or maybe he just trying to get out of his times where he won't have to share their troubles. One like that in every family. We Hoops had a boy run away from home during the depression. Shared the food when we had some but weren't willing none to share the hunger when that come."

Dorothy Jane's face took on the Palmer deep-eyed, thoughtful look.

Making the beds and straightening up, Honey worked her way around toward the closet. She dragged a filled but open red suitcase to the center of the floor. "When you fixing to light out?"

"Today. Keep your mouth shut, Honey."

"Dotty, is you in love?"

"What's your guess?"

"Deep in love?"

"You think I'd be eloping if I wasn't?"

"What your mama done you trying to get even about?"

"I'm not trying to get even."

"There couldn't be no other reason for lighting out on your papa's honor day."

"That's what you think!"

"That's what everybody going to think."

The girl crushed out her cigarette with a quick twist. "Maybe it won't be today." Her face was scarlet.

Honey put the suitcase into the closet. Her back was to Dorothy Jane as she spoke. "You the youngest. You always been the flightiest. And the sweetest. You been baby to us all. You been your papa's favorite. Reckon you ain't never going to disappoint us none."

"A girl has to get married some time, Honey."

"Not when she's seventeen. Reckon Mr. Jim kind of seen that. There he was, twenty-three and going to his death and you too young to be a widow. Reckon it shows how high he held you."

Dorothy Jane began to cry. She walked into Honey's arms for comfort.

When the sobs were calmer, Honey said, "That crying's the kind going to give you a headache. You just crawl under the covers. Honey'll bring you one of them aspirins of your papa's. Reckon Mr. Jim couldn't figure out no way to be fair to you, loving you the way he done."

It was Mrs. Palmer who insisted upon knowing how the table reservations were acquired.

Later in the sunroom she whispered to Andrew, "Honey is old Cuthbert's daughter! Worked for us twelve years and never peeped. And he's served us out there for twenty and never peeped. Makes me wonder what we could have said before one about the other. I never would have thought it of Honey! It's so—so—so kind of sneaky."

"Honey didn't say she wasn't his daughter." Andrew spoke vaguely, his mind on his speech.

"But, darling, she knows every single thing about us! That you wear a brace and that I tint my hair sometimes and that Bruce used to drink too much and that Junior——"

Andrew stirred in his chair. "I haven't seen Junior's letters lately. Well, now that I'm back in town, after today I'll have more time."

She knew it was a question: Could it be true that no letter had come in all these weeks?

She pretended to be thinking only about Honey. "It's rotten deceitful."

"You don't *have* to tell Honey our affairs."

"It's no use trying to hide anything from them. I found that out long ago."

"Honey never uses it amiss."

He seemed to have forgotten Junior. This was the moment to leave.

"I'll see if I can help Honey in the kitchen, but it makes me feel kind of different toward her."

The god made amused, tut-tut noises. "You could fix their cocktails and make their beds and then you'd know which one of them wore a brace and which one used the hair-straightener."

Mrs. Palmer giggled. She came back and rubbed her cheek against his. "Oh, darling," she sighed, "you're sweet."

"You're pretty sweet yourself."

Tears came to her eyes, but he couldn't see them, and she was able to keep her voice steady. "Darling, when this war is over and the boys all right, it seems to me——"

He patted her hand. "I know. I know."

"I'm so proud of you, darling, about today."

"Nice of them. Makes a man feel he's made a few friends while he's been out making enemies." Then the god smiled with distant amusement. "Some of those fellows who arranged this afternoon's meeting are the ones I've been battling with for years."

"You mean the men coming here for dinner today—are—are the ones who send you home from all those meetings with your bad headaches?"

"Tom Rusk's got about eighty of my headaches chalked up to his account, and Sam Smith along about one hundred and eighty—thousand!"

"Why, then——"

Andrew patted his wife's hand. "Just be sweet to them today. They're the most powerful men in the city. In a way they *are* the city. They've chosen to get up a meeting in honor of your humble husband. Ceremonies. And I'm to be the chief speaker. They're probably feeling very bighearted about all this—because they know our ideas don't just fit. It was nice of them, very nice of them."

Nancy Palmer saw only that he was happy. The honor was healing all the sore spots his spirit had ever suffered. His pencil moved across the sheet. She tiptoed out of the room.

While she was sitting at her dressing table trying to twist up her hair, Bruce came in chuckling.

"That Honey is a card!" His tones imitated Honey's way of speaking. "All them Palmers, they kind of like to worry."

Honey stood in the doorway. "Run along with your nonsense, Mr. Bruce. Let me tend to that hair! Ain't gonna look like nothing but a bird's nest 'less'n we gets it up in time to dry." Her fingers were taking down the twists Mrs. Palmer's had put up. With quick motions Honey dampened down the strands and pinned them into smaller and tighter rolls. "Mrs. Palmer, you ain't counting on me none for fixing supper?"

"If you could, Honey. I know we'll come home dead tired. After the ceremonies Mr. Palmer ought to have a plate of soup and—— Don't you want to stay?" She looked rebuffed.

"Reckon I can't stay after four. Oughtn't stay that long. I'll set the table and put the soup in a pan. All you'll have to do is light the fire under it. I'll fix some of them cheese sandwiches Miss Dorothy Jane likes, ready for slipping into the oven——"

"I thought you'd stay the whole day——"

"My mama needs me to help her."

"Oh, your family's having its Thanksgiving dinner tonight." It was part question, part statement.

"I done promised to help Mama this afternoon. I'll fix everything before I leave. I've got pie crust ready, the same I'm using for the turkey pies. I'll spice up them turkey pies some. I'll fill the other with something sweet. Mr. Bruce, is that colonel friend of yours out of bed yet? Likely it needs making."

"Getting rid of me, are you?" Bruce disappeared.

"Mrs. Palmer, you ain't got no call to go to worrying yourself about Miss Dorothy Jane. Not today nohow. Course she's aiming to fix up her pride, I reckon. Likely she figures doing something rash is going to fix it up. Reckon if she gives herself time she'll do something right sensible. Only if she's in a hurry she might go to fooling herself."

55

"You think . . . ?"

"I don't do no thinking. Only that today I reckon you can go right ahead and enjoy your parties. That's my doorbell."

It was both doorbells. Flowers for Mr. Palmer at the back, a personally delivered note on fine stationery at the front. The morning newspaper, which the Palmers had not yet had time to read, carried a long, praiseful editorial on Andrew Palmer, the man to receive this year's award at the ceremonies this afternoon. All the people whose hearts had warmed to him, despite their disapproval of his ways, found pleasure in discovering that they could yield to their hearts without damaging their reputation for propriety. The paper had the whole thing analyzed carefully. Andrew Palmer was a man of standards and a gentleman. More flowers came. More notes. More telephone calls.

I ain't getting anything did, Honey decided. She went to the second floor to see whether Dorothy Jane had dried her eyes enough to come down and put the flowers in vases. Mr. Bruce was in his mama's room talking all his jokes, trying to make her forget about Junior. Honey could hear them.

She found Dorothy Jane in the arms of the soldier boy from Maine. It was one of those long kisses the movies make so much of.

"Some folks cure up fast," Honey said as they pulled apart.

A quick look convinced her that the boy from Maine was handsome but scheming, the kind that was always taking in the Palmers. She stared at his stripes.

"You high up as Mr. Bruce? You learned to make a bed yet?"

They laughed at her, but Honey continued. "Reckon you better be making them beds. Honey sure ain't finding no time. Miss Dorothy Jane, you come down and help Honey with the doorbells and the flowers. Else I ain't going to get the dishes wiped off before the crowd pounds in on me."

Risking nothing, she motioned to Dorothy Jane to precede her down the steps.

Bad as Eulatha, Honey commented to herself. Eulatha got started that way with a broken heart. Reckon a good woman's only one ain't so dumb as to go giving in to her heart in the first place. Eulatha's safe when you keep her busy. Reckon it's right lucky I got work this morning for Dorothy Jane.

Dorothy Jane said, "If there'd been mail today, I'll bet we'd have had a couple of letters from Junior."

It's eating at the lot of them, Honey thought. Lawd Gawd, I sure hope that boy's all right.

Aloud she said, "My papa knows folks ain't heard for six months, and then they got enough letters to stuff a pillow."

"How do the colored boys feel about going into the Army? Wasn't there some——"

"Lamb, he ain't had to go."

"I don't mean your brother. I mean colored boys in general."

"I wouldn't know nothing about that, Miss Dorothy Jane. I just knows my business."

Dorothy Jane frowned a Palmer frown. "But Daddy says——"

"All I hears around our place is, 'Honey, I needs money,' or 'Honey, will you do this or that?'—except for that talk Lamb is saying all the time. Now Lamb he talks like that. 'We Negroes believe . . .' I ain't never seen how he can know how all them folks believe, black or white, even if he did go to high school, so I never pays him no mind when he's like that. . . . Course in our Ville papers I read about things. Appears to me half the time they dragging their heels about how our boys got to go to war, and the rest of the time they bragging about all the medals they got. . . . Reckon I'll put these relishes back in the box. Your mama done thought she bought salted nuts, and they turns out to be just plain nuts. Reckon I got to fry them up. And it's sure time to set my table."

6

HONEY IN THE HALL COULD BE HEARD INVITING THE LAST OF the guests to "rest their wraps."

They were Tom Rusk and his wife. The murmur of voices paused for introductions. The wives of the directorate had never met.

Standing in the doorway, the Rusks looked happy, as if pleased by the surprise their unlikeness to each other was causing. Tom was handsome as a magnificent animal is handsome, a vigorous and unmistakable example of a species. Above his massive shoulders was a hairy head and a lean jaw thrust forward. Mrs. Rusk was a little wren of a woman, a pallid blonde whose voice was a chirp and whose walk was a light skip. She was dressed in tan topped by an overlarge blue hat, as if the wren wore the headgear of a blue jay.

Nancy Palmer said to herself, A bird and a buffalo. I think I have them all straight now. The DuPrees are the tall decorative cranes. The Smiths are the little round growling bears. The Schneiders are the work horses, steady, thick-ankled Percherons wanting to be petted. And these last are the bird and the buffalo.

Andrew attended to the introductions. He was in high spirits. His young people in the dining room were having a good time, and now these men he had struggled with for so many years were showing a confidence in him he had feared they lacked.

58

It was warm and intimately friendly. The scared look had nearly gone out of Nancy's eyes.

All these years Andrew had wanted more time for friendships. A man rushed off in the morning, jockeyed from decision to decision, came home too tired to talk. He wanted to swap yarns, to be with people just because being together was wonderful. Rich and warm and wonderful. A man in a room with his friends was a man being reborn. The magic of it added another dimension to living. Too frequently men came together for a purpose—to get things done. Now and again Andrew couldn't go on like that. He would suddenly hunger for the random communion of friendship. Those were the times he would, without warning to Nancy, invite dinner guests, like yesterday, when Tom and Gus came blushing and stuttering to his office. How wrong that he had seen all these men a couple of times a week for years and knew nothing about them! Only that Tom Rusk had a couple of pretty daughters; that Sam Smith and his wife lived alone in a big stone castle; that Gus Schneider had a couple of sons in the Army and a daughter away at college; that Sterling DuPree had a son who was an officer in the Navy and a daughter cheated of a debut by the war. That was nearly all—well, Sam Smith's bad heart and good appetite; Sterling's fondness for golf; Gus Schneider's blush when his wife's name appeared in the paper; and Tom Rusk's fondness for plaid clothes. "Tom MacRusk" DuPree called him in those funny asides of his.

Andrew's heart expanded with its desire to like these men. His eyes sparkled with welcome. "Come in! Come in!" he said.

Seeing Andrew's pleasure, Tom Rusk decided there was no point in waiting. Seize a good moment when you had it! He stationed himself at the mantel, leaned against it with one plaid elbow. Plunging was easier for Tom than leaning.

He glanced around the circle. To catch their attention, he boomed out a sudden laugh. "Andrew," he began. "Andy,

Andy, what a man says on the day he receives the award is——" He hesitated to estimate his audience. Should he say "damned important" and laugh again or say "pretty darned important" and raise his eyebrows?

Andrew finished his sentence for him. After all, Rusk never before had called him Andy. Might be something up.

". . . is all written out and ready." It was Andrew who lifted his brows and squinted and smiled. From his inner pocket he brought out some note cards. His thumb snapped through them.

"Any chance of a preview?" Tom asked.

"None whatever."

Tom guffawed overloudly to signify that nothing was spoiled. He'd try again later. The others didn't laugh.

Nancy, always afraid of her own guests, wondered whether buffaloes were really vicious. She couldn't get at anything about Mr. Rusk that way, of course, but it was the best thinking she could do with Mrs. Schneider talking in one ear about her work at the ration board and all those organizations she belonged to which were doing what she termed a fine, civic-minded job. Mrs. Schneider was plump and wore a brown dress with large green buttons to match the frisky hat of green feathers over her right eye. She seemed to be a very solid citizen, but she made Nancy feel much less solid—in fact not at all solid; and Nancy wished she'd have a go at someone else.

At that moment Mrs. Schneider did turn to Mrs. DuPree, the tall woman in sleek black whose elegance set her apart from the others. Mrs. DuPree seemed to be a crane who had walked off a satin wall hanging and very likely was able to step among the water lilies without getting her feet wet. While Mrs. Schneider argued that Mrs. DuPree ought to believe something she had never thought about enough to doubt, Mrs. DuPree watched the steady treachery of Mrs. Schneider's too short belt. When

60

it finally popped off, Mrs. DuPree's coral-tipped fingers fanned a sheer handkerchief at herself as if the room were too hot.

Fortunately Honey came in just then with the cocktails, walking with the thoughtful grace of a dancer who approached the center of the stage for an introductory bow. On the palm of her right hand she balanced a silver tray with the drinks while her left palm presented tiny red napkins, green-scalloped, which Mrs. Palmer had forgotten she owned, Dorothy Jane's Christmas present last year to the household.

Honey had brushed her hair again and put on an organdy cap to match the fancy apron Mrs. Palmer kept for her best parties. Honey's broad brow was smooth with peace. As if performing a ceremonial, Honey's voice was hushed, her eyes half closed. When she withdrew to fetch the turkey pies, Mrs. Schneider whispered—yet everyone heard: "How fortunate you are!"

Mrs. Palmer explained, "She's just come back to help me for the day."

The woman in purple velveteen with powder around the neckline said, "Mine's in a defense plant too." She was Mrs. Smith and spoke in a voice which clanged loudly enough to remind Mrs. Palmer that Mr. Smith had caused 180,000 of Andrew's headaches! Her accent was southern, and unfortunately her words probably carried to Honey in the pantry. "My sister writes from down home that every nigger in Texas is rolling in money."

Wildly Mrs. Palmer tried to scramble to safety. Andrew's face was wearing the look that Nancy always assumed meant acid was gathering in his stomach. The only time he had ever whipped one of his children was the day Junior called Honey "nigger." Andrew had given strict orders that the word was never again to be said in his house, and now here it was ruining his good time!

61

Trying to halt the flow of acid, Nancy said firmly, "Honey's been with us for years. We're very fond of Honey."

Mrs. DuPree's cigarette holder paused midway of its arc of motion. Momentarily she left the water lilies. "Is Honey really her name? How amusing!"

"Down home," Mrs. Smith grumbled, "we had one named Bronchitis. She went with a buck named Catastrophe."

The laughing ended with a quick silence which froze faces as Honey brought the warm plates and platter of pies.

To soften up Andrew, Tom Rusk began to talk about juvenile delinquency and the need for playgrounds. Everyone agreed about that until Mrs. Schneider pinned him down about one on the edge of the Negro district, white for years, now demanded by the Negroes.

As soon as Honey left, Tom Rusk said it would be wrong to begin giving the darkies everything they asked for, no limit to where that might lead the city. He returned to the mantel. "After this clamor dies down about the playground—and we sure got to keep that one locked—that's all there is to it. But afterwards I'm going to see to it those pickaninnies get a place to play. I want those kids safe. I know a vacant lot—I can fix it with the owners by a telephone call—if necessary I'll buy them a trapeze or slide or something out of my own pocket. We got a lot of rentals in the district. Fact is, our Lions' Club might want to buy baseballs and bats." He put his cocktail down and wrote in a notebook. "I'm for being fair——"

Glancing at Andrew, he saw that Andrew wasn't seeing his side of it. Tom's neck turned red, and then his face. He wiped off his forehead and began to tell Andrew a thing or two. "Look what we're up against! There's a black real estate chap giving the association lots of trouble. Sells white property to coloreds every chance he gets. Not with any intention whatever of turning the whole block into Negro housing. He doesn't care

62

about the rest of the block. We're constantly having to go into court to get that property back into white hands!"

"Why doesn't the association put him out?" Mrs. Smith demanded.

Tom smiled at her. "We don't have colored members."

"Of course," she apologized.

"So what happens? The association abides by the neighborhood covenants. If people of a district get together and agree not to sell to coloreds, we keep their covenants in effect for them. This darky never asks whether a district has a covenant or not. Just let him get a chance to buy and, bingo, the block is black!"

Tom's wife looked up. "Do the others always move out, Tom?"

"They always want to." Tom smiled around the circle. "Mrs. Rusk isn't up on these matters. She's the artist of the family. I'm sending Mama to art school this year." Mr. Rusk somehow, without seeming to, was going at Andrew. "The black real estate fellow takes profits which rightly belong to the association!"

Nancy wished they would keep still and let Andrew enjoy his cocktail in peace. There he was with his brow all furrowed over Negro children's hitting one another with bats and no one to stop them.

Mr. Palmer said, "What we ought to do is open that playground for all the children of the neighborhood. The district is predominantly black."

Mrs. Smith's face bloomed nearly as purple as her dress. Her gold earrings trembled. "Mr. Palmer, you don't mean to tell me you'd let nigger children play with white?" Her voice cracked.

Andrew said he did. "They're dying together in the Army. Negroes are sixteen per cent of the enlisted men and only ten per cent of our populace."

63

"What on earth has that to do with it?" Tom came back. "Question is, do you want a race riot around here or don't you?"

Andrew smiled. "Up at the City Art Museum the other day I walked in on a pottery demonstration, very interesting too. A woman in a blue smock was showing the children—a lot of grown people there too—how to make a vase. Well, come to look around a little and I noticed some colored children mixed right in with the whites." He shook his head. His eyes twinkled. "I didn't observe any race riot."

After that everyone spoke at the same time, the women spoiling Tom's chance to swing the talk back to what Andrew should say at the Auditorium. Someone had forgotten to tell the women to keep still. His own wife was always getting off that nonsense about the beautiful color of Negro skin, just repeating of course what she heard that fool art teacher say. A man in a smock teaching art was Tom Rusk's idea of nothing at all! He hoped Mrs. Rusk wouldn't take the notion to speak up now. He hurried to take control again.

Sterling DuPree scented danger and got there first. He wove his finest courtroom phrases in loops, bringing them back at intervals to rhythmic repetition. Secretly Andrew's tongue ticked off the meter against his front teeth. "What is citizenship if not trustworthy service as a citizen to the place in which a man by the grace of fate or fortune was a citizen—and to the ways of that place . . ."

It went on and on. Andrew saw with a twinge of pain that Sterling DuPree was not satisfied with this year's choice of First Citizen. "I yield to no man in my admiration of Andrew Palmer's fine principles and high level of civic conduct. I admire Andrew Palmer's fine kindly spirit. I grant the validity of his concern over injustices within our community—injustices that are as they are of necessity and unfortunately must remain as they are and have always been." He was looking over his spectacles directly at Andrew. "At this tumultuous time in our history new paths must be tested with extreme caution——"

"You mean avoided," Andrew snapped.

"To avoid them wholly is certainly the course of wisdom."

The moment was tense until Sterling DuPree glided into praise of Andrew Palmer's way of life. The elegant mind produced an elegant tribute. Sam Smith and Tom Rusk, looking embarrassed, murmured compliments and their agreement. Andrew's joy in his day was gone.

Mrs. DuPree turned her heavy-lidded eyes from the cherry in the bottom of her glass to Andrew's face. Remote among the water lilies, she had not been part of the group. Now she looked at Andrew in the manner of a connoisseur determined not to yield except in the presence of the best. She took her time. She had seen Andrew once before, at the country club. She said, "Mr. Palmer, I'm glad you won the award."

Mr. Schneider sat forward in his chair. After all, a First Citizen was a First Citizen. He had not expected or wanted Andrew to be chosen, but now that he was chosen, the selection seemed finished business and correct. The honor wasn't going to give Andrew any more power. Might even make him watch his step. Maybe he'd stop advocating those silly measures the Negroes were always trying to get through the legislature in order to prove that they weren't second-class citizens when anyone could look at them and see that they were. He didn't like sitting here in Andrew's house and seeming not in favor of the award. Gus Schneider had got where he was—from plumber's assistant to head of a large firm—by looking up the ladder, not down, doing his job, and keeping his mouth shut. He'd told his wife plenty of times there was no sense in knowing more or being better than those above you. All that was needed was to make the whole question a practical one.

He cleared his throat. "I'm just thinking about things like Negroes being served in restaurants. What does the right to

65

go places mean, if they haven't the money, and if they have— I'm told there are some wealthy Negroes in this city—if they have money to spare, wouldn't they be better off putting it into savings?"

He hadn't finished, but Tom saw what he was after. Tom made the whole thing even more practical. "My wife has a birthday tomorrow. I've invited Mama to go out to dinner with me. Just a nice little celebration, see? I'm going to put on my best clothes, and so is she. Now suppose we enter the lobby of one of our finest hotels and come face to face with a Negro and his black wife going to dinner, doesn't that spoil everything?"

The issue was clear to everyone except Mrs. Rusk, who frivolously declared she would enjoy making little pencil sketches of them.

Before Tom got another start, Mrs. Smith dragged the Negro question back into the room, as if it were a dead rat which had to be disposed of by common consent. Andrew was getting that ramrod look to his neck. Once he stiffened up, there was no chance of getting anywhere with him. Something had to be done soon.

Tom bragged that he had suggested Andrew's name to the award committee months ago. It wasn't strictly true, but this was an emergency and a man had to accomplish what he was after. "Andy, I sold them a bill of goods. I said, 'For heaven's sake, what about Andrew Palmer?'" He swung around from the mantel to observe Andrew's gratitude.

Andrew didn't seem grateful. His eyes wore a distant look. Remorseful for his own scorn of his guests, he rose and re-filled their glasses. Before he sat down again he said slowly, "Boys, the way I see it, our city's sick. Got caught in an epidemic. Chief Negro problem we have to meet is in the hearts of white men. Negroes of this city want the right to move about as full citizens. Go where they need to go without question.

Eat where they happen to be when they're hungry—as their pocketbooks will permit, of course. They want to live where there's room and——"

Andrew had been talking in a gentle voice. Knowing him, the men saw his pain.

It was Mrs. Smith who seized the dead rat by the tail and swung it full force. Niggers, she said, were niggers and shouldn't be coddled. In the South, where she came from, men knew how to handle them and there was no problem. Up here there was too much nonsense and giving in to them. They should be kept in their place. It was a disgrace to permit them to sit where they pleased in the streetcars. Once when her chauffeur, a lazy darky, was playing ill, she boarded a car and a black nigger tried to sit down next to her. She raised her umbrella, and you just bet that nigger made for the door like greased lightning! All this talk about their rights was silly. She saw a fine brick building the other day, and nigger children were coming out of it. Didn't men have loyalty to their own any more? "It's all hypocrisy," she clanged. "I haven't yet met a man willing to have his daughter marry a nigger. That's the whole question! That's all there is to the nigger problem!"

Andrew stood up. He breathed deeply. "I've known many colored men and women. Educated and uneducated. They just want to stand as tall as the next fellow."

He turned to Nancy. "Mother, what time did you say we were due at the club for our dinner?"

"Now," she answered.

Honey in the hall, getting out the wraps, assumed deafness. She wore it prettily. Her black eyes were round with false innocence. She dropped Mrs. Smith's mink coat. Retrieving it hastily from the floor, she stepped firmly on the lining. Her heel came down hard and pivoted.

When the guests approached the coat closet, the mink was the only coat Honey held. Mrs. Smith was the only guest unembarrassed as Honey overgently put it on her shoulders. The other women were extremely polite in their thank-you's to Honey. They murmured to each other their admiration of this charming house and their surprise at the day's turning so wintry.

"Your money's up on my dressing table," Mrs. Palmer whispered to Honey.

"Thank you kindly." Honey's glance followed Mr. Palmer down the driveway.

When finally the cars pulled out, Honey walked through the rooms picking up napkins, emptying ash trays, restoring chairs, opening windows, clearing the dining-room table. When everything was back where it belonged, she walked through again. She seated herself where Mrs. Smith had sat. Talking out loud, she repeated the things Mrs. Smith had said and mocked her way of saying them. Her lips were Eulatha's, curved bitterly.

Then she rose and, as Honey Hoop, said down at the woman in purple: "You ain't no real true lady. You nothing but poor white trash fixed out in good clothes! You ain't got not any chance being invited in this here front door again—not if I knows Mr. Palmer, you ain't! No chance a-tall!"

Honey paced up and down waiting for the house to still her anger.

"Mr. Palmer," she scolded, and again she spoke out loud, "I done my part to give you a good time. I made my turkey pies right nice. I made them cocktails just the way you likes them. It ain't no use you trying to teach poor white trash to be Palmers. Come I was you and Mrs. Palmer, I'd just go ahead and enjoy myself. Give a party that wasn't all that talk. Give a party with jokes and laughing and a good time. That's what I'd do!"

As she spoke she stood in front of his picture. It was a large oil painting in a gold frame. The artist had caught that look of trying to live nobly which so often shone in Mr. Palmer's eyes.

Silently Honey looked at his face, remembering the years Mr. Palmer had served the Hoops as a sort of god. That time the police took Lamb. That time there weren't no money to bury one of Mama's dead babies. That time Eulatha had a baby and no papa to buy its clothes.

There he was on the wall, a man getting old and missing the fun of living. He was doing that for the sake of Honey's people.

"You a damn fool!" she said to him. "You a damn fool! You the finest damn fool I ever met up with. . . ."

Standing still like that, her legs stiffened. They pained from last night's dancing and today's work and yesterday's. Up and down her thighs the muscles stung and twitched and along the calves lumped into hard knots.

7

MRS. PALMER'S ROOM WAS ALL RIGHT. MRS. PALMER HAD Mr. Palmer's bed turned back, the sheet on a nice slant, the way Honey used to do it. She had fresh pajamas laid out, and the electric pad ready for his feet. Honey felt to make sure it wasn't turned on. The tray-table was there too. Mrs. Palmer was fixing to give him his supper in bed.

Honey found her pay on Mrs. Palmer's dressing table. And a note. "Please, Honey, clean up Mr. Bruce's room before you leave and give that other bathroom a good going over." Huh, a fine time to tell me, when I'm all dressed! Honey put back one of the dollars. Mrs. Palmer was an awful one to think folks were cheating her.

Halfway down the stairs she thought of what Eulatha would say about that dollar. "Tell her you got you a job now—with holidays!" Good lawd, this here pay wasn't nothing alongside what she earned out to the plant. She went back and snatched the bill, stuffed it into her purse. To Mr. Palmer's bed she whispered, "It won't mean nothing to you one way or the other. If it was your bathroom or your bed, I'd do it. But not for no one else."

From below on the street she heard Ben's horn. As she went out, she slammed the front door hard.

Mama was in the back seat of the car, fixed out in her best. In her lap was the purse Honey had given her last year for Christmas. Black suède with a crystal clasp.

Honey sat next to Ben. He looked fine. His black satin face shone from being washed right good. His eyes were proud of Honey.

"Rest yourself," he said. "Reckon you're tired."

Honey put her head back against the seat top and thought: He'll make a good husband. What a girl needs in a husband is someone with sense, someone to stick by a woman all her days, someone to count on forever and ever. She stole a look at Ben. You the nearest to a Mr. Palmer a black girl ever going to get, she thought, slipping her hand into his. They drove along happily in silence.

At the streetcar loop there were a dozen or more brown women with big bags waiting for the car the way Honey usually did. Driving past, she felt *dicktee* and liked it. She sat up straight.

Without knowing why, she began to feel angry. Angry at the old women who had so little pride that they carried their scraps of food and their servant's uniform for everyone to see; angry at the white men driving who saw the car of black folks and smiled; angry at the pain which stabbed at her back! Angry at Mama too!

They were out of the beautiful residential region now. The houses were smaller and closer together and as smoke-scarred as if they had been in battle. The streets were lively with automobiles and people and children playing running games and shouting to one another. As they turned in Mount Vernon Avenue they heard an ice-cream vendor's bell clapping dully. At once the block was cleared of children. Then back they rushed with pennies and nickels. Mothers in war-plant slacks shouted commands from doorways. Stooped old women stared from windows.

"They ain't got nothing much to be proud of," Honey said, "but they ain't going to want us none."

Fear drew in her heart. Then her anger swept back and she

told herself: The Hoops, they got a right to live where they please, Smiths or no Smiths.

Ben found the number. The house was just like all the others in the row. Mama handed him the key, and he opened the door. Inside, the room was dead cold and roaring with echoes. It was a house which had once been fairly good, but now was run down and dirty. It had been lived in unlovingly. There was a tiled fireplace with some tiles missing, and a mantel whose shelf was split and ringed with marks.

Honey saw that Mama was dead set on liking it. Well, it could be fixed up. The Hoops knew how to paint and paper and polish. They weren't helpless like white folks.

From the porch came hollow thuds. Ben leaped to lock the door. White children peered in the window. They shouted insults. They licked at ice-cream sticks and shouted and licked.

"Let's go upstairs," Ben said. Honey saw that he too hated and feared this Mount Vernon Street notion of Mama's.

On the second floor there were four bedrooms. Wallpaper drooped from the ceiling like burned skin, hanging. The side walls were water-stained and moldy. The smell was like that in the Palmer basement. There was a dark bathroom with a cracked bowl.

"Mama, these walls is a sight."

"Somebody done dinged them walls. That ain't nothing. They'll clean up right nice."

"Oh, Mama, they're awful."

"This is a classy house, Honey. Got itself dirty on top, but clean her up and she sure a queen!"

The doorbell rang. Fists banged on the windowpane.

Mama ignored it and admired the closets. She had never lived in a house with a closet.

Honey sat down on the window sill. She whispered to Ben, "Come Mama takes this here house, Honey's going to have enough scrubbing to do to wear her fingers white."

"Your house in the Ville is so nice and clean. Looks a lot better than this."

He hadn't wanted to say anything against the new house, yet in the end he had.

Stubbornly she answered, "Lamb could hang the paper and paint the floors. Ben, when you phoned me about Lamb, you ain't said much."

"Wasn't much to say. He stood in front of your house and he looked right pleased. . . . I met a man this morning never was in this town before, but he knew all about the Urban League and the N.A.A.C.P. and the March-on-Washington. He knew lots about how things are with us. Seemed to me he knew more about the Ville than I do living there." He didn't say who the man was.

"Mama," Honey called, "where-at is Lamb?"

"Lamb, he come home early," Mama answered. "Got the place full of white folks. . . . Plenty bedroom here. Except for the babies, wouldn't not more'n two or maybe three Hoops got to sleep to a room. This house sure is grand!"

Honey sighed and went back to the window sill. Downstairs children were hooting. A rock crashed through the glass above her head.

Startled, Honey jumped up and ran into Ben's arms. He brushed the specks carefully from her face.

"It may be the Hoops have the right to live on Mount Vernon," he said, "but they wouldn't get happiness from it."

He'd make a good husband, Honey told herself. But she answered sullenly, "Hoops been rolling to white man's tunes long enough."

Ben kissed her on the cheeks; then quietly on the mouth. She wriggled out of his arms.

"When are you going to say 'yes' to Ben?" he asked gently.

She gave him a smile of dew and dreams, but she didn't speak. To herself she said, Honey's going to say "yes" all

73

right, but Honey's going to wait a piece until she wants to say it more'n she do now. Come I set my head to it, I'll be wanting to, like when I went to the Palmers to work. I ain't wanted to work out none, but trying to like it, I got so's I did.

Standing concealed by the shadows, Ben peeped out the window. "I don't fancy the looks of this," he kept saying. His hands rattled his car keys.

"I'm right glad you parked up a piece or they'd be smearing your car."

Ben mumbled, "How are we going to get out of here? The porches across the street are crowded with people. I don't fancy the looks of this!"

Slowly Mama creaked in from the other rooms. "It sure grand! The Hoops sure going to roll to glory! No more sleeping all over each other like a litter of pigs."

"Mama," Honey said, "listen to that out yonder. We can't go to living here. Get that out of your heart right now!"

"Can't live here! Why, that white man what brung the key, he said we could. He owns the house, don't he? He say we can live here. Carmen, she talked to him and he say we can. We got the cash money to pay the rent." She was a little girl hysterically clutching a doll. She wouldn't let Honey wrest it from her. "We Hoops going to live right here! I'll break their——"

"Listen, Mama——"

"I'll break their necks!" Mama shouted. "I'll sure break their necks, 'cause I going to live here!"

The noise outside changed.

Honey said, "A police is down there!"

Ben brightened up. "He'll make them stop."

Ben knew everything! The police was white, and Honey hadn't expected him to side with the Hoops.

"Ben, you reckon he's going to make them let Mama live here?"

"He'll fix it so she can't," Ben answered calmly, "but he

74

won't let them throw any more rocks or cut my tires. He'll make them keep order."

They looked down on the policeman waving his hands in a get-going gesture at the children. He was lean and young, with long arms.

As they watched, a car drove up. A spry, red-haired man hurried out.

"That's him!" Mama said. "That's the man brung the key! Now we'll see can the Hoops live here or can't they!" She was already mumbling through the bedrooms, saying, "Honey and Eulatha sleep here. Carmen and . . ."

While the real estate fellow and the policeman talked, a crowd gathered to listen. Scrawny old men and full-breasted young women, thin women, children, a youth with an empty sleeve. They talked on. They were angry.

Ben said, "They don't look like pleasant neighbors."

Honey smiled. "They don't look none like neighbors."

Mama came to see. She snorted. "Look like borrowers. Reckon the Hoops with all they war money is going to be borrowed bare."

When the red-haired man knocked on the door, Ben and Honey went down. Mama followed as quickly as her stiff joints permitted.

The man drew a notebook from his pocket. "I've got a pretty little place likely to be vacant next month. Not on the market for showing yet. About a block from where you live now."

"How large is it?" Ben asked.

The white man turned the pages and turned and turned. Finally he said, "Four, counting the kitchen."

Honey sniffed. "We're doing that good now."

From halfway down the steps, Mama spoke. "We going to live right here!"

The red-haired man coughed. "There's been a mistake."

"Ain't no mistake," Mama told him. "We got the rent money. You got the house. Everything, it's set!"

The man coughed again. He looked pleadingly at Honey and appraisingly at Ben. Then he handed Ben a card. "I'm with Rusk & Rusk Realty Company. Mr. Thomas Rusk had some kind of an idea about changing this property over, but when I just spoke to him out at the country club after the police phoned about the disturbance, Mr. Rusk says we can't run counter to the wishes of the neighborhood. See, he owns several houses on this block, so he'd like to do it——"

"How much were you fixing to increase the rent?" Ben asked quietly.

"Ten a month on each place. In time it would permit improvements. You see the property needs repairs——"

"You weren't planning to paper now?" Ben pushed on.

"Not under our former program of rehabilitation——"

"Not if you rented to colored, you mean?"

"That's it," he said and then hastily added, "Folks like you, used to a nice home, wouldn't be satisfied in a run-down place like this. No, no, this wouldn't do for you at all. I thought that the minute I set eyes on your pretty little place——"

Mama interrupted, "Honey, is that man talking sense?"

Honey answered, "Mama, he saying this ain't for colored."

"I done listen. He ain't say no such thing!"

"He saying it," Honey sighed. "He saying it right polite."

The white man blushed. "Well, I've got your name and address and phone number on my card, and you're going to be the first family informed when I get a fine piece of colored property on my list. . . . Course if you want to buy I've got a dandy to show you now."

Ben chuckled unhappily. "Maybe this whole thing was just bait to fetch customers for property you're trying to sell."

"No. No. No. Nothing of the sort in Mr. Rusk's mind!"

Honey said, "Reckon if we do buy, he'll pull the trick again."

"That piece over north of here sure is a dandy. Buy your own place, I always say, then you're fixed forever. Nobody can take your home away from you."

"How much is it?" Honey asked.

Maybe that was a way to help Mama out, to stop her from standing there bawling in front of a white man!

The red-haired man smiled benevolently. "I could let you have it for eight thousand."

"The Hoops ain't got no eight thousand," Honey answered.

Ben said thoughtfully, "You wouldn't have to pay it all. Put a loan on it and——"

The white man coughed again. "Not in that particular section. Not any more. Real Estate Association forbids us to put a mortgage on property in that section. The members have agreed to that."

Ben asked, "What section?" and though the white man only named streets, it was clear he was telling them it was the section where most of the colored people lived.

"It's not considered safe property for mortgages," he explained.

Honey asked, "Ben, what do it mean?"

Ben's black satin face was lumpy and frowning. "It means that a colored man with three thousand dollars can buy him a home for three thousand but a white man with three thousand dollars can buy him a home for ten thousand."

"Let's get out of here," Honey said, walking angrily to the door.

"While the getting's good," Ben added because it said itself. He moved slowly with the weary resentment of a man whose anger had grown cold and was not in this moment a torment to him.

Mama said she had to go through the house once more. They heard her mumbling over the names of the children, placing them in this room and that. At first her voice was

77

broken with weeping, but by the time she came back she was as she used to be just after a baby was born and the pain of its coming gone, stiffened for the troubles she knew were born along with the baby, suffering only a little from her own pain, mostly from the pain the baby one day would have to bear.

Mama shouted, "Mr. White Man, that there torn paper up yonder, it ain't to my taste. I wouldn't live in no pigpen like this. Not a-tall. We Hoops too good for your filthy house!"

The white man went off to stuff paper in the broken pane. He didn't answer. By the time Mama had stiffly plugged down the steps to the first floor again, he was at the door ready to take the key from Ben and lock up.

He scanned Ben's face again and then handed him another Rusk & Rusk card.

"It's got my name on it," he said. "Any time you're in the market for property, let me know. Rusk & Rusk is fair to everybody. And I always say service is what I'm here for."

At the wheel of the car again, Ben sighed, "They'll always make money from a black man. That never seems to hurt their pride any."

Mama whimpered, "Ain't no use for the Hoops to earn, come we can't buy nothing."

The policeman stood beside their automobile, his face set. White people were on the porches. Their resentment hazed like smoke from porch to porch and down to the sidewalks and into Ben's car, the shiniest and finest car at the curb.

Ben drove away rapidly. At first they didn't speak to each other; then they spoke crossly. Mama blamed Honey for not sticking up for their rights. Honey snapped back. Ben scolded at Mama and then Honey at Ben.

As they turned into the Ville, they eased into laughter. It was good to be in the Ville again with black peace in the streets. The houses were smaller, but when a man felt like painting his front door blue or his fence yellow or his house purple, he

78

could do it and not be ashamed. In the Ville a man's spirits rose.

Honey couldn't shape what she felt into words, nor could Mama or Ben.

They wanted to part. They had been together too long, seeing something ugly which turned them ugly too. Honey didn't ask Ben in, and he remembered he had a funeral to get ready. Tonight there would be the Celestial Choristers at the Tabernacle. Loraine wanted to go, and his mother. He'd be glad to call for Honey about nine, and Mama too was welcome. Then he said something which silenced the thunder in Honey's back.

"Ben, you mean I got a right to go to see Mr. Palmer get his honor?"

"Everybody's got a right to go to everything in the Municipal Auditorium. It's built with our taxes same as theirs. They might send you up top, but they can't keep you out. Today they're coaxing our people to come. Don't know why. Some say there's something special to be said to us about the war. I hear the place is likely to be half empty——"

"Mr. Palmer, he'd be right ashamed."

"Might be."

After Ben drove off, Honey said to Mama, "We Hoops got to roll downtown and set in them empty seats."

"My stays, they hurt," Mama grumbled. Her anger was on the way back.

"Your stays don't got to go," Honey said. "Just you!"

"I ain't going!"

"Then you going to look to all the babies by yourself, because every grown Hoop except you is going to go!"

"You got more mule in you, Honey, than any child I ever had!"

Honey was already at the door. Snake was waiting to draw her in. He was alone in the hallway except for a crawling baby.

79

He grabbed Honey and kissed her as he had kissed her last night. He didn't free her until Mama was at the door.

Honey shoved Snake away. "Where's Lamb?" she asked. Lamb, looking as proud and important and happy as if his skin weren't black, came to the door of the front room. Beyond him were white men looking kind of holy. One had a wart on his nose. A younger man had large gray eyes and a hard mouth. A third had bulldog jaws. A fourth was still scribbling in a notebook.

Honey's eyes demanded an explanation.

"These are CIO brothers," Lamb explained. "I'm going to get our plant union to be CIO too. CIO sticks with us on not holding to a colored union with no voting rights on strikes and wages and the real——"

"They with you?" Honey demanded coldly. "Who going to throw the rocks? Reckon the black man got to do that!"

The one with the gray eyes explained that this union wasn't AFL. The one with the notebook said they were doing this for their own sakes because there was no choice; either they took the Negro in or forced him to try to get their jobs. To scab. Acting selfishly, really, but it turned out to be good for the Negro too.

Honey blinked before so much sun.

"Reckon it'll be Lamb getting into trouble——"

"CIO doesn't put Negroes on the picket line where there are white workers or white police who are anti-Negro——"

"Reckon you saving our boys to picket heaven."

They laughed at that. Then they all went back into the little front room. They tried to explain the whole thing to Honey. The one with the bulldog jaws said it was important because she worked in one of the most reactionary plants in the city. They tried to explain, but they kept saying they had to hurry because they wanted to get to the Auditorium in time for the talks, especially Mr. Palmer's.

Honey looked up at Snake, standing there back of the fellow with the wart on his nose. It was easy to see that Snake was all evil.

Honey asked, "What he got to do with this?"

Mr. Williams, they answered, was the one who prepared the colored employees for a union.

"Needs educating in union thinking," the one with the hard mouth added, frowning, "but he's done the cause a service in bringing the men together."

"Snake, he ain't never worked for nobody but Snake," Honey answered, and Snake, remembering Honey in his arms, laughed Whee-ee-ee, a laugh wild with scorn and prophecy.

Hearing him, Eulatha, in the next room with Jo-Jo, laughed too. The children took it up, and Mama in the kitchen, and the big boys and girls upstairs. The evil laugh writhed through the Hoop household.

The white men rose to their feet and shook hands with Lamb. They told him that was a magnificent speech he had made this morning to his men. The labor movement needed orators.

"As probable head of the new local," the one with the wart said, "you'll come to the regional meeting tonight, at eight."

The fellow with the hard mouth added, "And that doesn't mean C.P.T."

Wart-on-the-nose looked baffled and then remembered. "Colored People's Time," he mumbled. "That's two hours later, isn't it?"

"Only an hour, brother, only an hour!" Lamb answered gaily.

Snake getting drunk on liquor; you getting drunk on white men, Honey thought.

Then they were gone and Honey shouted at those who had laughed, "We Hoops is going to hear Mr. Palmer. Get ready fast!"

81

It was something to do. The high-school ones began to run back and forth, shouting their pleasure. The girls quarreled over combs and hair ribbons and socks. The boys took sweaters away from one another. The front room was filling with little Hoops and their friends.

Carmen came in wearing white-rimmed glasses. They made Honey think of skeleton bones. Carmen made her think of skeletons anyhow. Thin and sharp at the edges, kind of dead inside and out. It had come with getting raised up higher than her own heart felt she belonged. Seems like she was scared someone was going to find her out.

Honey knew Carmen was soft on Ben and that no man, not even Ben, was going to want Carmen until life beat him down to the place where he didn't much care what happened.

"Carmen," Honey commanded, "you go put on your new hat and come with Lamb and me."

"*And* Snake," Snake said.

Carmen eyed Snake with Judgment Day in her stare. "I have a date with a teacher friend," she said, "to meet at the Auditorium."

Honey knew Carmen was lying. Yet, waiting around in the lobby, Carmen would likely manage to see a teacher and talk some of her fancy talk and then have someone to sit with. She didn't want Carmen to have to be alone.

Honey stalked through the drawn portieres. "Eulatha, you and Jo-Jo get going," she commanded in a voice everyone knew had to be obeyed. Honey went on through the house "dusting Hoops out of corners."

"Them what's in school can go," she answered to the little ones and paid no attention to their crying. "Them in grade school, they got to walk with them in high school. You hold their hands at the crossings and you wait to buy pop and gum and stuff until Mr. Palmer, he done made his speech and you back here in the Ville." She distributed money for carfare and treats.

The household had been drowsy with body love and scornful jesting about the city's ways. Honey's orders aroused it. Soon everyone but Mama and the babies was gone and Mama was still growling, "Honey, you got mule in you! You got mule in you! Honey, you all mule!"

8

LAMB AND SNAKE STOOD OUTSIDE WAITING FOR HONEY. ON THE way to the streetcar Lamb told Honey about Snake's brother.

"Before he went into the Army he was high up in the CIO. He said he's just gone from one fight against fascism to a bigger fight. Says Negroes can't make a private little world for themselves. Got to help make one good world like Mr. Willkie claimed. Says white and colored got to learn to work together in the labor movement or both will get licked."

"Why-for he make all that speech, then run off?"

"He had to round up his soldiers. He's a great man, Honey."

"What is that, a great man? Ain't nobody great. Only good."

"He's great. I can feel it."

"A colored man ain't great."

"A great man isn't a colored man. A great man is a man first, then a colored man. A great man lives with the world——"

"You mean he passes over?"

"Only a little man passes over. A great man is what he is, but he lives in the whole world, naturally. Because his thoughts are world thoughts. And his ways are world ways. And his hopes are——"

"Lamb boy, don't go to letting it hurt you none! You as good as that great man. Maybe you great too."

Lamb laughed at her. They laughed together. Lamb had always been one to let her into his life.

84

Snake laughed too, but differently. "My brother, he's got enough learning to make him dumb all over. Right *dicktee*, Emery is, right *dicktee*. Whee-ee-ee!"

Snake was drunk. Earlier he had seized the bottle from Jo-Jo and divided, but he gulped down what was left, enough to make him talk loose and walk loose.

Honey's drink had taken the thunder out of her back and the lightning out of her legs. She felt heavy and swollen. When Snake pawed at her arm, she turned with anger, with more anger when he didn't. She thought: Lamb, he drunk on dreams instead of liquor, and dream drunk harder to get over. All his black life, Lamb he been getting drunk on dreams. Used to be, right after high school, he was going to ride to glory on a job. Going to do good work and get him a white man's high-up place. Then there was that time he got drunk on religion. Honey's heart moaned. She could see the sweet look on Lamb's face that cold Easter morning. The minister in rubber boots marched Lamb without boots into the icy Mississippi. The minister's hired men dragged Lamb 'way out past where the minister stood, as far out as the rope let them go. Honey shouted at Lamb to come on back. Lamb, with his eyes shining, kept on going. He let them duck him all the way under. A rat crawled the rope from the boat the Angel Chorus stood on, right past Lamb's head, and Lamb never noticed! He came out in a shiver that lasted a week, coughing up blood. Lawd Gawd, it wasn't as if you could ever say nothing to stop Lamb from what he believed. Seems like I can't stand no more of his dreams, Honey thought; seems like I can't stand to see him roused out of them no more.

Lamb was still talking. "Way it is, I got to sign up four hundred more men. Then we'll have strength in numbers——"

"Numbers!" Snake sang out, turning the meaning evil. "Numbers is what Snake's going to get rich on! Snake's going to win big! Then he's going to buy out every diamond in that there Shylock Castle yonder and whee-ee-ee, Snake's going to put diamonds in Honey's hair and in her teeth and on her hands and on her toes."

"Shut your face," Honey said. "Lamb, how you meet them white men?"

The question was meant to stir Lamb's suspicions.

"I looked over the unions. I chose CIO. I asked them to work with us."

Honey saw that they weren't white men to Lamb, just union men. His faith had built a world where white men and colored men would walk to work together. Every colored man would have a job, not just elevator jobs or porter jobs but jobs back of machines, those wonderful new machines where all a man did was push a button and the machine performed the work of twenty men.

"Where-at those twenty men?" Honey demanded. "Outside throwing rocks?"

"They are in another building making clothes. Every child, black or white, is going to have good warm coats for winter——"

"White men making clothes for black children?"

"They're doing that now!"

"They don't think about it none that way," Honey answered.

Lamb took off again. White men and black men would get along fine together. White men would build houses right along with colored men for colored folks to live in. Everybody, white and black, would have enough to eat and wear, enough for their children to be well and strong.

She told him about Mount Vernon Street. The anger of it dried her voice. "They was nothing but poor white trash! White women on Thanksgiving wearing same kind of slacks I wear to the factory! They didn't want us none, Lamb, they didn't!"

Lamb stopped waving his hands around.

"It'll take a long time," he said. Sorrow seemed to have crawled into his heart.

"We'll be dead," Honey answered.

"Don't you care, Honey, how the world's going to be after you're dead?"

"Reckon, Lamb, I don't. Reckon that way you like Mr. Palmer. He all the time caring about what's going to be after we-all is dead. I never did understand no such talk. Saying it, he ain't talking none about angels, only just about other folks not born yet, nobody we know a-tall, and what's going to happen to them."

"That's what counts!" Lamb answered. "What's going to happen to them!" He was up on the glory wagon again. Honey was too tired to talk about it. The car was coming. If they didn't run, they'd get left.

There were no vacant seats. Standing where everyone could see them, Honey was ashamed of Snake in his sweater with those crosswise stripes. He slipped when the car stopped or started, a tall man made of rubber twisting and turning, evil in every twist.

As they got off the car a cold fine rain slanted into their faces. The gray rock station crouched in the mist. In the waiting room Snake took a few swift steps forward and slammed his foot down hard on the toes of a colored officer. The officer was caught off guard, so that when Honey first saw Emery's face she also saw his disgust for Snake.

The men had similar features and, when Snake straightened up, were of the same height. Their skin was the shade of coffee; their eyes of the same brown velvet. Emery's eyes were steady, honest eyes, and his mouth firm. He was Snake's brother and he wasn't Snake's brother at all. In a way, Honey thought, he's the man Snake could have been.

Emery was thinking of Honey with less approval. That she

was with Snake was an accusation. His eyes studied hers and then looked at his brother in some surprise.

Earlier, with the white men present, there had been no talk brother-to-brother, not even a hello. Now Emery said quietly, "You've been staying out of jail?"

That were his way of stomping back on Snake's foot, Honey thought. It didn't hurt Snake none. Then she saw that it did. Between the brothers was a need to see each other and a need to hurt each other. Like I'd feel to Eulatha, come I hadn't made my heart give in. The stranger's voice was full of deep and familiar rumble, but the way he said things was the way the Palmers spoke.

Snake chuckled, "Emery, he went to college. Highest educated black man ever steered an elevator. Got him so much learning the Army said he'll do. Good enough to go out and get killed. Give him a gun too. Snake don't need no gun. Snake got him a switchblade."

"Keep that in your pocket!" Lamb said. Then, as if his thinking had been interrupted only momentarily, he asked Emery what he knew about the CIO in the East.

The question changed everything in Emery's face. "It's the Negro's great opportunity," he said. "CIO's not out for the purpose of fighting the battles of the colored man, but it's treating him fair. Giving him his chance to fight his own battles——"

"Let's walk," Honey said. "I cold."

The station was divided lengthwise into three parts, a long building, a train shed, and, between them, this wide, glassed, tunnel-like esplanade, thronged with people. The rows of crosswise benches were filled. At the gates crowds gathered waiting to entrain. Another crowd watched the huge blackboard as unseen hands recorded news about incoming and outgoing trains. Soldiers, sailors, girls with babies, old men, women in slacks, families huddled; black folks, white folks. Coming.

Going. Waiting. People jogged out of place. Strangers staring into one another's lives.

The four paced slowly. Often they had to separate for a moment but Emery and Lamb never stopped talking.

Honey sighed. They up on that there glory wagon together. Funniest thing how two men far off from each other get them the same dream. Reckon a woman to be a good woman, she just got to be without evil, but a man to be a good man, he got to have him a dream. Lamb always was one to have a dream.

Looking at Emery, listening to him, Honey lost her heart. His body tempted her as Snake's tempted her. Her glance roved his cheeks, his forehead, his mouth, hungrily. He was Snake cleansed of evil. Her mood swelled with sweetness and faith. They were engulfed by the glow of her body. This was what she wanted to feel for Snake! Or Ben. This was what could never be.

You ain't got no more chance with him, Honey Hoop, than . . . You ain't got as much chance as Carmen got with Ben. He as high up over Ben as Ben is high up over you, and— Lawd Gawd!—you'll have trouble enough standing on your tiptoes for Ben. This here Emery, he a white man, a high-class Palmer white man except for his skin.

The stranger, steering Honey through a knot of people, discovered that she was shivering.

"You seem chilled," he said. "How about a cup of coffee? It's cold in here. Damp. Come to think about it, I haven't eaten all day. I could do with a dinner."

Honey said yes, a cup of coffee.

The station lunchrooms were crowded. They went out on the street. Walking toward the tall buildings, they soon reached a region of restaurants. Lamb started to lead them one way, Emery another.

"In here," Lamb said.

The black white man answered, "I saw a nice place back there."

"Ain't for smokes," Snake tittered, enjoying the change which came into his brother's face.

They had entered a lunch-counter restaurant adjacent to the dining room Emery had selected. Both were run by the same company. The dining room sent colored customers next door.

"Sorry," Emery said crisply. "I never accept segregation. I'll wait for you outside."

Lamb followed him through the doors.

Honey said to Snake, "Ain't no use waiting. Won't be able to get past all them people nohow. Ain't going to be no seats."

"Taking a fancy to Emery, is you?" Snake scoffed. "Whee-ee-ee!"

His sneer echoed her own contempt for herself. The feeling had begun when she had stepped on Mrs. Smith's coat. She had never before revenged a white insult. Remembering, she was angry and ashamed and surprised. The whole day lay festering in her thoughts. She heard Snake's whee-ee-ee with hate.

"I wish you was dead!" she told him.

"Thought you ain't wished nobody evil! Now you go to wishing me dead."

"You the onliest one I ever wished evil," she answered, trying not to think of Mrs. Smith and the red-haired man from Rusk & Rusk. She breathed rapidly. Her bosom was tight with anger.

"Evil's more fun than good, just like I'm more pleasure than Emery. Reckon we'd better tell Emery how you're feeling." He pulled at her arm and tried to drag her toward the door.

"Snake, you more'n half drunk. You better go back home. Please, boy, go home!"

"And leave a pretty girl like you here? Leave——"

"Please go, Snake!"

His eyes shone at her hungrily. "Little Virgin of the Ville!" he mocked.

Emery saw how things were from a distance. He started toward them. Then he stopped as if recalling that Snake's girls always made scenes.

Lamb came rapidly. "Cut it," he said to Snake.

"Hush, son, hush your baby talk!" Snake scoffed. In his voice there was a threat.

Honey thought: Snake's jealous of his brother. Not jealous on account of me. Just jealous.

"Go back home, Snake," she pleaded, "till you sober." It was the Ville habit speaking, the matriarchy mothering its men.

"Snake the soberest man in this whole world!" he shouted, waving his arms.

People were watching them.

She wheedled Snake. "Go back, please go back." Pleading, her heart pleaded also with herself, begged her to stop bothering about what happened to Snake, to stop caring.

Before slinking away, Snake growled his hate at Emery, who stood near by, unsurprised, unpained. Honey pitied Snake. An angry man had the right to rouse up anger. She rubbed at the glow Snake's touch had left on her arm.

Without speaking, they returned to the station.

"I'm right ashamed," Honey told Emery. "I done spoiled your visit with your brother." Her lips trembled. "Snake, he evil. He all evil."

Emery's face was of rock.

Gradually his low voice and quiet manner pushed the noise of the station away. They drew Lamb and Honey into a closed room. He seemed a man able to create his own world.

He spoke to Lamb. "You've got the chance to lift up your people. No man in this world, white or colored, has a better chance than you have. The future of this whole country, the future of the whole world is going to be made—or broken— by what happens to the colored man in industry. Snake took the discontent of the fellows in your plant and led them into a union. You've got them now, and you can make strong union men of them or let them remain only malcontents. The difference is a matter of where you're aiming for and why and how. If you make union men of them, you'll have to see to it that the union sticks by. CIO has some fine leadership. Also some Quislings. Sometimes I think historians searching for a name for our age will call it the Quisling Era. Quislings everywhere. Quislings in the Army who can't bear to treat a soldier as a soldier—rather lose the war than give up treating a black soldier as a nigger. . . . It's that way in the unions too. I like to think that, by the time this fight is over, it won't seem like the Quisling Era any more. Might really have democracy. We'll have a chance at it anyhow. It's you fellows in the unions who've got to see this thing whole—and lead your men honestly. No matter how tough they treat you as Negroes, you've got to go on. Democracy, like peace, is indivisible. You've got to fight for the whole thing. You can't win any other way. . . . You've got to behave as if you know you are men of destiny."

Lamb said, "You mean that Negroes must fight for their rights as men, not as Negroes?"

"Exactly. They must line up on the side of freedom. Wherever that is. Sometimes the other side holds out plums. Special little prizes for Negroes. They never last. They can't."

Lamb nodded. "That's the way I've been figuring it out. That's where my puzzling has been leading me."

Emery's face returned to rock. "Snake can't be trusted. Courts everything good for the fun of ruining its goodness, ever since our mother died. His father was afraid of the South. Snake tried to stand up to the South. He lost the fight too often. Said he was going to be what they thought he was. After

that he went bad. He was done for. . . . He can't be trusted."
Emery looked at Honey coldly. Her face was disorderly with
shame.

He turned toward Lamb. "You're the one who counts. Get
rid of Snake. Report him to the police if you have to. . . .
Once they find out who he is, they'll arrest everyone within
a mile of him." He glanced at his watch. "It's been fine to have
this talk."

Lamb had been nodding happily as Emery spoke about the
union. Now he asked in a troubled voice, "You believe in this
war?"

"It's the opening act. Has to be won before Act Two can
come. If I hadn't believed that, I wouldn't have broken my
rule about not accepting segregation. I didn't like going into a
segregated army, but I saw that it had to be this time. Act One
has to come through to a sane conclusion. In Act Two you'll
be the leading man. It's a great trust—a very great trust, sir."

Then he was gone.

Lamb's lips repeated, "A very great trust, sir." Joy widened
his eyes. He spread his shoulders, a good man vowing to be
strong.

Honey shuddered. If this here union business got sense to
it like Mr. Emery said, if Lamb gives up his dream this time to
something do got sense to it, then Lamb he might be on the
right glory wagon at last. Lamb, he might!

She tried to feel pleasure in it. Hadn't she loved and suffered
and done for Lamb all these years? Hadn't he turned out
good? She could take pleasure in nothing.

Outside, Snake leaned against the building, waiting. He had
been drinking again. His eyes were bloodshot and his breath
strong, but the last drink had quieted him.

He's solid mean, Honey thought. She expected Lamb to
chase him off, but Lamb's thoughts were with Emery up on
the glory wagon, making plans for driving it the way Emery

93

said it should go. He had forgotten the part about getting rid of Snake.

Honey said, "I'm through with you, Snake—for good."

Snake slid his hand up her arm. They walked the several blocks to the Auditorium without speaking. At first they were surrounded by crowds leaving the station, then by crowds approaching the Auditorium. Furious anger pummeled Honey's heart. She walked in fear of herself, fear that she might not be able to pull free of Snake, that she could not go on wanting to.

At the Auditorium corner they were delayed by a steady stream of traffic. The policeman in the center of the street, answering a motorist's question, forgot to change the direction of the flow. The crowds joked about it. The laughter made them one crowd, happy-hearted with the pleasure of Thanksgiving Day.

It ain't been no Thanksgiving Day for me, Honey thought. It filled up with hate. I ain't never done nothing to fill it with hate. It just been that way.

Snake knew a short cut into the building. He led them along a side street. They entered by a door marked PRIVATE. Down the hallway a sweaty-faced white man in a business suit ran toward them. He shouted commandingly, "You boys come in here and help! Fast! This thing's giving trouble."

He hustled them off. Snake went meekly, Lamb with a frown.

From the doorway Honey watched. It was the strangest place she had ever seen. The sides were of brick and extremely tall, with an unfinished look, as if this part of the building had never been completed. Tangles of black wires hung on hooks near the distant ceiling.

Huge, flat walls stood about as if they had strayed from a monstrous house. To Honey the scene was grotesque and frightening and without meaning.

She bent her head far back, trying to see the top of the

hundreds of ropes which rose like the pipes of a giant organ. Far overhead were two railed iron walks, the first higher than the Palmer roof, the second again as high. A man stood on the top one.

At her elbow a large instrument board sparkled with lights of various colors. Levers of red and orange and green were guarded from casual hands by an iron cage painted gray.

Staring, Honey thought: That thing with all them lights, it ain't nothing but white man's talk. It's something they learn each other. Lamb ain't had no chance to learn it. Or Snake.

Just don't go to feeling sorry for Snake, she warned herself, only for Lamb. Once you felt sorry for Eulatha, and now Eulatha, she's just kind of trash. Then you went to feeling sorry for Carmen, and now Carmen, she's too stuck up for the Hoops. Then you went to feeling sorry for Mama, and now she ain't sweet no more like she used to be. Lamb, he's the onliest one you can hold to in your heart. And Snake don't mean him no good!

Lamb and Snake were helping a half-dozen stagehands tug at a rope, trying to swing it under a wheel for fastening. Snake panted hard. His feet slipped. After that he stood near by, not helping.

Soon he began to walk about, swaying and staring and mumbling. Once Honey thought she saw the switchblade flashing, but the next second it wasn't. Very likely it had only been suspicion flashing in her heart, accusing Snake.

I believe you crazy, Honey Hoop, you plum crazy, she told herself. You sure crazy.

When Lamb finished, he rubbed his palms with his handkerchief while he, too, looked around, amazed. Snake had gone outside.

The policeman in the passageway told them to enter the Auditorium by the front door.

Honey said to Lamb, "That place in there, it's high like heaven."

"Secret to us like heaven," Lamb answered.

Honey thought: Lamb, he's in a baptizing spell again. She spoke gently, "It looks right mixed up, like as if it don't make sense. That's not like heaven. That's like living on earth."

Lamb thought out loud: "Those hands in there were AFL. I could tell by their buttons."

"Don't go to letting your glory wagon hurt you, Lamb boy!" she warned. Yet within her heart she could feel his hope stirring her own. He was a mighty good boy, Lamb was, and that Mr. Emery shared his dream. Somewhere there must be a better chance stored up for their people. Maybe this was it. She didn't have to wait to understand it before she could believe in it and defend it. She just had to go on sticking by Lamb. Ever since he was born, Lamb had had something special in his ways.

They hadn't seen Snake, but he stepped forward and took Honey's arm.

Soon he ought to have his revenge against the uppety white man. More than once his switchblade had cut men in fights. This time it cut ropes. Two ropes. A wide rope and a thin rope. Not clear through, so that all that weight it took a half-dozen men to pull up would fall down right away. The big fire curtain too. Just little cuts. Neat little cuts. An expert's wrist turned so far, no farther. Snake knew ropes well—sawmill ropes; steamboat ropes; all kinds of ropes. Nearly every job he had ever worked on had ropes in it. A cut rope could ruin lots. Stop a factory. Free a boat. Rope was fine for getting even.

A cut in a rope was like a dead mother in a family. Put weight on, and it pulled apart. One strand would tear. The next, tear further. When? Well, nobody could be right sure. Snake could be almost sure. A cut rope gave a fellow time to get away. He'd cut ropes before.

96

9

THE GOLD DECORATIONS, THE LIGHTS, THE MARBLE FLOOR, the handsome wide stairway, the spacious magnificence startled Honey. A world polished and pretty and, Lamb said, hers.

She mourned: I wish I felt nice inside so's I could enjoy it. I wish I felt like as if I was good. Like I done this morning.

Aloud she said, "Mr. Palmer, he ain't got nothing to be ashamed of. Looks like they ain't going to be no empty seats."

Lamb answered, "Reckon CIO got out a crowd. They and Mr. Palmer are agreed about black skin—that it's the man inside that counts. In the CIO constitution it says color mustn't rule against a man."

"That sounds just like Mr. Palmer."

Others who entered the lobby, gaudy with life and lights, were slapped into speech. The sudden chatter. Black men and black women with happy eyes. White men and white women with solemn eyes.

Mostly the costumes of the black women were handsomer than those of the white women, their heels higher, colors brighter, garments newer. Their hats and earrings and gloves matched. The white women had come to disavow superiority, the black women to disavow inferiority. Persuasively, the fine clothes of the black women—not really black, but brown or tan or white-to-look-at—spoke to the white folks, assuring them that their wearers were clean, intelligent, decent people.

The black women could see the argument succeeding. They wore their bows and beads triumphantly. On their bodies a flower, a fur coat, a glittering ornament, like castanets in the hands of a Spanish dancer, came to life.

Inside the lobby there was a web of voices weaving across their greetings, talk of the future, that things would be better, that this meeting was one of the steps toward a better world. Those from Enright Avenue could prove that it was already better; they gave examples; they were the leaders, and they had led more efficiently than the grumbling Ville would admit. The Ville said it believed what it could see with its own eyes. The more money it earned, the harder white people pushed in the streetcars. This was just a place to go, nothing to turn dizzy about.

White men in the lobby, talking to each other, spoke of good will between the races. White women talking to each other said the city had some fine-looking colored people, but the cleaning women who came these days were so grudging that they ought to be called the measure-for-measure women.

On her way to the Auditorium Carmen drew her head down deep into the fur collar of her coat. She walked with her shoulders lifted. Her hat had been selected for its power to conceal. Her cheeks were heavily powdered.

To further disguise her color, she walked alone in preference to joining a group of brown girls on the other side of the street. They had been her classmates at high school but later became maids and then defense workers and from those realistic vantage points laughed at Carmen Hoop's *dicktee* ways. They were snickering now. Carmen heard them say something about Deep South niggers. She knew they were referring to Big Mama's cotton-picking days.

At the next corner Carmen turned to escape them. In so

doing she nearly bumped into a girl as brown-skinned as herself and without benefit of powder.

After a second of hesitation, Carmen greeted the girl effusively.

Let that show the gigglers! They made faces and went on their way.

The girl was Loraine, Ben's sister.

Momentarily lowering her shoulders, Carmen asked, "Are you going to the Auditorium?"

Loraine frowned. "I reckon not," she said. By a succession of excuses and fibs Loraine concealed her mother's banning of the world beyond the Ville.

"You haven't applied for a teaching position."

"I help my brother in his business."

"Brother Ben?" Perhaps Loraine didn't know that Ben came to see Honey. Very likely he was ashamed of Honey, who had never gone to a city school, only to that one-room thing down in the cotton country.

"He's going to take Mama and Honey and me to hear the Choristers tonight."

Primly Carmen drew in her lips. "I don't fancy spirituals. I like Beethoven and Verdi."

"You don't like 'Motherless Child'?"

Carmen shook her head energetically. She had often thought that were she a motherless child she'd be better off.

" 'Swing Low, Sweet Chariot'? "

Carmen shook her head again. "They're not to my taste."

"I like 'Joshua Fit De Battle of Jericho—Jericho.' " Loraine was almost jigging it.

Carmen cocked her head shrewdly. "Does your brother like spirituals?"

"He likes 'Precious Lord' and 'Beautiful Garden of Prayer' and 'When I Have Done My Best' and 'Face to Face.' We use them at our services."

Carmen's expression stumbled from acuity to bewilderment. She wasn't sure whether those were spirituals or whether they weren't. She drew her shoulders higher.

"I like those songs very much," she said finally.

"I don't," Loraine answered.

A mischievous twinkle brightened Loraine's eyes. Was Loraine making fun of her? Why?

"I'm afraid I'm-I'm late," Carmen stuttered. "I'm afraid I must-must be g-going along n-now."

Her embarrassment nearly shed tears. She walked away. Her head drew down deeper between her shoulders. Her feet minced more elegantly. Loraine was queer. Not up to her brother.

Very likely Ben was not much either—or he wouldn't have picked an uneducated girl like Honey. The only one of the Hoops who had never finished grade school. Even Eulatha finished.

Carmen's outing had lost all pleasure. She wanted not to go. She stood still. She didn't want to return home.

You have to go, she told herself. When Honey gets set, she's set. Makes a god of her old Mr. Palmer. If he's so much, why does he want to bother with black folks? Why does he?

The question and its lack of answer restored her confidence. She might not be able to powder away the dark in her cheeks, but she could think as white people thought. She knew she could! She'd learned it! It was what made her supervisor call her "valuable to the school system"! Outside the Ville, she wasn't laughed at.

The elegance of the Auditorium always made Carmen feel good. It made her feel as if she was a nice person going to a lovely place.

She wanted to be nice more than she wanted anything except being treated as a nice person. That would be best of all. To be able to walk along the street, lady of refinement with white skin, of course. Then everyone would see that she was respectable and treat her with deference. A nice person was a person whose body was of no importance to herself or to anyone else. A colored skin somehow made the body most important of all.

It had been lonely in the Ville until she had discovered the Library. In the borrowed books she met lots of well-bred children. All of them were white. The Five Peppers. Elsie Dinsmore. The Twins. Because they played with dolls, as a little girl she had written to Santa Claus for a doll. Bitterness still poured like slime down her throat when she remembered that the doll he had brought was black.

There were other betrayals. Carmen learned to expect them. She learned that the only important betrayal was betrayal of herself. And that she never did. She kept on looking around her, studying the heroines in the movies, studying the faces of important people in the newspapers. Important people were white. The rule was invariable. By the time Ville papers got around to the idea that tan-skinned people were beautiful, it was too late to convince Carmen.

She wanted to live out there in the big river Emery had talked about to Ben, but she wanted to be the only colored person there, so it was after all not the sort of river Emery meant. Her desire was a very simple one. She just wanted to move about the world as a fine person. Some of the colored teachers were satisfied to be accepted as fine for colored persons. But Carmen accepted no modification. She wanted to be a fine person, and that meant first of all being white.

She never carried it so far as wanting to marry a white man. It wasn't her husband who had to be admired. It was Carmen. So that if a man rich enough to let his wife live like a lady, even a man with a skin as black as Ben Boston's, should ask her to marry him, she would. She'd be a little ashamed when she was with him on the street, but she'd be kind to him when they were alone. Let him see she was being kind. Forgiving the blackness of his skin. They would marry as white folks married, with tulle and a long satin train and white flowers in the church and candlelight so soft that people would whisper to inquire whether the bride was really part Negro. She'd have a house as elegant as the most elegant white houses, like the pictures in the magazines which showed glamorous white women sitting on luxurious chairs in handsome rooms. In the afternoons she would go to white movies, her powdered cheeks slipping her by the ticket taker, or she'd read novels about white women.

For some time Carmen stood in the dusk of the passageway between the inner and outer doors of the Auditorium lobby. She stood far back in the corner, so that a time or two those coming through the westernmost door glanced in her direction, peering, she thought, to see whether she was white or Negro.

She admired the white men and women walking past. The women wore tailored coats and low-heeled shoes, showing that all this was no great affair in their lives. They came mostly in twos and talked soberly.

Negroes were making a party of it. They had come five or six to an automobile and entered the lobby together talking gaily, proud of the fuss the city was making over them, chattering softly, fluffing their fur-clad shoulders, tossing their bristling hats.

The men were calmer about it. This wasn't a zoot-suit crowd. The men were dressed like prosperous businessmen, shoes highly polished, coats neat, letting the women make the show.

When her feet grew cold, Carmen went into the lobby too. She looked around for one of the teachers from her school. There was only one she'd care to sit with. Then a white woman bowed—"How-do-you-do, Miss Hoop!" It was that supervisor who was cordial to all colored people, the refined and the unrefined. A silly woman, but white, and she had spoken just as in Carmen's dream white women were always speaking to her on busses and streetcars and in stores.

She rushed forward and shook hands with the supervisor and called this a charming event and forgot that it was Honey who had made her go.

Now she felt good all over. She didn't care much whether she met anyone to sit with or not. Walking up the wide marble staircase to the upper lobby, she was sure she was a lady.

The best seats would be on this floor, but here the lobby was only a well, a big square hole where people stood and looked down upon the crowds still coming in. All Carmen could see was the black and white tiles of the floor, that terrifying floor waiting for her to crash through the balustrade. Several times she tried to walk near that railing. Even watching others stand there dropped her stomach until she was dizzy and sick, all the world a murderous floor and she herself smashing toward it. Careful not to look back, she hurried up the next flight of stairs. She could feel, back of her, the hole, the hungry hole, longing for her, hating her, tempting her.

Upstairs Honey stood near the entrance of the balcony. Carmen tried to conceal herself from Honey. There was a laugh which contained a curse. Honey saw too much and too fast! Carmen pushed through the crowd.

Inside, the balcony was steep and frightening. Cautiously holding to rails and people and seat backs, Carmen approached some vacant places in from the aisle. There were two. She took the one next to a white lady, a white lady who didn't look up to observe her color. Then some nigger spoiled it all by sitting down next to her, a shameless black hussy, likely as not a washwoman who didn't know Shakespeare or the *Ladies' Home Journal* or anything that was admirable. Carmen sat as far away from her as she could, far enough to proclaim that they hadn't come together. Those who watched couldn't be sure it wasn't she and the white women who were friends.

Once Carmen looked over her shoulder and saw Honey watching her. Honey's head was bobbing like a weight on a spring. Her eyes babbled of dimes and dollars fetched from Mrs. Palmer's kitchen. Her mouth in a grimace accepted defeat. It said that Carmen had won; yet Carmen, trying, could not feel the joy of victory.

"Their hair, it looks right nice," Honey said. "The ladies' hair, it does, and the men, they look clean and neat."

The last part was a rebuke to Snake, spoken before she saw that Snake had fixed himself up a little when she wasn't noticing. Buttoned his coat and put a gray muffler around his neck, so the striped sweater no longer showed. He looked better and different.

But he was still high on liquor and behaving as if he knew a good joke. Lamb stared with excitement at the audience. Snake, leaning forward, stared at the stage. He kept counting the empty chairs and hissing in time with the music.

Snake banged one pink palm down on top of the other. "Ever see a flying-high white man go boo-oo-oom?"

"They got a good crowd," Lamb said, ignoring him.

Snake laughed, "Whee-ee-ee. All these people start yelling at one time, whee-ee-ee, it make a powerful lot of noise!"

"Snake, you shut up!"

Honey's left hand wandered fretfully along the edges of her hair. Honey thought: Carmen were ashamed to know me! Lamb, he's sure all I got left. He ain't ashamed none, Lamb ain't. Lamb, he's all right.

The music played louder. A dozen men in business suits crossed the platform and stood before the chairs. Gray suits, blue, brown.

"He's there!" Lamb said, meaning the CIO man.

104

Honey watched Mr. Palmer, all excited about his honor day. She couldn't tell whether he was happy or just trying to be.

Once he looked toward the box where Mrs. Palmer sat with Mrs. Smith, and the fat lady with the green hat and green buttons to match, and the beautiful tall lady, and that little birdy one.

Mr. Palmer, he can be right proud of the crowd. Everybody and his sister is here.

Her heart twisted. Sister! Carmen was a few rows away, sitting there looking like an umbrella folded up for a sunny day.

I ain't going to feel sorry for her. I ain't, Honey thought. I sure ought to bust in her head with a chair.

The orchestra played the "Star-Spangled Banner." Lamb's pretty voice rang out, and people looked around and sang louder and smiled.

The black minister with his eyes scrunched up said his prayer. Then Mr. DuPree spoke, and the mayor, and then the head of the award committee. A string quartet played. Some school children sang.

The sounds entered Lamb's ears, but he heard nothing that was said. He was listening to Emery's voice even more attentively than the first time, trying to make out not only what had been said but beyond that what was meant and what he, Lamb Hoop, could do about it. The whole deal had got entangled with his loyalty to Snake. Didn't a man first have to be loyal as a man before he could do anything for his people?

Very likely Snake was a bad number, but Lamb couldn't shove him off into the jaws of the police to be chewed to bits. Yet if he didn't shove Snake into the jaws, would Lamb ever again feel right inside, and if not, could he go on believing in himself enough to serve his people?

Snake wasn't the sort you could shove off and not turn over

to the law. Whenever Snake had too much, he began to talk about "Oswald," meaning his switchblade and its fights. They were always with someone who had turned on him—"dealt double" with him—as Lamb himself would be dealing double if he told Snake to get going—and the stories always ended, "Then me and Oswald hit the road, and no white man's law never caught up with us none." There had been a lot of those stories.

Perhaps it would be best just to let him go on living at the house and wait. When the union got wise to him, the men would edge him out. But that would be playing double with the men. They took Snake to be Lamb's friend. They had no politics in them yet, except being for friends and against enemies. All whites were enemies and most Negroes friends. They had a lot to learn.

Lamb boy, Lamb said to himself, you can't be a leader of your people and a coward at the same time. You can't do that, you sure can't. . . . And come you're dead, you can't be a leader at all. . . .

Reckon the best thing is to let the law take him. . . . But watching his drooling interest in what went on up yonder on the stage, Lamb only saw that poor Snake was having a nice innocent time watching the show, and the sin of sins for Lamb, no matter what it was for anybody else, was the sin of snitching on your own people, heavily laden as they were, snitching to the white police. Even if a colored police took him to jail, it was only to turn him over to the white avengers.

Lamb remembered the time the police ran him in. Some guys rolled a fellow and stole his money. They ran away. Lamb, knowing he had done no wrong, stood still. The policeman, too fat to catch the others, took Lamb to the station house. In the courtroom a white man told him to plead guilty to get a light sentence. So Lamb said, "Guilty for a light sentence." The judge laughed, "Plead guilty or not guilty!" Lamb answered,

"Guilty, but I never done it." The judge gave him four months in the workhouse. Mr. Palmer fixed everything, but Lamb could still recall the loneliness and the fright. It wasn't any fun to be a black boy with white police. He couldn't do that to Snake.

He began all over again. Began where a decent black man had to begin, standing by his own. Maybe Snake would decide to move, though the way his fingers lusted for Honey . . . Maybe a brother to Honey ought to stick up for her. Seemed silly after all these years of Honey's sticking up for him, for all the Hoops. Kind of funny, anyhow, the way Honey had been a good girl all these years, pretty as she was. He was proud of Honey.

Again he started at the beginning, this time forgetting Honey, who could look after herself. He tried to fit his loyalty to the union and his loyalty to Snake together.

There was loud applause. Lamb realized that he had missed thinking about the award while it was being given, though he had seen it with his own eyes and clapped at the proper time.

Now Andrew Palmer was about to make his speech.

Funny how Mr. Palmer had played god all these years to the Hoops, yet Lamb had never before laid eyes on him. Strange that he looked so much like other white men. Lamb had thought he'd be larger and grander, but there he was at this distance looking like a little man as astonished by the ways of this city as Lamb himself.

Mr. Palmer's voice was deep with trouble, smooth with faith that he could solve that trouble, steady with loyalty.

First he said briefly and firmly that this war had to be won, that winning it meant even more to the Negro's future than to the white man's. He said about the same thing Emery had said about Act One and Act Two, though in different words. Everyone in the hall now understood why the award was being publicly given. Andrew Palmer was the man the Negroes would believe. What he was saying wasn't what Mr. Smith would have him say, but Mr. Rusk and Mr. DuPree looked satisfied.

Then Mr. Palmer changed his tone.

People leaned forward. They were quiet and looked down at Andrew Palmer thoughtfully. He stepped nearer to them, out from the row of men on the chairs.

He didn't stand next to the table where there was a light. Didn't sneak any looks at a piece of paper. There wasn't any piece of paper. He was a man searching inside himself for a speech, finding it there, and now that he was well started he was gazing up at the balcony box where Mrs. Palmer sat, though as if he wasn't seeing her at all.

Then the disaster occurred.

Wild clatter of metal. Roar of giant things smacking the floor. Andrew Palmer struck down, blood gushing from his head. Then he was still. There was rushing about on the platform. A woman's piercing scream. Hundreds screaming. A cloud of dust on the stage hid everything even before the tall purple curtains came rushing at each other. Then the heavy fire curtain fell swiftly, slowing as it neared the floor.

Someone dragged Mr. Palmer's body out of the way. A man yelled words meant to quiet the panic. Lights came on. Eyes glared into eyes. Some were crying. Those which didn't weep had the flat look of eyes which had witnessed the helplessness of man, even of the greatest man. They knew now that every life, though filled with important little pieces, was itself fragile, a struggling second in endless time.

Snake was the first out of the balcony. Lamb remembered later that Snake had pushed by him.

Lamb rushed away from the hall in a daze. Nowadays he knew better than to stand still because he hadn't done wrong. When murder happened, a black man had to run. And not toward home, where they would look for him. When the police freed him again, his body would still suffer from all those blows. His body and his pride.

Back of Lamb klaxons moaned and shrieked. Bells clanged. Huge tires, whining, turned corners short. Lamb slowed to a walk. To run was to be guilty. To loiter was to need locking up. He would walk as if he were going somewhere, not in a hurry, just trying to be on time.

Soon he was downtown. He had been there only a few times before, looking for jobs. The buildings towered unevenly above him. The wide sidewalks were holiday-empty. The manikins in the store windows, pleading for admiration, were white women, coldly inhuman.

Seeing a policeman talking into a corner box, Lamb hurried to the next street. What could he say if they growled, "Where you running to, you?" To buy—on Thanksgiving? To enter one of the tall buildings, locked, and consult a white lawyer who wasn't there? To eat where there wasn't a counter which served Negroes? To see a movie—in a white show house?

"Sir, I heard about a clean-up job on the levee. Friend told me."

"What friend? Boats laid up for the winter. Come along and tell that one to the Chief!"

Lamb pinned his factory badge containing his photograph on his overcoat. That proved the FBI hadn't found anything wrong!

He slowed his pace.

"Where you running to, you?"

"Sir," touching the badge, "I'm on my way to union headquarters."

"O.K. Keep stepping!"

That's what he would say! Somewhere was the building where the union brothers would meet tonight, not on C.P.T. time either, on real time, as it had to be when you turned on your favorite radio program. On the nose!

His steps were steadier now. He was nearing the levee. The buildings were lower. The streets narrow. The sidewalks gone. The cobblestones rounded and slippery. The downhill steep. This was where the city began in place and in time. It was rotting with age.

At the foot of the hill a freight train halted him. Chug-chug-chug-clackety-clackety-clackety. Likely Honey would be worked up about Mr. Palmer. She would have taken on plenty if he had just passed away. Crying off by herself. Quietly. Going out there to help. This way she would—— What would she do? He couldn't remember that Honey had ever lost anyone she loved. Nobody she loved had died. Those she lost—like Eulatha and Carmen—had gone on living.

When the train ended, Lamb crossed the tracks and the street and looked down the levee slope to the tawny water waltzing by. He was standing only a block away from a bridge. The black iron bars formed a huge geometric pattern, formed it again and again and again until it ended in a mist as a sound ends retreating.

It was a stern structure. Once Lamb had seen a bridge which reminded him of a dancer leaping. This bridge didn't leap. It lay flat in mid-air, a sensible bridge with a toy tunnel for trains, another for automobiles, another for those who walked. Tunnels on top of each other.

From the water, pushing up to prop the bridge, rose square rock posts as large as houses. The largest grew at an angle from the levee cobblestones. There a man might find shelter from the wind and from other men, from the police.

Lamb eased toward the place, walking slowly, ostentatiously unhurried. Beneath the bridge he watched the sliding waters and thought about Mr. Palmer, dead.

A man died fast, too fast! Alive-dead. It made life seem not to count for much. Maybe a single life never did count. Lamb's, Mr. Palmer's, Snake's.

110

But the life of a union counted! All its lives could die and the union could go on living. A union counted. More than Lamb's life. Or Snake's.

More than Snake's. Snake should be given to the police. Lamb looked over his shoulder and saw a cop passing on a motorcycle. He moved deeper into the shadow.

Snake's life might be a menace to the union. Or it might not. Until he was sure, Lamb couldn't turn Snake over to the law and still feel good inside, ready for his work. He couldn't. Whatever a man did, he had to see to it that it left him feeling good inside himself. Feeling decent. Clean.

It was time now to go to his meeting. He touched his badge. He moved away from the shadow of the bridge. He climbed the levee with deliberate steps and walked into his city.

10

A POLICEMAN GUARDING THE ENTRANCE TO THE STAGE TRIED to send Honey away. Mrs. Schneider called, "Let her come, she's Mrs. Palmer's maid."

Mrs. Palmer opened glassy eyes. "Oh, Honey!" she moaned. She wept dry, soundless, terrified sobs.

They had carried Mr. Palmer into one of the dressing rooms. Mr. DuPree had a broken arm; the mayor, a sharp cut on his forehead. They were out of sight, receiving medical attention.

A policeman was questioning the stagehands. One was crying and saying things over and over, defending himself. Plainclothes men took notes.

The talking, crying little stagehand in the slack suit seemed to feel the blame was on his shoulders and didn't belong there.

"I was leaning against the guard when he walked out onto the maple. I remember particular he was staring up at the balcony rail of lights—just staring blind-like—and I looked up at the grand traveler up there"—a stubby finger pointed to the looped curtain—"because we'd had a bit of trouble earlier with the sheave to it. Works on a winch steel cable. When I looked it was all right—still all right, it is!" He pointed again. "Ain't nothing wrong with it."

"What hit him?" the officer asked.

"See for yourself. The pipe batten hit him. Had it hung on cable ready for tonight's show, and why that there rope bust I can't tell you——"

"I can tell you!" Mr. Smith, scarlet of face, shouted. "You fellows want your pay and don't want to do a damn bit of work for it!"

The little man blinked. The sense of guilt hovering in his eyes cowered. His mouth was defiant.

"I been on this job twenty years, been flyman, sound man, done every part of it, and I ain't never had so much as a counterweight slip from my hands when I was loading a carrier. I ain't had accidents, I tell you!"

The other stagehands said, "Jim's a good man, he is."

Jim drew a deep breath and went on. "We're used to working in a black-out, come tearing on with them units, and I tell you we ain't had accidents—none of us ain't!"

Mr. Smith shouted, "You had one this time, didn't you?"

"All I'm saying is, I look to them ropes as if they was babies. Ain't a day I don't go over the pinrail as if it was a baby. That rope what broke was five-eighths manila! They were O.K., them ropes were."

"O.K. except they broke!" Mr. Smith yelled, and gasped, and nearly strangled on his rage.

Tears poured down the little man's face. "I tell you I couldn't have been more careful if I'd known my own mother was going to stand right there on the maple where he stood— I couldn't have been more careful!"

"Careful!" Mr. Smith scoffed. "Leaning against something, weren't you?"

"I was waiting to give the signal for the red plush traveler!"

"If you can explain so much, why did the big curtain come down too?"

"I dragged him out of the way of it, didn't I? Out of the way of thirty-seven tons!"

"By that time he was dead!" Mr. Smith shouted.

Honey thought: Lawd Gawd, stop being a Smith! You're bearing down as hard on a white man as if he was a nigger.

Then she remembered when she had seen Snake fooling with those ropes. But how could she turn him over to someone like Mr. Smith? Trying to, she took a step forward. . . . It's Lamb I might get in trouble. . . . Snake'll lie out of it! But Honey, you got to tell! You got to!

"Step back! Step back!" Mr. Smith bellowed at her.

The women grieving, even Mrs. Palmer, wanted to see. They wanted to listen to the little stagehand sobbing out his defense.

"I went over them ropes yesterday morning. Ben, he was lamping the house, and I went up there to the fly floor and the catwalk above, and I looked to my ropes and they was all right!"

Mr. Smith said directly to the policeman, talking past the stagehand's nose: "You can't believe a word they say!"

Anger and panic and grief entangled in the stagehand's face. He turned to the other hands. "What gets me is how come something happened to the steel curtain too." He pointed to the broken cord dangling far above their heads. "That cord ain't nothing but a safety device. It's there for cutting in case of fire. Cord holds the control on the motor and hydraulic cylinder, see? It's the cylinder, oil it is, makes the curtain come in slower at the last. You saw how it done. Comes in fast until the end. Then it's the oil what holds it."

"So two ropes gave?" Mr. Smith shouted.

"The rope to the batten. And the cord to the steel curtain. I don't get it. . . . I don't get it. . . . I just don't get it!"

Mr. Smith turned on his heel. "You deserve to get it! Rank carelessness! Sloppy, filthy work!"

The other stagehands shouted too. "You can't be putting this off on us! Not on Jim——"

Honey thought: They're white men. They can sass their way out. Ain't nobody can prove nothing on them. Ain't nothing to prove. But Snake—— Reckon I got to tend to Snake myself.

She rubbed both her hands upward along her cheeks with

114

hard pressure which dragged the flesh. Her eyes were black and wild.

Mrs. Schneider whispered to Mrs. Palmer, "Your Honey looks as if her world has come to an end."

Mrs. Palmer called, "Honey! Honey!"

Honey knelt at her side. "Mrs. Palmer, I'll be there in time to sleep tonight. Might be late, but I'll come. I'm going now. I got something I got to do."

"You'll stay with me, Honey, until—until afterwards? You'll stay as long as you can?"

"Yes'm." Tears drained down Honey's cheeks. "Poor Mr. Palmer! Lawd Gawd, it weren't right! Oh, Mrs. Palmer, this awful for you! I wouldn't have had this happen none—not for nothing. Not for nothing, I wouldn't."

She rose. Staggering a little, she went away.

An officer led her through a twist of long, narrow halls to an outer door.

A Ville cab was passing. She raised her hand for it and climbed in.

You got to do it, she said to herself. You got to. Your heart got to give him up. Snake's evil, it got to die.

She looked down at her hands lying upturned in her lap. She spoke to them: You got to have the strength. You got to. For Mr. Palmer's sake. For Lamb's sake.

A wide calm now entered her heart. She was in a land of beautiful distant hills. She stood in sunshine. It caressed her, and she wasn't lonely. The birds sang and the flowers smiled and the clouds were soft patches sliding happily across a friendly sky. Her heart forgot Mama's bawling, the children who wanted things tied and untied, Eulatha's sinful, tearing-up ways, Carmen's *dicktee* face sneering at her own sister. In Honey's heart there was no longer any weighing: Ben or Snake, Lamb or Snake. Peace.

She roused up as the cab drove across the last car track into the Ville. She saw the Ville as if it were a far-off place.

115

Mr. White Man, she thought, you can't do it. You done tried and you can't. You just thinks you keeps us separate. You can't keep us separate none. We knows all about you, how it is you live, what you feel, and what you say to each other, when it is we can make you die. You fooling yourself, Mr. White Man, that's what you doing. You can tromp on us and tromp and make us like Snake is, but it ain't good for you neither. . . . You ain't even living private. We got that much. We living private. . . .

I done wrong ever since I set foot in Mr. Palmer's house. 'Cause I ain't never been sure which one I loved most, Mama's house or a white man's house. I ain't never sure. I thought likely I could do right by both. I never were smart enough to know how. I ain't been fair to nobody, not to Palmers, not to Hoops, not to Ben, not to Honey, not even to Lamb.

When she entered the door, they stood back in a wide, dark circle. The little children were crying. The big were fidgety. Mama had heard, over the radio. She sobbed for Honey's grief.

In Honey's face there was no grief. Her eyes were dead, but there was no grief. And no excitement. Honey was quiet, fierce quiet. And steady.

Eulatha said, "Snake, he's in the basement."

Carmen said, "Mr. Ben phoned his sympathy. He said . . ."

Honey walked through them. She dropped her coat on the floor.

She went to the kitchen. They heard her pull out the knife drawer. Eulatha saw her click at the blade with her thumb.

They saw her open the inside door to the basement. They heard the key turned from the other side.

In the dim light Honey could see only the green gleam from the radio, faintly shining, faintly babbling. Babbling about Mr. Palmer, dead.

116

For a moment she wept for love of Snake, wept because even now she half wanted him.

She told herself she must be strong enough to kill his evil. She told herself she was strong enough. It was nothing the white man's world needed to know about. Here, in their city apart, black folks, pushed aside, were left to struggle and suffer, private. They could kill private, too.

Breathing deeply, she hurried toward Snake's cot. On the pillow was the hollow made by his head; on the floor glinted a smashed bottle. Along the wall the row of nails was cleared of his clothing. Snake was gone.

Making herself strong, Honey had knotted her feelings into readiness for action. Now there was nothing to do with them. Of a sudden they fell apart, frantically beating themselves against one another, leaving her weak and weary. She sobbed and shivered and tried to look into the dark cavern of her own heart, which loved Snake and yet wanted him dead. She saw only that Lamb was safe and Snake gone from her forever. Briefly she pitied Snake, fleeing always, always from his own evil.

When at last Honey roused herself, the black of night had come not only to the basement but to the outdoors and to the Hoop house except for a light in the kitchen. It cast long thin shadows, sharp with elbows and knees, through the other rooms and into the hall.

They heard Honey climbing the stairs with the steps of an old woman shaken by fatigue. They heard her unlock the door. They were afraid of what they saw in her eyes.

Mama sobbed, "My Gawd, Honey, what you done? What-for you done it?"

"I ain't done nothing. I ain't had to. Snake, he lighted out."

Mama wept, "You always been the bestest of my children!"

Honey spoke hoarsely. "I'm going and I won't be back."

117

Tears streamed down Eulatha's face. She pleaded, "Ain't nobody going to tell! Nobody!"

"That's right, ain't," Honey answered. "Ain't nobody going to tell. Ain't nobody know what there is to tell. . . . I'm running out on the Ville. Seems like I seen my share of wrongs and hating for wrongs. I'm going to do like Mrs. Palmer wants."

"Why-for you don't marry Ben?" Mama begged.

"I'm going to live in Mrs. Palmer's basement. I'm going to live there alone. I'm going to be what comfort to Mrs. Palmer I can." She no longer looked angry. Or sad. Her face had the swollen blankness of a little girl's.

Mama rocked her shoulders in anguish. "My Gawd, Honey, you ain't did nothing to deserve being laid away from your people alive! You can't have no pleasure living in Mrs. Palmer's basement——"

"It's what I'm going to do," Honey said. "Tell Lamb . . . tell Lamb not to come to see me. . . . Tell Lamb particular I want he should live his best."

Her shoulder stiffened and shoved away the wall she had been leaning against. She walked past them as if she could no longer see them or feel their woes.

11

THE JANUARY TWILIGHT STRETCHED LAVENDER SHADOWS across the fresh snow of the Palmer back lawn, making it look like the Christmas card Honey had saved from Mrs. Palmer's wastebasket.

Standing at the window of the unlighted kitchen, Honey watched the dark spread until the only white remaining was a streak around the iced lily pond and another along the lip of the birdbath. A shawl of snow hanging unevenly over the trash can turned purple where it trailed the driveway.

Hearing Mrs. Palmer's step creak the landing, Honey flipped on the light and hurried to put the chops in. There were two chops, both for Mrs. Palmer. Honey could have ordered some for herself. The Palmers had never been like those people who bought treats for themselves and trash for the girl who cooked them.

Sometimes Mrs. Palmer would say, "Why, Honey, what are *you* going to eat?" and Honey would answer, "I'll take some the soup left from last night and maybe a biscuit with my coffee." Then Mrs. Palmer would answer, "Be sure you have enough. You know you're welcome to buy the same." Honey would say cheerfully, "I know that, Mrs. Palmer. I'll enjoy the soup. And the biscuits." While she said it Mrs. Palmer frowned at the strange tastes of colored folks. Honey couldn't let her see this was punishment self-inflicted.

119

The two women lived together in a mist which was neither grief nor happiness, but only static melancholy without peak or cessation. After the condolence callers had stopped coming and the thank-you cards for the funeral flowers sent out, Dorothy Jane, quiet and frowning, left for some strange school of her own selection where girls who didn't have to went to work on purpose, calling the jobs education. Then Mrs. Palmer and Honey were really alone, as encased in the house as Mr. Palmer in his coffin. The days became beads on a string, each rounding in the same way as the others toward the night and into the morning.

Honey got up early and cleaned quietly. When Mrs. Palmer was ready, sitting up in bed with her pink wool shawl across her shoulders, Honey carried up her breakfast on the four-legged tray. She would ask, "How did you rest, Mrs. Palmer?" and Mrs. Palmer, looking as yellow as chicken fat, would tell how often she had heard the clock strike and which numbers and what she had done between times to coax herself to sleep —an aspirin or a drink or a different pillow.

Sometimes Mrs. Palmer, sipping the last of her coffee, would suggest the evening menu, but mostly she would say, "Anything, Honey. Anything will do." On those days Honey would rub Mrs. Palmer's back and pull down the shades for another nap, or say she'd be so much obliged if Mrs. Palmer would mend that curtain which came to pieces when Honey washed it.

Sometimes Mrs. Palmer went downtown to "the box" or to "take some papers to the lawyer" or to have those oil treatments for her hair which Honey said were needed to stop its falling out. When Mrs. Palmer returned she was always exhausted and needed to nap. In bad weather Honey fixed her a pretty lunch, prettier than formerly and more to eat. Mrs. Palmer was getting fatter. These days she ate faster, as if she had to have her dinner hour over with because the

120

empty places at the table were too empty, or perhaps it was only that her secret self demanded pleasure, any kind of pleasure.

Tonight as she ate her chops she and Honey talked, as they did every evening, Honey standing near the swing door to the pantry, leaning lightly against the jamb, her hands folded ashamedly beneath her organdy apron. She had stopped using polish on her nails.

Mrs. Palmer was saying, "I hate January. So much snow."

Honey said, "Yes'm. Snowed all afternoon. But the lawn is right pretty."

"Mr. Palmer always used to say snow was like powder on a woman's face. Covered up all the blemishes and made what was ugly, pretty. He didn't know I used powder."

"Mr. Palmer, he loved the lawn, didn't he?"

Then they began the do-you-remembers with which they were wont to live Mr. Palmer's life over again: the time he washed Junior's face in snow; the time he stuck his cigar in the mouth of the snow man Bruce built; the time he forgot his overshoes and caught that dreadful cold. Or the way he used to say, "Soon as I saw this snow, I knew Honey'd have soup. Funniest thing, the way that girl can turn snow into soup!"

"For a long time Bruce-y believed that," Mrs. Palmer said, staring into the dimness of the living room as if she could see Bruce-the-believing-little-boy in the shadows.

Honey hurried in to turn on more lights. She lighted the white porcelain lamps next to the pair of love seats facing each other beside the fireplace. One was where Mrs. Palmer always sat; the other where Mr. Palmer used to read his newspaper. Then Honey went into the sunroom to turn on the light beneath his picture.

Unmoving, she faced him for a moment, then snapped on the piano lamp under which Miss Dotty Jane used to practice. Honey turned the lamp off again. Quickening her steps, she lighted the one on Mr. Palmer's desk and spread out some stationery.

Back in the dining room she asked, "Has we wrote to Mr. Junior this week?"

Mrs. Palmer cleared her throat. "It's so hard to write when he never does."

"They don't let them prisoners write."

"I know," shaking her head. "I'm planning to write soon."

Honey returned to the living room and stood Mrs. Palmer's knitting box next to her lamp.

With just this much illumination the room was prettiest. The floors shone, the table tops glowed; the picture frames had bright lines along their gold. Honey looked up at the urns on the mantel.

"Mrs. Palmer," she said as she brought the dessert, "it would be right nice to have some greens in them urns. Maybe next time you buy flowers for the cemetery you could get us a few branches of something."

Mrs. Palmer frowned. Honey tended the house as if it were a shrine. Sometimes Mrs. Palmer was almost jealous. Sometimes she felt as if Honey were trying to marry her to the place now that Mr. Palmer was gone.

"Mr. DuPree says I ought to give up the house——"

Honey nearly dropped the cup of coffee she had refilled. "Reckon you done told Mr. DuPree to stick to his lawyering?"

"He says the house is most of what I own."

"You don't need much else."

"Oh, he says I could stay, but it hardly seems worth the sacrifice."

Honey wasn't leaning against the jamb now. "What sacrifice do he mean?"

Mrs. Palmer's fork pushed at the last bite of pie on her plate. It was a rich pie, an overlarge individual pie made of Honey's flakiest crust with lemon filling. Mrs. Palmer gave the fragment another jab. She frowned at it and drew her lips in and licked at them. She had on a black dress which sagged down and showed the top of her plain white slip.

"He says I ought to live at a nice residential hotel where I'd be with people."

"I been telling you to have your cousins in to dinner."

"At the place he means you don't have to bother with inviting and all that. You live upstairs in a nice apartment, and when it's time for dinner you go downstairs and you're bound to meet people. You don't have to eat alone. Each one pays for her own dinner. You don't have to make any effort to invite and all that. You're not alone. You're with people."

"What people?"

"Oh, they're nice people. I don't know them, but living there you get to meet them and you're never alone."

Honey, breathing fast, walked out into the hall and switched off the chandelier, which was four candles hanging in a glass tube. She polished that tube every other day.

"Reckon we don't need this one," she said and in its stead turned on the green-shaded lamp under the mirror. She kept at the house as if it were a pretty bow to be lovingly arranged and pridefully rearranged on the head of a beloved child.

When she returned to the dining room Mrs. Palmer had cleared her plate and was folding her napkin. Honey picked up the soiled dishes and started toward the kitchen.

Midway she turned around and asked, "Where-at is going to be the home for the boys and Miss Dotty Jane to come back to?"

"Mr. DuPree says it's cheaper to rent a room when you need it."

Honey went on out into the kitchen. She heated the soup and cut two biscuits open and spread syrup over them and poured a cup of coffee. She sat down on the stool too high for the kitchen table.

She knew Mrs. Palmer would come and stand and talk to her the way she talked to Mrs. Palmer while she ate.

They lived together in a separateness the neighborhood would have approved. She showed Mrs. Palmer the respect the world expected her to show. She knew Mrs. Palmer liked her for it.

But now Honey could see that, even so, she wasn't anybody much in Mrs. Palmer's life. All her efforts to please Mrs. Palmer hadn't made Mrs. Palmer feel as if she were being with anybody. She'd feel better with those strangers she didn't know, people who never had met Mr. Palmer but were just nice people. . . . Who would say the do-you-remembers with her then?

A stiff place in Honey's throat blocked the soup as she tried to swallow. When she heard the swinging door whine, she stopped trying.

Mrs. Palmer said, "You oughtn't to pour out good soup like that, Honey. My father always use to say, 'Waste not, want not!' "

"Yes'm."

"If you'd eat what you dish out for yourself, you wouldn't be so thin."

"Yes'm. I'm about to begin on my biscuits."

"Has the janitor been around for the walks?"

"This is the day he said he wouldn't be coming no more, beginning today. He got him a job in a factory."

"They don't look ahead to when the war's over and those factories close up."

"I'll try to do the walks in the morning."

She could see that Mrs. Palmer didn't really care about the walks. She had forgotten them already. She was asking Honey's advice.

"There's a hotel near the park. In a very nice neighborhood. It has everything right under one roof. Everything. Two dining rooms, the little one for lunch and breakfast, or they'll send trays up. They've got the best maid service in town. Everybody says it's remarkable the way they've kept up their service even in wartime. Their beauty shop is run by the brother of the girl who runs mine. I hear he's even better. And they've got Swedish baths there for my back."

"It sounds right handy."

Mrs. Palmer was touching her palms together. Primly she smiled a little toward Honey's shoulder. "When I give up, there'll be lots of things for you to take home."

"Yes'm."

"Of course I'm just thinking about it. In some ways I don't like the idea. You don't have to worry. Mrs. DuPree will be glad to take you. Says she'll pay whatever I've been paying."

The doorbell rang, a sharp, firm r-r-r-r above their heads. The two women looked at each other in surprise.

"Maybe it's someone wanting to clean the walks," Mrs. Palmer suggested.

Honey straightened her apron. Stepping with something of her former swing, she said over her shoulder, "The men don't need to beg none for work no more."

She peeked between the glass curtains and stepped back quickly.

"Who is it? Why don't you open?"

Honey didn't answer.

"Shall I call the police?" Mrs. Palmer whispered.

Then Honey opened the door for Lamb. She couldn't speak to him. She hadn't seen or heard of any of the Hoops.

"I'm Honey's brother," Lamb said to Mrs. Palmer's frightened face.

The fear left, and now the face was empty of everything but inquiry as to why Lamb had come to the front door.

Honey said, "Mrs. Palmer, my brother, he won't be here but a minute. He come to get something; then he's going right on back."

"To get something?" Mrs. Palmer's tones inquired what was to be taken out of her house.

"Ain't nothing but a note I wrote to Mama."

"Why, Honey, I would gladly have addressed an envelope for you. You oughtn't to bring your brother out on a night like this."

Honey was at the top of the basement steps. "Mrs. Palmer," she said, "I'll be doing my dishes in a few minutes. Lamb, you come down here with me."

Mrs. Palmer moved closer. "Maybe your brother would do the walks."

"No," Lamb said good-humoredly, "her brother came to talk to Honey. He's going to be here a good long while, and he's not going to have time for anything but talk." He smiled and patted Honey on the back and was too much at ease to seem entirely respectful.

As the door closed after them, Mrs. Palmer assured herself that Honey couldn't have had tears in her eyes. It must have been the way the light shone in that back hall. Though you never could be certain of anything with those people, for, even agreeing with Andrew that they were a good race badly treated, they were certainly hard to understand, even Honey.

Lamb paced Honey's room, looking at the snowy Christmas card stuck in the broken mirror, at the rickety chair, and right through the mattress to the sag in the springs. He rattled the coins in his pocket and gave Honey time to get over her gasping. He stamped his shoes, though he had cleaned off the snow outside.

Honey sat down at last on the edge of the bed and asked, "Anything wrong?"

"Lots—all of it with you."

"Lamb, you best go on home. What I'm doing I got to do."

He crossed to his overcoat, hanging on a nail. From the

pocket he took a bag of candy. He put it into Honey's lap. "It's good," he said to her silence. She didn't move.

He waited. Then he said, "I missed out on my supper."

She opened the bag and pulled out a slab of peanut brittle. It was too large for one bite. She broke it in two and handed Lamb one part and then the other. She kept on feeding him, handing him pieces and waiting until he had eaten the last before giving him another. He watched her and ate and teetered on the back legs of the chair and then stood up and said, "You've got to stop this."

She told him she wasn't ashamed of what she was doing.

Lamb pretended he wasn't listening. He whistled and teetered. He smoothed his hair away from its part. Lamb was the only Hoop who had Indian hair, straight and blue-black.

He said, "I'm not interested in ancient history," watching Honey to see whether she knew what he meant.

They were silent for a long time. Then Lamb said, "I got plenty of trouble making history for the future."

"You in trouble, Lamb?"

"I'm in trouble."

She sat still to show that his troubles didn't mean anything to her any more. She sat still for a long while. Lamb sat still too. He put his hand on his stomach as if to soothe its hunger and reached out for another piece of candy.

Giving it to him, she asked, "What you in trouble about? What you done?"

The front legs of his chair plunked down against the concrete. Again Lamb paced the floor.

A slow smile spread his lips. Secret gaiety brightened his eyes. "I've got a half-dozen bosses, one working me harder than the other."

"You lost your job?"

"I've got the most wonderful job in the world!"

He was still working at the plant, he said, though he might

127

be stopping soon. His good job, the one that was swell, he got that when the men voted him head of the plant union. The CIO office downtown was the beginning of a new world. That's what those guys—his other bosses—were trying to do: to build a new world. A world in which a man was treated as a man without regard to his color. He might be working full time for the union pretty soon.

"It's part of the CIO constitution not to let color count against a man. I'm not claiming the rank and file understand it as yet. But the men running things understand it. They know race hatred's a rotten timber in the foundation. They know they have to put in a sound timber before they can build a——"

"How you in trouble, Lamb?"

"This thing's going to change a hell of a lot. The men who run the factories have been used to running them their own way. They're beginning to take orders from those of us who do the work. From Uncle Sam too. They have to let a man have a man's job if he can do it, no matter what his color. They see a big change coming—and they don't like it. They ——"

"Lamb, you look different."

He threw out his chest. "I am different." He slapped himself proudly.

"I reckon I don't understand being happy about being in trouble."

"It's sweet trouble. Sweet—like being in love."

"You in love, Lamb?"

"I'm in love. That's trouble too. Glory's sick. Caught a cold, and it gets worse."

"Is she a—a good girl?"

"Best organizer we got. It's tougher to organize women than men. Don't want to part with their dues."

Honey laughed down at her hands. "The war'll close up one

of these days and all them women'll come back and be cooks."

"Maybe they will and maybe they won't. Nothing wrong with being cooks—if they demand wages and hours and decent conditions—not this!" He waved his hand scornfully.

"Mrs. Palmer's right nice," Honey said.

"They're all nice, I reckon, but the girls ran out of their kitchens like from a plague, first chance they had. You too."

"They'll run back."

Lamb stood up to go. He frowned and seemed to forget Honey. "These are exciting times! If you want to bury yourself alive, I guess it's your business. I've got work to do. . . . Tomorrow's your day out——"

"I ain't been taking no days out."

"Tomorrow's your day out," Lamb repeated slowly. His stubby forefinger, pointing at Honey, stabbed out each syllable. "Glory needs somebody to come in and do for her. Make up her bed and fix her some food. Poor kid's coughing from her heels."

He stopped abruptly and waited.

Honey stood up.

"God, but you're skinny!" he said.

She wet her lips and then didn't speak.

Lamb handed her a piece of paper. "That's where she lives. It's a filthy kind of a rooming house, but all she could get. If you don't go, I'll have to hustle around to find someone else. I haven't time. I've got something big cooking."

"I'll do for her this once. But not no more." They were upstairs before Honey asked, "How's Mama?"

"Yelling around like always," Lamb answered.

Startled, Honey looked at Lamb again. He had never been one to speak against his own. The remark showed that Mama wasn't much in his life now. His words moved the Hoop household far away where Honey could look at it as a stranger might. Her heart raced and pounded.

129

After Lamb left, Honey stood still for a long time trying to see Mama only as an old woman who yelled a lot.

On the streetcar Honey kept thinking of the Bible. "Whither thou goest, I shall go." It was a pretty thing for a girl to say to a mother-in-law. In Honey's head it kept making itself over into something she was saying to Lamb: "Who thou lovest, I shall love."

But when she saw Glory she was too frightened to love her. The girl's skin was greenish, her eyes bloodshot, her lips blistered white.

Honey phoned the doctor. She found his name across the bottle of medicine standing on the marble mantel. He was a white doctor and busy, but he said he would come.

Then Honey hurried to make the room fit to be seen. On every window sill there were plates of uneaten food. Hamburgers brought from a nearby tavern. Lamb's idea of a meal always had been a hamburger sandwich. Empty coke bottles everywhere. Three half-filled milk bottles.

The girl's wardrobe was neat with skirts and suits and blouses carefully ironed. On a chair stood an overnight bag with toilet articles, opened but not unpacked, as if Glory intended to move.

The house was below Grand Boulevard, in the region the Ville scorned. It was tall and thin like an aged, shabby spinster, part of a row of houses which once had contained grandeur and pride. The ceilings were high. In Glory's room there were three beds. She had slept in all of them.

Wanting clean sheets, Honey searched for the landlady. All the doors were locked. The halls were dark and smelled of wet carpets and cooked cabbage and sleep. Honey went back to the second floor and with the cleanest of the sheets made up one of the beds fresh. When she moved the girl into it, she opened her eyes. "Bob send you?" Glory asked.

"Lamb sent me."

The blistered lips smiled sweetly. Honey saw that she loved Lamb.

"Who's Bob?" Honey asked.

"Headquarters." The voice was dry.

Whatever that place is, Honey thought, they take care of their own, come they're sick. That's something in their favor. Come Honey was sick and not part of Big Mama's family no more, what would happen to her? For a second Honey, wide-eyed, saw herself sicken in gloomy solitude and die, alone.

Tidying the room, Honey learned that Glory's name was really Gloria and that she was a graduate of the same college Miss Dorothy Jane was at now. Honey stood still and stared at the green-tan skin and shiny, straightened hair and tried to encompass that fact.

When the doctor came, he listened to Glory's chest and said he couldn't understand why Bob hadn't let him know sooner. He said he was a friend of Bob's, but he said it as if he wanted to be, though something held them apart. Bob was the best in the world. This young lady here was the best in the world, too, and he would send some medicine which ought to do the trick. Might make her sight blurry for a while, but never mind about that. Ought to be in a hospital, but every hospital had a waiting list.

He was a plump, jolly man who kept singing under his breath: "All's right with the world." He said he'd be back and he'd expect Glory to be well enough to tell him about the convention at which she caught this cold. Honey should stay with her, he said in going.

"I can't stay after dark. I got to get back. I got someone afraid to be alone after dark."

"Tell her to come on down and sit with you."

Honey smiled a little. "I can't stay," she said.

"I'll phone Bob."

Honey did everything the doctor told her to do and a lot of cleaning up besides. Gloria slept most of the time, moaning and coughing and waking up and sleeping again.

About five o'clock there was a knock on the door.

The girl in tan slacks had worked at the factory when Honey was there. She remembered Honey.

"You were always sweet to everybody," she said, "but you never came to meetings."

"I don't remember nothing about meetings."

"You never took any interest when we announced them." It was an accusation.

Honey answered, "This is how to give the medicine."

The girl listened attentively. When Honey was ready to go, she helped her on with her coat. "I didn't mean any harm." The bright red lips in the dark face twisted into an embarrassed smile. "You older ones aren't used to it, I guess. Lamb Hoop's doing a wonderful job!"

"What he doing?" Honey asked.

"Building a swell union. Largest in the city. Bob says he's good on negotiations too."

"Bob knows a lot, I reckon." Honey spoke sarcastically, hating Bob.

"Bob's doing a lot for the colored workers in this city."

Honey raised her head quickly. "This Bob, ain't he colored?"

"Bob Jensen? He's white."

Honey looked toward the sick girl to whom Bob, white, had sent a doctor, white too. She had figured out, when the doctor said Bob was a friend of his, that all he meant was that Bob's brother worked for him as a chauffeur, or something else like that.

On Wednesday night the phone rang, and Lamb asked Honey to go down to Gloria again. He was in a hurry and didn't seem to hear her protests. There was the hum of nobody-on-the-line.

This time the room was neater and Glory was sitting up in a chair with a quilt around her legs. She didn't recall Honey's former visit but told her Lamb's sister was welcome.

For a little while Honey just sat with her hands folded like company. She stole looks at Glory when she could. Lamb hadn't picked a pretty girl. Her eyes were too excited for that. Pop-eyed, with long black lashes. But it was a face Honey liked. The head was neatly shaped, the mouth always smiling. In Glory's ways there was a swagger as in Lamb's.

Gloria leaned forward and took Honey's fingers in hers. "You love him very much, don't you? You love Lamb."

Honey hadn't expected the question or her own tears. She got up and began to tidy the room. "Tell me about Gloria," she said.

The girl laughed. "Once upon a time there was a black family in white America. It lived in Massachusetts, where being black wasn't so different from being white as it is some other places. Little Gloria was the one and only child. Her mother was a trained nurse. Her father was a mail carrier. Glory went to school with white boys and girls and sometimes topped her class. Her mother and father began planning to send her to college before she was born. By the time she was five, they had the money put by for it.

"Glory did go to college. She went for one year to Wellesley and learned enough to know there was something wrong with just wanting to get ahead in the world. She tried another college. She studied some and thought some and held some jobs. She learned that you had to decide how to be black. You could let it sink you. Or scare you. Or spoil you. Or stimulate you. Glory decided to be stimulated.

"She met a white girl who thought the labor movement had been eating the only vitamins on the American market. They

133

argued a lot, Glory saying the future was being shaped by the Y.W.C.A. and the white girl saying it was being made by the unions. After they left school the white girl took a job with the Y.W.C.A. and Glory took a job with the union. She came up the easy way. She hates to have people find out she never went hungry or worked in a factory because she had to. She counts herself lucky. She's met the grandest people in the world! She's happy all day long."

Coughing slowed the story a time or two. At its end the coughing was very hard. Honey made Glory lie down.

They didn't talk much more, but they became friends. Their feelings met and were satisfied.

When Honey put her coat on, Glory said, "Come next Thursday."

"You won't need me. You'll be well."

Glory had been lying on her abdomen, ready for sleep. Now she turned over and opened her eyes. They fluttered. She smiled. "I won't need you. I'll just want you."

Spring tinged the shrubs green before Mrs. Palmer phoned an agent to say her house was for sale. Honey knew nothing about it until a tall, pale woman with a parrot face and a dove voice came to the door one morning twirling her folded eyeglasses on a silver chain and said she had her notebook with her and was ready to take down the facts. Mrs. Palmer at the top of the stairs called for her to come up. After that there was low talk and every closet door opened and the next day a sign on the front lawn.

"It might not be for a long time," Mrs. Palmer said, but Honey could see that the parrot-faced woman meant business.

Nearly every day she brought someone to "look." They would say things against the house. Honey thought they had no manners. She hated their talk about old-fashioned fixtures and walls awful in color and windows which were hideous. One couple said the partition between the back sunroom and the living room would have to be torn out, but even then Mrs. Palmer didn't object.

At last it happened. After the parrot-faced woman left with Mrs. Palmer's signature on her papers, Honey stood in the dark of the pantry, shivering. She could hear Mrs. Palmer at the telephone telling her cousin that she was "rid" of the house at last.

Selling the furniture was worse. Mrs. Palmer put an ad in the Sunday papers, and the doorbell rang before she was out of bed. Wartime shortages and newcomers in town and a fine June morning brought a steady procession of people in search of dishes or rugs or silver. The well-dressed, older ones asked for antiques. Nearly everyone asked for electric irons and carpet sweepers and vacuum cleaners. Honey heard them praise a little table which had never given anything but trouble, a leg coming off every time she dusted. As each piece went out, its going thinned Honey's desire to live. Her eyes were moist as she packed Mrs. Palmer's nice dishes for those strangers.

At last she protested: "When Miss Dorothy Jane gets married, she ain't going to have nothing to prove that she came from people."

"Dotty Jane wouldn't want any of my old trash. The young folks want everything modern."

Lots of those who came in—not the war workers in slacks, but the ones who knew about Mr. Palmer—would look at the urns on the mantel, take them down and turn them over and snap their fingers at them. They would say they looked as if they were good but they weren't really.

Later Honey would mutter, "Them urns is good. If they look good, they is good. Got to be! Ain't nothing else to them but how they look and can they hold water. Them urns ain't got a crack!"

"I'll be lucky if I get ten dollars for them. I'd give them to you, Honey, but I think you ought to have something more practical."

"I don't want nothing practical."

"Then take the urns. I hate to see you behave like that, Honey, when you could have that bed in Miss Dorothy Jane's room."

Honey carried the urns to the basement.

All week long Mrs. Palmer accepted money in exchange for things whose very nicks recorded the lives of the Palmers: the chair Bruce-y used to sit in to practice his saxophone, the bookcases Junior built at school, the dressing table Mr. Palmer bought to surprise Dotty Jane on her twelfth birthday, the bed he slept in, the dining-room set he gave Mrs. Palmer for their anniversary. She was selling the lives of her own folks! Once in the middle of the night Honey said out loud, "There's more'n one way to cut a throat!"

The next Sunday Mrs. Palmer ran another ad to get rid of the odds and ends which were left. The bare floors clattered under the shoes of women war workers in slacks: skinny women and women too big in back. Honey, not trusting them, tried to keep an eye on what they did. She was running up and down stairs all morning.

Once when she came down not expecting anything but more war workers or more dealers with their trucks outside ready to gobble up all they could, she opened the door and there were Mr. and Mrs. DuPree and back of them, taking the steps two at a time, Lamb—Lamb looking clean and good and not afraid of anybody.

Mr. DuPree and Lamb knew each other. Lamb said, "How do you do?" and smiled the smile he used for people not above him. It was Mr. DuPree who reached out to shake hands. He was trying to please Lamb; that was easy to see.

Lamb was in a hurry. He said he had come to look at the desk which was advertised.

136

Mrs. Palmer said, "It's for sale, you know."

Lamb laughed out loud. "I fancied that." To Mr. DuPree he explained, "We're opening up larger offices. Taking the suite next to that one you were in the other day. We need a couple of desks."

Mrs. Palmer led him back to the sunroom, and Lamb pulled out each drawer in Mr. Palmer's desk to see that it wasn't broken. He laid the money in Mrs. Palmer's hand and asked whether she had any more desks or maybe some files or some straight chairs. He said the war made it impossible to get quick delivery on new things and what he needed, he needed now.

Mrs. Palmer closed her eyes to think; then she whispered, "We can't keep Mr. and Mrs. DuPree waiting. They haven't even a nice place to sit down out there. They've come to see about taking Honey."

Lamb said quietly, "They're not taking Honey."

"But I promised. Mr. DuPree's been lovely to me, and I promised——"

Lamb put his arm around Honey's shoulder. "Here's one piece of furniture you can't dispose of. I need Honey." He looked down at her. "Glory's found a nice little flat. She can't swing it by herself. She says she can't live with just anybody and get her work done, but she'd like to have you."

Honey was silent for a long moment. Then she said, "I'm tired. I'd like a few days off. I reckon I could come for a while." She didn't want to work for the DuPrees. He, with all that talk, couldn't take Mr. Palmer's place.

Lamb said, "This isn't for a few days. We're buying furniture and fixing up the place right."

So it turned out that Lamb bought Bruce-y's bed and desk and chairs and paid Mrs. Palmer what she would have charged anyone else. He hurried outside and arranged to have a dealer deliver the stuff for him. He behaved like a man who knew how to get things done. When Mrs. Palmer saw the pieces being lifted in, she said to Lamb in her being-generous voice, "Take this sewing cabinet too. For Honey. It's my present to Honey."

Lamb looked down at its fragility, opened the miniature drawers with their tiny compartments filled with buttons, and inquiringly raised his eyes to Honey's.

"It's nice, right nice."

Lamb said dubiously, "If Honey wants it, out she goes!" He tossed the dealer another coin and himself carried out the cabinet. On his shoulder. Lamb had become heavier. He wasn't fatter, just wider, stronger. He no longer looked like a schoolboy.

Mrs. Palmer didn't say that she gave the cabinet because after all there wasn't going to be any place for Honey in the DuPree home. Mrs. DuPree was sick about it, but while Honey and Lamb were upstairs, Mr. DuPree had explained the situation to Mrs. Palmer.

"I'm the attorney for a whole brace of industries negotiating with CIO. One of them has to deal all the time with this Hoop boy. Lots of my phone messages at the house are private—very private—and it wouldn't do to risk anything. It wouldn't do at all. On this occasion the welfare of the moment must be sacrificed to the welfare of all time."

He laughed down at Mrs. DuPree, and she made a pretty little face.

They agreed that Honey wouldn't have any trouble getting work. Mrs. Palmer needn't have that on her mind. Faintly, Mrs. Palmer kept saying, "Honey never has been one to carry tales."

Suddenly she wanted to give Honey the sewing cabinet. There was another one, the real mahogany one which stood near the desk in Mr. Palmer's sunroom, for downstairs sewing. That one would do at the hotel. It would be all Mrs. Palmer needed.

138

12

Rooming with glory was for honey like moving to another land, yet it was in the same city and in a colored neighborhood, though not in the Ville. The flat was furnished in accordance with Lamb's idea of an office and Gloria's memory of the tuberculosis ward where she had once spent a year. Everything was there because it was needed, except the garnet-colored urns Honey stood on top of the bookshelf where Glory kept neat stacks of pamphlets. Against the tan paper instead of the green of Mrs. Palmer's walls, the urns appeared dull.

"Maybe them urns ain't good," Honey conceded.

Glory explained what good could mean. She played with the idea as a singer plays with a musical phrase. Good could mean when a thing was made, or by whom, or how. Good could mean beautiful or useful or expensive or stylish. Or it could be like the words: "A good nigger." "A good nigger" was what the CIO office would call a bad man, bad for the labor movement.

They talked about it for a long time. Honey thought being good was doing what you knew you ought to do—even if it was a sin and nearly killed you—and Glory thought being good was doing what was good for the new world she and Lamb and the CIO were trying to build.

"Out there at the Palmers' seemed like them urns had something to do. Here they ain't got nothing to do. Like me, I reckon."

139

The next day Glory came home from the office with some vines in little pots. She stood them inside the urns, and behind them she stood a pair of green plates.

"It's like as if them urns was dead and come to," Honey said happily. All evening she looked at them, and when it was time to go to bed she rubbed Glory's back and gave her some warm milk and a hot-water bag for her feet. Glory was still coughing.

After the lights were out, they talked.

Honey said, "I never knew it could be like this. I thought you had to live where everybody used your things and—well, yelled at you, but you was loved and felt at home. Or if you really wanted peace, you had to work for white folks and be kind of ashamed. Ashamed of being black and ashamed of being born." She hadn't been able to forgive Mrs. Palmer for those last weeks.

Glory's deep voice mumbled, "I wouldn't want to be anything but black."

"You want to be black?" There was silence as wheels sizzled past in the street, brushing lights and slanted shadows across the ceiling. Then Honey's voice jested, "Is you maybe got fever?"

"If I'd been born white I never would have had to think. I would have grown up bored by all my good luck. I probably would have——" The flare of a match lighted the room for a second.

Honey said sharply, "It ain't right to smoke in bed. Likely half that cough is all them cigarettes you eat instead of food."

"I would have married a rich man who hated 'niggers.' Might never have got into the labor movement. Maybe I never would have found out what makes the world go round."

"You wouldn't had to do all that hanging on when it went to turning, neither. You wouldn't had to do that."

140

Honey could hear her putting out her cigarette. "I'm going to sleep. You're too defeatist—too——"

"What is that what I am?"

"You haven't any faith or hope, Honey. No faith in the future. You believe nothing can be done to improve the world. You don't believe in trying."

"I reckon I seen too much——" Honey's voice was asking Glory not to be angry.

Glory was angry. "I know! I know! I know all about it! Lamb might just as well stop trying to make something of you."

"Lamb ain't been asked to try."

"Lamb wasn't trying for your sake! He was trying because the movement needs—— Well, never mind."

"Lamb was trying for my sake."

"Lamb wouldn't have anything to do with me either if I turned on the movement."

"Don't that hurt your feelings none?"

"It's the grandest thing about him!"

"I'd want a man to love me for myself."

"What is yourself? Bones and hair and skin? Or what you think and feel?"

Honey laughed. It was a soft sound in the dark. "I reckon you ain't nothing but that membership card you so proud of."

Glory sat up, about to argue. Then she stretched out again, pulled herself tall like a cat yawning. "That's me. A membership card. Lamb's name on it in purple ink! But when it comes to love—Lamb hasn't said a word, damn him!"

She went to sleep, but Honey stayed awake listening to footsteps and a whistled tune outside, to angry voices across the alley, to the things she wished she had thought to say to Glory. She didn't want Glory to think hard of her. She liked Glory, liked her little-girl eyes, excited as if from too much play. A serious girl who would be full of pep on her deathbed; that was Glory.

141

The next morning, as they drank their coffee from a table Honey had tried to make pretty enough for Mrs. Palmer, Honey said, "What is that bad word I am?"

"Defeatist. Rather give up than go on." Glory approved the phrase. Her eyes rounded out even as she said it again. "Rather give up than go on."

Honey's eyes were solemn. "I don't want to be that. Not if it's bad for you and Lamb."

"It's bad for the whole labor movement. Bad for all colored people. Bad for everybody, black or white."

"I can't care that far out," Honey answered. "Reckon I can only care for you and for Lamb."

"For the Ville?"

Honey sighed, "I reckon I can care for the Ville too. Maybe you can teach me to be so as I——"

Glory considered the idea, rolling smoke around inside her mouth.

"Can't undo defeatism just by learning some principles. Defeatism is a way of living. Trusting your chance to shape the future, that's a way of living too. . . . You'd have to go back to the factory."

"I got to do something. My money's giving out." Honey didn't look up at any of the things she had bought to take away the cold look from their rooms: the rugs and the little tables and curtains. She didn't let her fingers touch the pretty tablecloth, nor her eyes rest on the new dishes.

"I reckon I ain't any more tired than you is," she said to Glory.

"I'm not tired," Glory answered.

"You tired and you don't know it. Reckon I'm not tired and I don't know that."

"When will you go back to work?" Glory asked.

The corners of Honey's mouth tried to smile. "Same time you cut down your cigarettes to one pack a day."

Glory opened the big red pocketbook which was waiting for her on top of her coat. She tossed the unopened pack to Honey. "You surely learned something from those Palmers you worked for," she laughed. "You drive a hard bargain. Go over to the plant in your slacks, ready for work. They're hiring all they can get. It's a good factory."

"It used to be good. It——"

"Good for us to get into, I mean." She slid into her coat and hurried off.

Honey could hear her tap-tap-tap down the steps as fast as Bojangles ever went in the movies. She saw her running toward the bus corner. Something about the swish of her coat proved that Glory was happy. Glad to be colored. . . .

Glory and Lamb got off the bus on Jefferson Avenue and walked toward People's Hall. The day was sunny and the air drowsed against their faces.

"Too nice to go indoors," Glory said.

Lamb laughed down at her. "You got to wait until sundown anyhow—before I propose."

Glory giggled. "I gave up hope. Gave up a long time ago."

"Gave up too soon, Sugar."

"I figure you're just not a marrying man."

"My, my, girl, aren't you ignorant!"

"You're a poor educator," Glory sparred.

"Want to give you lots of time to be sure."

"You don't care what I want."

"There are about two hundred other girls I could make out with. They're all CIO—and about half are pretty. . . . You happen to be first choice."

"Sure?"

"Sure."

"Why didn't you ask me before?"

"I'm not a college man——"

143

"You're the——"

"Sure I am. I know it." Lamb's head was up, and his walk was proud. "Want to be sure Wellesley knows it."

"Looks like to me as if you proposed in broad daylight."

"No, no, no! Wouldn't do a thing like that."

"You got yourself accepted too."

They stood still and laughed at each other. Lamb squeezed Glory's arm. "The meeting's in here," he said.

The hall was on the top floor of a building built more than a quarter of a century earlier by Negro business and professional men who believed the road to racial equality was lined with successful financial enterprises. They had lost ownership and come out of the venture with smaller bank accounts, but the offices continued to be occupied by Negroes, and the building still seemed their own, more their own than any other in town.

As they passed colored couples, well dressed and sedately mannered, Glory whispered to Lamb. "Seems like a visit home. These are the sort of people my parents go with."

Lamb winked at her. "The deal's off."

When Glory paused for breath midway of the climb, Lamb said, "I always was one of these guys needed something to believe in. Part of trying to believe in myself. I always have been a sucker for a crowd and a man up in front——"

"Now you're the man up in front."

"You kidding? The reason I hold them is because I remember what all the Lambs want. They want a place to hang their faith. Like me they've been putting it on one nail after another. Nail pulls out from the rotten wood and down goes everything! Hurts like hell! I tried every religion in the Ville. I tried a few outside."

Glory frowned. "You wasted a lot of time before you found the labor movement."

"Reckon a man has to search before he finds. . . . Maybe it wasn't all wasted."

144

After the "Star-Spangled Banner" had been sung and a prayer spoken, the man in charge of the meeting said they were going to interrupt their program at this point to permit Brother Lamb Hoop of the CIO to speak. He was an elderly black man with trembling, ashen-purple hands and a voice which quavered. "We expected the speaker to be a white man from the CIO office, but he has sent us Brother Hoop."

Lamb saw that the words unintentionally expressed the lack of cordiality in the audience. He did not mount the steps to the platform. As he walked toward the center aisle, he walked with the slow, light tread of an athlete. He rubbed his hands as if to warm them. His black face smiled. His lips were spread; his eyes drowsy. With his first sentence he made the audience laugh.

"My! My! 'Pears like I'm mighty welcome!" He spoke in accents more southern than his own.

As the jollity thinned into silence, Lamb peered from face to face, as if he knew everyone in the audience. "Looks as if all Enright Avenue turned out!"

Flattered, the audience again laughed.

"Just to hear me, little old Lamb Hoop from the Ville."

He continued to smile at them until they were smiling back. He faced educated men and women, professionals who had served their people selflessly; professionals, too, who had served only themselves. He shifted tempo. "No, no, you brothers and sisters are too up and coming for that. Never would have come out just to hear a little black boy from the Ville." He shook his head with a serio-comic motion. "You came today to hear an organization. Word's got around that the CIO is doing what all the other organizations you ever belonged to tried to do and failed. This very building was put up by men who wanted to claim their share in America." His voice rose. "Got cheated out there, didn't you? Reckon you did."

A few in the audience shouted: "That's right! That's right!"

"I wouldn't ask you to take my word for what the CIO's doing. Wouldn't do that." Abruptly he straightened up and clapped his hands. "Let her go!"

With that, there was a sound of a movie machine, and on the white screen back of the speaker's chair a film began to flicker. It showed factories with flashes of moving belts and turning wheels, of black men bent attentively over electric drills, of black men going into massive plants, of black men, great crowds of them, going through opened work gates. There were quickies of individuals, black men skilled, responsible, dignified by what they were doing.

As they came on, Lamb called out their names. Some were known to the audience; some were sons or brothers. The film ended with a black man stroking his CIO button and laughing into the camera.

Lamb let his powerful voice out into a roar. "Anybody around here want to stop that? Anybody around here want to take those buttons away?"

A voice from the audience sneered, "How about the unions that won't let us join?"

As if he were swiftly returning a hard-hit tennis ball, Lamb shouted back, "They're dead! Done for! Need burying bad! Stinking up the world! Want to go off in a corner and bawl about them? Want to go to their wake? Me? I haven't the time" —slowly his smile broadened—"though I'm feeling right comfortable in my heart about the *rigor mortis* setting in. I'm feeling right comfortable about that."

He waited for the chuckling to cease. "I reckon I've got news for you. Good news. I didn't expect to be able to bring any information to an audience as *dicktee* as this! But it seems, after all, I've got news. I'm living out where I get it." He cupped his hands and shouted to the movie operator, busy now rolling his film: "Sam, stretch out your neck. Let these folks see the color of your skin!"

146

The man was a white man, a blond white man. "Hurt your pride any to show a film for black folks?"

The fellow hadn't expected the question. He blushed and drawled, "I'm a union man three generations back. Glad to show a union film anywhere. Especially to union folks."

"They didn't hear you. Shout it so they can!"

When they heard, Lamb yelled up at Sam. "What do you mean by insulting my audience! These are high-up folks! Business people! Lawyers! Social workers! Doctors! Too *dicktee* for unions!"

Sam retreated, and Lamb lowered his voice. "Poor Sam up there. He's AFL. Poor Sam. Hey, Sam, we offer sympathy!" Sam grinned, and the audience roared.

They knew Lamb was managing their feelings as an actor manages the feelings of his audience. He had come, a labor-union man, to speak to people whose pride pivoted around the fact that they had lifted themselves above the labor level. He was trying to engage their loyalty to his union because it was taking in Negroes of the very level they scorned. Even those who gripped their scorn most avidly enjoyed watching the game. The young fellow was an amusing actor and had a warm, ingratiating manner. He was giving them a spot of fun.

"Me?" Lamb pointed a stubby finger at his chest. "Me, I feel today as if I've come slumming. No, I'm not joking. I feel so sorry for you *dicktees* I don't know what to do." He looked around slowly, watching the good humor drain from their faces. "You're fine folks. Capable folks. Worked hard. Got to be lawyers." His voice was climbing the hill of passion. "Isn't anybody black gets to be a lawyer without working harder than the white boy who gets there! Isn't any black lawyer opens up an office gets to be a success without slaving harder than the white man who goes to lawyering! You're better! Much better! So what? So what? So what?"

The eyes which watched him now were heavy with the

147

memory of hurts: the no-Negro-wanted stare they saw in some eyes and imagined in the rest.

Lamb's voice became natural and serious and steady. "We're in a war." Their eyes deepened with grief and resentment. "Some of your boys are out there playing a risky game—playing it for keeps. You ought to be tickled to pieces to see them go. Some of you were. Some of you were too busy being Lot's wife. Looking back over your shoulder won't help you! It won't help your boys! If the fascists win that war, we're done for! Democracy will be done for, the kind of democracy that works and the kind that is only a dream and a promise; both will be done for. Both will go under." He looked around slowly and then stabbed his finger at their doubts. "And you with them! Bingo—down you'll go! Down everything worth living for will go! All the gains you've ever made! If we win, well, brothers, we'll have a chance! The best chance at getting our share of democracy we ever had——"

A voice called out, "They promised that in the last war!"

Lamb walked toward the interrupter. "That's right, they did. We weren't ready." He waited a long time. Then he resumed. "We weren't organized to take it. It's nothing the Negroes can take by themselves. It's something the peoples of the world—— Some of you have read Henry Wallace's *The Common Man*. The common man has to seize that democracy and hold to it. It's his life preserver on a stormy sea. Who is the common man? You? Oh no, brother, you're not the whole show! You call this the People's Building. You call the Art Center the People's Center. You call everything Negro the People's This and That. You're not the people, you're just part. The common man Mr. Wallace talks about is labor and Negroes and Jews and every other minority. We've got to work together. We've got to stop lining up with the enemy! We've got to know the enemy when we meet him. We've got to stop being the enemy!"

148

Lamb had been shouting at his audience. Now he whispered, "I know I'm talking to a Republican audience. I know why most of you are Republicans. I'm not going to ask you to become Democrats. I know what the southern Democrat is. I'm just going to ask you to think. I'm going to ask you to stop looking back over your shoulders. Keep your eyes on the road ahead. My organization is going to make some recommendations this year. Nobody knows yet what they're going to be, but a lot of us know how the candidates will be chosen. They'll be picked because they have lined up with the future welfare of the common man. With your children's welfare. That's how they'll be chosen. All I ask is that you remember there's a way of life at stake. That's what you'll be voting for this time: a way of life."

He walked off as slowly and undramatically as he had come. For a few seconds the audience did not realize the talk was over. Then a little scattered applause sounded. It spread across the hall.

The old man called to Lamb, "Thank you, brother. Will you come again?"

Lamb stood on a chair near the door. He looked around. His warm smile won warm smiles. He frowned as if sternly, "Believe I will—but not to talk to a lot of pillars of salt!"

They laughed at that. Then Lamb and Glory were running down the steps. Back of them the applause was loud.

Glory said, "You took the stuffing right out of their shirts!"

Lamb drawled, "Next time I'll aim to take the shirts!"

One evening as Honey was walking home from the plant she thought she saw Ben drive past in his car. She had worked the eleven-to-seven shift and now at seven-thirty the light had faded just enough to play tricks.

Ten minutes later she was sure she saw him coming from the Ville, this time with Carmen and her white-rimmed goggles by his side. The car came to a sharp, grinding stop, and then Ben was standing before her with hands outstretched. Tears glazed his eyes.

"It's Honey!" he called back to Carmen, but Carmen was busy polishing her glasses.

Ben looked back and forth. Then he took Honey's hands in his. "I didn't know you were back in the Ville," he whispered.

"I ain't in the Ville. I ain't living at home, Ben."

"You—you——"

"I'm living with another girl." Part of Honey was raging: Carmen never looked at me! Carmen's got to be made to know I can get Ben away just by crooking my finger. My little finger. All I got to do is crook my little finger.

She crooked it. She gave Ben her address. "You'll be right welcome."

He wanted to take her home in his car. Wasn't she tired? He'd be glad to drive her there.

"No, Ben. Not now. You go back to Carmen."

When she turned the corner she stepped differently. Had Snake seen her, he would have said her walk again had panther in it.

At CIO headquarters they were getting ready for a conference with management. Mr. Smith would be there, and his lawyer, Mr. DuPree.

Bob Jensen was explaining how things stood. Bob was a long-legged, sandy-haired bachelor, of Swedish ancestry. He had a slow, farmer's way of talking.

"Fellows," he said now, though several in the circle around his desk were women, "fellows, I've called some of you in who haven't anything to do with today's negotiations—to let you see what it's all about. We'll be up against this same thing again and again."

He waited while they settled their opened notebooks on their

150

knees. Then he spread some papers on the desk—Mr. Palmer's desk.

"Smith Company, as you know, is reactionary. CIO got their Plant No. 8 by a big vote. Grievances won for us. Workers out there are hillbillies, anti-Negro."

He looked as calmly at the colored faces in front of him as at the white. "Smith himself thinks southern, but he blames the prejudice on his employees. That prejudice is about the only thing they agree on. Smith says his employees won't stand for having Negroes working there. Might be they won't as things are now. Personnel out there has been turning colored men away. Said they didn't need men—on the same day they ran this ad." He picked up a clipping headed URGENT—MEN WANTED! "If we make an issue now of opening that plant to Negro skilled workers, we'll very likely have trouble. We'll lose the chance to educate those fellows. If we don't make an issue of it, we've got to go into, through, and out of this conference today without making management any promises along those lines, because sooner or later we will make an issue of it."

Someone said, "They know how we stand."

Bob tapped his pencil thoughtfully. "DuPree might know."

Lamb said, "Smith doesn't know anything except that he's sore."

Glory asked, "What's the conference for?"

"Management requested it," Bob answered. "They say they want to explain their production problem."

"They've got a problem. More bottlenecks in that place than bottles."

Bob turned to the man who said it. "How come?"

Nobody knew.

Lamb suggested, "Maybe management doesn't know either. I've got a couple of men who could sure find out for them."

"Have to be white men," Bob answered.

Lamb shook his head. "I'd like to take Smith with me now

151

to some of the plants where Negro and white are working in the same buildings, calling each other by their first names, and no trouble whatever, plants which a year ago said it would never work."

Bob said, "I called you together because I don't want anyone forgetting the over-all picture. CIO has more than a half-million Negro members. We aren't going to agree to anything that results in HELP WANTED signs with a second line reading: FOR WHITES ONLY. On the other hand we might have to fight that part of the fight when it suits us best, after we get this local really going, educated to trade-union thinking. We've got to have solidarity."

Some thought the issue ought to be made clear now. They argued the point.

Bob interrupted. He said it was time to go to DuPree's office, and after all there wasn't much preparing could be done for these conferences. You never knew what those babies would spring. He smiled. "This is their turn for putting the cards on the table—for giving in, too. We're sitting pretty. We can afford to play Great Stone Face."

Lamb added, "Just sit still and watch Smith pop a gut."

13

M<small>R. DUPREE'S OFFICES WERE LARGE. THEY FLANKED A WIDE,</small> carpeted corridor hung with oil portraits of the deceased members of the firm. One room was walled with lawbooks and called the library, though its large central table was frequently used for conferences.

There Bob waited alone, looking down upon the wide, muddy Mississippi and its bridges. Across the nearest one ant-like trucks were crawling from the smoky mist of the far shore into the tangle which was the edge of the city. Bob could see freight trains moving along both banks. The scene was handsome, prodigal with natural abundance and man-made wealth: tall buildings, huge electric-power chimneys, squat banks with vast vaults. Cross-hatching it, Bob discerned a civilization having more faith in success than in character.

He thought: The whole show's been built on the suspicion that the man who isn't afraid of starving won't work. It's built on distrust of mankind. God, what we could do with faith!

He heard his secretary come in. Hilda was a pale, round-shouldered girl with big spectacles and too short skirts. She was always hurrying him. Sometimes he hated her for it. Today she wore a red topcoat and red beanie to match her painted lips, making her look even paler.

"As soon as we can finish here," she said as she reached into her brief case, "we've got to get ready for tonight's meeting. Sign these letters so I can get them into the mail."

He took the sheets but remained at the window. "Want to see twins?" he asked slowly. His wide thumb indicated the office buildings, stores, Produce Row, and with a circular gesture followed past the markets to the massive factories beyond. "All that is the dog-eat-dog stuff. Here"—he leaned forward against the pane—"down where the cleared area is, that's to be a park for the people. Something we own and can use and take pride in—with no price tag on it. Twins: Competition and Co-operation."

Hilda laughed her short, shrill laugh. "They're kicking each other's brains out most of the time."

She had made up her mind about the past and the future a long while ago. It irked her to have Bob forever discussing it like a schoolboy sitting on the edge of a fraternity bed.

When the conference began, Mr. DuPree made a ceremony of the introductions. Bob Jensen was the "brains and the brawn and the busy executive of the labor movement of the Middle West as we find that labor movement here in one of its newer, more experimental branches called the CIO." Bob's secretary was the "lovely little lady who gave him orders." Lamb Hoop was a "boy of sturdy, dependable family, a background to be remembered with pride, a background not to be lightly deserted." Mr. Smith was a "prominent citizen widely known for his philanthropic past and present, head of the Smith Company, one of those men who by their superior capacity become the soul and heart and spirit of any city they live in." The others at the table were "union gentlemen" and "union ladies."

As Mr. DuPree finished, his long fingers still tossing his watch chain, Bob made the introductions over again. He said, "Mr. Hoop, Mr. Smith is owner and management of the plant we know as Plant No. 8. Mr. Smith, Mr. Hoop is a CIO organizer. Coming in the door now is one of his assistants, Mr. Arthur."

154

Mr. Smith's face flushed when he recognized Lamb's assistant as the white leader of the union at his plant.

Through the sullen silences and the sparring, the purpose of the meeting soon became clear. Mr. DuPree hadn't been able to convince his client that Executive Order 8802—forbidding industry to refuse to hire workers because of their color—had to be obeyed or that the union men he would have to deal with were men sure of their legal rights.

For a long time Mr. Smith made only one remark. He made it again and again. He said, "Nobody's going to tell me how to run my plant."

At last Bob leaned forward and said, "Enforcement of the law isn't our business——"

"What is your business?" Mr. Smith snapped. "Making trouble?"

Bob smiled. It was a calm, condescending smile, and it circled the table, crossing colored faces as well as white. Slowly Bob replied, "You've a good deal to gain if production is what you're interested in. We have a no-strike pledge."

Mr. Smith looked at his watch, "It's twelve o'clock. I eat at twelve."

Bob laughed. "It's twelve twenty-one, Mr. Smith. CIO eats when we have time."

Mr. DuPree raised his brows. "Food is famous as the way to a man's warmer sentiments. Let's reassemble here at one-thirty."

"Why reassemble?" Bob asked. "You can explain the law to him."

"You must give Mr. Smith time to get used to the new laws. Now if you fellows will do the sensible thing—keep the Labor Board and the FEPC and all that newfangled nonsense out of this——"

"You're asking us to renounce law and order. Without

the 'newfangled nonsense' we have nothing to resort to in a dispute but a strike. Without that nonsense we wouldn't have taken the no-strike pledge. The new laws are good laws. CIO plans to stand by them."

Mr. DuPree glanced across the room at his client. "You can't ask Mr. Smith to negotiate with colored men. He can't do that."

"Maybe not. Maybe he can't live in the U.S.A.—and like it."

"Why not just forget that part—about colored employees? I don't ask you to renounce it. Just forget it for the time being."

"Forget a little thing like democracy," Bob smiled wryly and put on his coat. "From our point of view there is nothing more to talk about, but we'll be back after lunch. We'll stay only twenty minutes. We've got work to do. There are employers in this city, lots of them, honestly trying to understand the new laws and live by them, men who put production for the war effort first—before their own prejudices."

It was in regard to such an employer and his proposed labor-management committee that they wanted to talk during the noon hour. Prior to the evening session with him, they needed to work out plans adapted to his factories.

Going down in the elevator, they tried to think of a place where they could eat and talk at the same time. On the sidewalks the crowds were lunch-hour crowds. Girls without hats. Men with toothpicks. Young boys slapping peanuts into their mouths.

Lamb said good-by.

Bob stopped him. "I want you there." To the others Bob said, "We'll have to go up to the restaurant at Union Station. Only place serves colored."

Hilda shook her head. "That's twelve blocks west and three to walk over. We won't have time."

Lamb frowned. "I'd better meet you later."

Bob said, "We're going over there." He nodded toward a large department store. "We're going together, the eight of us."

Hilda narrowed her eyes. "Then you better go to their best dining room. The higher you go, the less chance someone will raise a fuss."

Jim Arthur asked, "Are you right sure?" His voice was southern hillbilly.

"I'm sure," Hilda answered. "Prejudice is nothing but insecurity and fear and ignorance. The masses have more of it than the tops."

Lamb agreed. "The crackers would take on more."

Hilda looked up at Bob. "I thought you were going to forget the color clause——"

"Can't do it even when you want to. It's one with everything we're after. Giving it up puts us into one illogical position after another. DuPree himself made that clear when he asked us to keep still and therefore forget the FEPC, the Labor Board, and all the rest."

While Bob said "Eight" to the woman holding the corded gate of the gilded tearoom, the others stood back among the waiting crowd.

She looked over her shoulder. She didn't see Lamb. "I'll have something in a few minutes. That table 'way over there near the window is for eight. They're about to go."

When she summoned Bob, all, including Lamb, walked through the dining room and sat down.

Lamb chose a place with his back to the crowd. That way his color would be least likely to be seen. "Brothers," he said, "and sisters too, you're making history today. Pretty history."

Jim Arthur blushed. "I never ate with a black man before. I never come to such a swell place before."

Bob drew out an envelope and pencil. "To make a labor-management committee really work in that setup, we——Hilda, you order for us. Something that'll come fast."

"Anybody got ulcers?" Hilda inquired.

"For Pete's sake!" Bob snapped at her.

"Some people do have ulcers," Hilda persisted.

Lamb chuckled. "I'm getting them." Then they saw that Lamb was the one carrying most of the burden of their courage.

Hilda frowned at him. "Stop perspiring and look natural."

Bob, trying to put Lamb at ease, joked, "In the CIO we have to ask Hilda when we may perspire."

They were laughing while Hilda summarized the order for the waitress. No one could be sure whether or not the girl in the green uniform observed the color of Lamb's skin. Those who were eating seemed too busy to be aware of his presence.

That evening Lamb told Honey and Gloria about it. The three frequently had dinner together at the flat. After Honey got home from the factory she would finish preparing the meal she had started earlier in the day. Trying to please Lamb and make Gloria strong, Honey was regaining her weight. She was beginning to be pretty again. Her eyes were wide with wistfulness, and her well-shaped head seemed too heavy for the long slender neck. Her way of being pretty now made people look from her eyes to the grace of her neck and back to her eyes again.

Telling about his lunch at the department store, Lamb pretended he wasn't pleased. He just said, "So I got the chance to pay a dollar for a two-bit feed."

Glory asked again, "And nobody said anything?"

"No riots. Nobody fell dead."

Glory's eyes roved his face. "It isn't as if your skin was light.

158

They must have known." Glory patted at her lips with her napkin. "At first all their talk about democracy made me mad. Then I began to see just talking it was good. Some was bound to cling."

Lamb agreed. "They'd have to be dumber than they are not to know this country's sending black men out to fight for democracy who'll never be satisfied to come home and not have any."

"Just you two don't get yourself in trouble," Honey warned.

Lamb scowled at her. "We're in trouble. Even you. Only thing you don't know it."

"I got promoted today," Honey answered. "I take the supplies around. I wheeled that baby carriage a thousand miles this afternoon."

"That's a swell job!" Lamb told her. "You can make friends that way. You can get to be an influence."

Then there was silence. They knew Honey hadn't decided that she wanted to be an influence.

She kept trying to want to for Lamb's sake. It was all mixed up with whether she wanted to stay alive. . . . She couldn't go on forever on the scraps from Glory's life and Lamb's. She had to have some sort of life of her own. Then she might want to be an influence too. Help Lamb build his new world. Help him against that Mr. Smith who wouldn't give in, not even after a good lunch.

Trying to understand what Lamb meant, she spent long, dim, dawn hours thinking of Emery. In the quiet she could see his face, watch him walk, hear his voice. He was Snake purified. He was Lamb's new world come to earth. He was a black white man. She dreamed of him and talked to him and finally listened to him.

He was hard to understand, yet she could discern some things he wanted her to do. He wanted her to be satisfied that Lamb ate in the white man's restaurant.

159

Because gasoline was rationed and because the flat was midway for everybody, it became the late-evening meeting place for those who needed to confer or deliver literature or report on progress made. On a boulevard which paralleled Enright, the street for several blocks had only colored residents, but it was not colored as the Ville was colored. There was no one place where it began and ended. It fringed off gradually into white neighborhoods.

Hilda fell into the habit of coming to leave notes for Bob, who would come later. Jim Arthur and other organizers came to get used to thinking of colored people as people. Bob had asked them to come. They would be overjolly shaking hands with a colored man for the first time. They would stare around the room as if amazed to observe how tenaciously a pretty chair remained a pretty chair in a Negro home. They would at last sit down in it and peer through their past and its fog of darky stories at the urns, vine-filled, above bookcases containing their own union pamphlets. Many times they would be caught not listening when spoken to. They were listening instead to insistent words said by part of themselves to another part. Punch was berating Judy; Judy berated Punch. A man first had to get used to the din.

To Honey they were not so much organizers as company. She would serve them a cold drink, quietly standing it on the nearest small table. Each evening the beverage was different. She would mingle tea and ice and orange or lemon juice and a carbonated drink of one brand or another. Once she put in peach syrup she had made, once grape juice. Sometimes Bob would look up with surprise and say, "This is good! What is it?"

Lamb or Gloria would answer, "Honey made it," and go on talking. Bob began to call Honey "Velvet" because of her soft ways. If she saw that his coat was ripped, she would mend it as she sat listening in the doorway nearest the kitchen. She mended any coat needing mending, any pair of gloves needing a stitch. She would reach into Mrs. Palmer's sewing table and, without looking, find her thimble and scissors.

The summer was a hot one. When the girls came, they looked wilted. Honey would scrub their white pocketbooks. If they tried to thank her, she would say, "I just wanted to do it."

One evening as Bob stood up to leave, he said to Lamb, "Tomorrow's going to be a heavy day for Hilda. Meetings and letters. We've got a lot of material to mail out and no one to fold and stamp. What about Velvet?"

Glory said, "Too defeatist."

Lamb said, "Not any more, she isn't." It was a question and an exhortation too.

Honey said, "I reckon I can fold if Miss Hilda will show me. I go on the night shift tomorrow, so I've got the day free."

When she finished folding, she washed off the desk tops, sharpened pencils, mended a wastebasket, and repaired the roller on a shade.

She was slipping out the door when Bob called her. He began to talk about the CIO and "what the colored people in this crazy town want."

Honey stood near the door the way she used to stand while Mrs. Palmer was eating dinner. She said, "I don't know nothing, Mr. Bob, about the CIO, but I knows there ain't no such thing as the colored people in this town all wanting the same. We ain't all alike."

"The problem's the same."

"Nothing ain't the same. Some colored folks is rich and uppish just like some white folks is. Some is poor. Some is like me and Lamb and Glory, not up, not down. Some has got learning, some ain't. Some is down on their own, all the time raising up a fault; some is all the time bragging about their own. Some fusses against segregation; some segregates themself. Ain't any colored folks, except maybe Lamb and Glory,

161

who is just about the same with their own and with white folks. I been listening to you talk lots of evenings. Mistake you make, Mr. Bob, is thinking because a man's skin is dark, he'll stand by his own people. That ain't so. Most of us, I reckon, is just trying to get along in the world like white folks is trying to. Everybody black and white, he wants his children to come out ahead of the rest. They ain't no one colored people in this city. They is lots of colored peoples. Fighting each other. Hating each other. Jealous. Tell me where-at a man lives and what shade skin his wife's got and what church they send their children to and what places they go to on Sunday, and I can right off name the kind of folks what turn up their noses at them, color or no color."

Bob paced up and down, thoughtfully. "I suppose that's the reason Lamb says he needs a highbrow to help him reach the professionals."

Occasionally Honey wondered why Ben had not come, but mostly she went through the summer, a leaf in a high wind, indifferent to the direction of her going. The gale of Glory's and Lamb's life carried her forward. When they had company, she listened. When the wheels of the factory turned, she trundled supplies. At the end of the day she came home to cook. She tried not to think back to Snake and the Hoop basement. Her thoughts never strayed toward the future.

Then one evening, late, Ben did come. Honey was alone, waiting for the return of Glory and Lamb and the others who were at a meeting. The cool drink was in the icebox, ready.

The building of which their flat was the upper part had been owned and occupied a half century ago by a well-known white family. From the outside it looked as it always had, except that it was dulled by smoke. It was a wide house of red brick with a sloping slate roof and, for proof of elegance, an arched front doorway. Inside, under the arch, there now was

162

an enclosed entry with two doors, one leading from the upper apartment where Glory and Honey lived.

Honey came down the steps slowly. She had changed from her factory slacks, which she considered an unwomanly garment, to a yellow dress.

The evening was pleasant in temperature. July had worn itself out in a fury of heat. With August came cool evenings, fine nights for sleeping. The downstairs tenants had gone to bed early to "catch up." Honey was alone on the porch.

She sat on the top stone step with the brick of the railing to lean against. She stretched out her legs level, crossed at the ankle, and leaned her head back. The tall cottonwoods were tossing a little, loosening leaves which crackled as they fell. Lightning bugs were floating in and out the shrubbery, and a cricket was scolding irascibly.

Honey closed her eyes and listened to the city. Down the block some children were singing. Across the street a radio droned. Beyond, on the boulevard, streetcars clanged and hissed along the rails. The engines of the busses bleated as they stopped and started. She tried to sort out the whirring of the automobiles.

Overhead the evening mail plane throbbed across the sky. She parted her lids to watch it wink alternately its green and white eyes as it came, its red and white as it left. Poor Junior, she thought, and sighed. She returned her listening to the city. To footsteps back and forth near her house. For some time she heard a walker pacing, worried.

"Why, it's Ben!" she breathed as he came closer.

Sitting next to her, he tried to keep his eyes on the hat he tossed in his hand.

"Perhaps your heart might feel better, Ben, if you didn't come."

"My heart made me come."

"You ain't proud to be here?"

Ben was silent for a long time. Then he cleared his throat, threw his hat into a nearby chair, turned to look fully at Honey in the dim light, and said, "I came here a long time back. I saw white folks and colored going in. I heard talking and laughing. I've seen it lots of times. The neighbors are suspicious. I know something's wrong, but when I look at you, Honey, you don't look wrong. Not to Ben, you don't. You look to me like the finest woman I ever met."

"Ben, I don't feel evil no more. Lamb ain't evil. Glory ain't evil. Our house ain't evil."

Just then Bob's car drove up.

Honey reached out and touched Ben's arm. "The best way, Ben, is for you to come up and see. See for yourself. I never was a good hand at explaining."

Once during the evening Lamb came to the kitchen with glasses. He whispered, "Ben Boston's eyes are bugged out about as far as they will go!"

In the beginning Bob asked Ben if he was a trade-union man. When Ben said "No," Bob ignored him. The talk—between signing things for Hilda and planning the schedule of meetings —was of the demands these days upon labor.

"Now that we're getting recognition we're getting too much," Bob lamented. "Can't go to all those meetings and have time for our own work too."

"Labor has to have community contacts," Hilda said primly.

Bob answered, "Labor has to have time to tend its own fences."

He began to pull letters from his pockets. The first was from the Tuberculosis Society. The League of Women Voters would like a CIO official to participate in a panel. The Good Will Circle of the Congregational Church was planning a round table. The Colored Y wanted a CIO speaker against the poll tax.

"Very important," Hilda said.

"Hush, woman!" Bob laughed. " 'You are invited to give the address for our annual luncheon——' " He tossed them across the room to her.

Nearsightedly Hilda read through each one. She began to name people to send to this one and that. She handed a list to Bob. "O.K.?"

"Do what you please," he answered.

"But this is important."

He tugged at his ear. "Believe you're right." He scratched her list and made additions.

"You're too tired," Hilda said, "else you'd see that it's important. You know the policy as well as I do."

"The policy is Hilda's newest club over my head," Bob told the group. "She went to the regional conference and came back with more policies than Phil Murray ever heard of."

"One of the most important," Hilda persisted, "is overcoming the ignorance of the white worker on the color question. Labor divided is labor enslaved."

"Let up on the quotations," Bob grumbled, but the others said she was right. Labor, color, tuberculosis, voting, good will, each problem was in the whole problem, and the whole problem was in each.

Bob agreed to that. He was in a straight chair. He tilted it back against the window sill. He began to think out loud, laying down his words slowly like blocks carefully chosen, cautiously placed. Gradually they shaped into a structure which could be seen. Bob said the white people were unwise. They acted as if a nation could tie up part of itself and not be mule-kicked in return. Democracy meant freedom for individuals, but it also meant over-all unity. Like in the labor movement. Everything came back for comparison to the labor movement.

When he finished, Lamb said, speaking to Ben, yet not speaking to him too: "Take the crackers up on Mount Vernon Street who don't want colored people living near them. That's

O.K., but when times are different—the war over, and too many men for the number of jobs—then what? Wages go down. Mount Vernon Street crackers go out on strike. Colored men rush in to take their jobs. Nothing to prevent. No loyalty to worry them. Swell little way to get even."

"Both sides are ignorant," someone said.

It was then that Ben spoke for the first time. "It's odd to my ears to hear white men and women speaking of the unfriendliness of white folks. It's something I've thought about. Every colored man's thought about it, but it never would have seemed possible to talk about it before people—people like you." He meant white people, but couldn't bring himself to say the words.

Bob looked up and asked, "Do you think the colored people are as divided among themselves as the white?" Without saying so, he quoted what Honey had said.

Ben stirred in his chair. "All that's true, but we have one issue on which we are agreed. Whether we're rich or poor, businessmen or porters, we agree that the discrimination has to stop. The unfairness of it has been brought home by this war. Seeing the colored boys go off to fight. Hearing white men condemning themselves——"

Bob looked at Ben levelly. "If the colored people are in agreement about any one important issue, then they're a long step ahead of the white. We don't agree on much."

Ben got ready to leave when the others did. Honey could see that he was happy. What was going on in Honey's flat was good. Unbelievably good!

In an undertone he asked whether he could come tomorrow night. Tomorrow would be Wednesday. Perhaps they could go——

"Not tomorrow, but——" she began, and then stopped, unable to speak.

Across the good-bys Bob was saying to Lamb, "I got the name today of the new organizer National is sending in to work with you, the highbrow you said you wanted. Emery Marshal."

Lamb frowned. "Thought he was in the Army."

"Was. Left an arm over there. Back working for us. Gets in Saturday."

"When?" Ben asked Honey. "When may I come?"

The next morning while getting dressed Gloria startled Honey by saying, "Saturday's going to be an important day around here."

But the words, after all, had nothing to do with Emery's coming. Glory was standing in front of a mirror putting on make-up. Her lips weren't staying thinned out. They were pushing forward into the sort of smile which had to do with Lamb.

"You two getting married?"

"Right the first time!" Glory laughed. "Thought we'd take the jump and then go on up to the Regional Conference together. It begins in Chicago Sunday morning."

Honey took Glory into her arms. "You right welcome as Lamb's wife. I'll move out while you're away. I'll fix everything nice before I go."

But Glory wouldn't have that. Honey was to stay. What was wrong with that day bed in the living room? Hadn't Lamb slept on it many a night?

"I've got a better idea," Honey answered. She didn't say what it was.

On Saturday afternoon Honey reached the pink, spired City Hall a little early. She stood outside at the top of the steep steps watching for Glory and Lamb. It was an exciting place to stand. Here the street was broad, and beyond it, where blocks of slums once stood, green lawns were edged by rows of trees. Dark specks here and there were men lying on the grass. On a pair of benches sat some colored girls eating lunch.

The plaza was oblong and walled by buildings of all sizes. Over the roofs of the low ones could be seen higher structures stepping up towards a bright blue sky, so brilliant today that no one could see the planes droning past. The finest of the buildings were ones which belonged to everybody. To Honey too. Her heart was proud today of her city. Once she thought she saw Mrs. Palmer, but what would Mrs. Palmer be doing here? People came to the City Hall to pay taxes, but not people who had lawyers to come for them.

Then she did see Mr. DuPree, tall and imposing and graceful, coming down the inside steps. At first he didn't seem to remember Honey. Perhaps he didn't know what to do about his hat. He couldn't tip it to a colored person and he couldn't *not* tip it to a woman. He removed it to scrub his cuff against a spot on the brim, and asked Honey whether she had seen Mrs. Palmer lately. "You are Mrs. Palmer's Honey, aren't you?" he asked, looking down at her.

They agreed that Mr. Palmer was a fine man and that his death was a great loss to the city. They shook their heads.

Surprising herself, Honey blurted out that she was feeling proud of her city today, loving it. "Seems like a body has to have a place to love. That's bound to be the place you live, I reckon, or where-at you was born."

Mr. DuPree, who wore his own love of the city proudly and at times ostentatiously, blushed, for he was astonished to hear that Honey believed the city was hers too and felt for it the love of a native. He mumbled some words which didn't reply to anything she had said and hurried off.

Then Honey saw Lamb and Glory coming arm in arm. On Glory's shoulder tossed a corsage of pink roses. Honey was glad Lamb hadn't forgotten that. His work made him like a man with his nose in a book, not knowing what was going on. But today both he and Glory looked unworried. They walked as if rejoicing that the land they walked would as readily accept their footprints as any others. They were light of heart, courageous—and dressed up. Their clothes were still store-stiff.

Honey sighed. It might be that the CIO gave them hope, but they were giving the CIO their youth. They were never carefree. Perhaps it was an even exchange.

Honey too had dressed up. Her way of being dressed up was different from Glory's. When Glory was dressed up, it was as if she had trimmed her body to conceal its faults. When Honey was dressed up, her clothing merely emphasized her grace.

Lamb said in a level voice, "Emery will be here soon."

He was taking away the shock of it for Honey. Emery's train had arrived, and he had agreed right off to be the other witness to Lamb's marriage. Lamb also said he was now married, but his wife was not here yet.

Emery had forgotten Honey. Lamb said, "This is my sister. She's a member of our local at Plant No. 24. Her name's Honey."

Afterwards Honey could only vaguely remember what had happened: a white man telling Lamb and Glory to sign things, some tall windows in need of washing, and her own heart pounding cruelly at her throat while her thoughts, staggering with grief and fear, tried to fight off Emery's—or was it Snake's?—terrifying fascination for her.

Because Glory and Lamb went off alone in a taxi, Emery and Honey were alone in another. Honey sat far back in her corner. Emery didn't speak. He looked old, as though the pain from his injury had made lines which now rushed back to his face.

Finally he said, "Lamb is carrying a heavy load. Are you sticking by him?"

169

She nodded, and suddenly she told him everything, about Snake cutting the ropes and how she had gone down to the basement to kill him, only to find him gone. Emery's expression didn't change.

"You won't have to worry about Snake any more," he said softly. "He won't be back. He's in jail again. In Chicago."

She wanted to ask him more, but he quickly changed the subject. He told her that the new flood of women in industry was slowing things for Lamb. Bad enough to have to deal with men not used to unionism, but now there were women, women not used to working in a group, women not used to living in a white world, women who fought for today, not for tomorrow. Lamb was building for tomorrow.

How many women were in her union? How many CIO women in town? How many AFL? How many women in her factory who never went to union meetings?

"Let me alone," she murmured. "I don't know."

He told her that she who was a Ville woman should give the Ville to Lamb.

His real hand tapped at his other. "At first this stirred up all the meanness I ever had in me. Hated everything. When I was being invalided back, our hospital train came through a station in the South. The lunchroom wouldn't give breakfast to us Negroes. Through the glass we watched a whole dining room of German prisoners gorging on the best. Bacon, eggs, coffee. The krauts were getting fed all right, all right. That day I wanted to cut a lot of throats. I saw I would only be cutting my own. The captain—a medic in charge of us—raised hell with the lunchroom. Risked his hide plenty, because the colonel stationed at the field hospital where we were delivering some of our men was a southerner. I decided to stick around and team up for the rest of my life with fellows like the captain! A phony arm wasn't the worst. It wasn't going to bother me any more than I let it bother me. That's the way what you did will have to be with you. . . . You can lick it. Sure, you can lick it."

Leaving him at the door, she felt a great gladness that he was back, even though he had brought a wife.

When Lamb and Glory had eaten the supper Honey cooked, and were at last packed and ready, with a cab waiting at the door, Lamb said to Honey, "Drop by home and tell Mama about it. Tell her when I get back I'll bring Glory around to be looked over."

"I ain't been home since November," Honey answered thoughtfully.

"Time to go. Don't stay long. See you here when we get back."

Because the war in Europe was pleading for planes, Honey's plant was working seven days a week. That Sunday afternoon she left the factory at four and took a bus which let her off at the Ville corner.

She walked with the short steps of a little girl too tired to take a real stride. No one heard her come into the house. She could smell corn bread and greens.

In the kitchen several of the children were helping themselves from the stove. Honey had often begged Mama to have a mealtime when everyone sat down together or when two tables were served, one after the other. She used to say it was wrong for the children to run free. There ought to be one time when it was their duty to come home. The way Mama did it, just cooking the food and leaving it there for taking, the children behaved like animals running in to feed. She saw at a glance that Mama hadn't improved her ways. The kitchen wasn't as neat as it used to be.

When the children saw Honey they ran and hugged her and shouted their love. She told them they had grown, and she

171

kissed each one. She took the little ones on her lap. Then Mama came to the door, an old woman angry at Honey's desertion. She stood silent, her mouth chewing at its own emptiness. Her eyes poured tears. She opened her arms, and Honey walked into them.

Honey spoke first. She said, "Lamb asked me to bring you his good news. He married a right fine girl. He's fixing to bring her around to see you, Mama. He wants you two to be friends. You'll find it right easy to be friends with Glory."

She didn't tell Mama that Glory had a college education. She didn't tell Mama any of the things which would have raised up a barrier. She tried to show Mama she would need to be kind to Glory. "Glory isn't strong. She don't take care of herself good. Lamb, he still one to forget to eat."

By the time she left she had given Mama something to tell the neighbors in explanation of why Honey and Lamb had run out on her: In the work Lamb did there was need for a place to meet. Her children lived on the place, kind of like janitors. They took care of it for the boss. They couldn't do that and live at home. They lived out. Like lots of other Ville children. That's the way it was.

Restoring Mama's children to her, Honey saw that she was mothering Mama again, but this time it was different. She was mothering herself too, freeing herself from Mama.

By the time she got up to go, she knew Mama would never be able to boss her again, but Mama for her would never be just a yelling old woman. She was Mama doing her best, Mama needing new teeth, Mama come up from the cotton fields and all mixed up by the city. Mama was 'way off from her, but Mama's arms were still there for comforting. A person couldn't love her mother all the years Honey had and then turn against her with a rested heart.

Honey said, "Mama, you get you some teeth. I'll pay for them."

172

Mama writhed her lips. "I ain't fixing to go no place where-at I'll need teeth."

"Teeth ain't just for show."

"China teeth sure ain't for eating. But I could use that there money——"

"No, Mama, you don't need no money for nothing else. All the Hoops is earning big."

Mama grinned guiltily. Then worry flattened her features. "Honey," she whispered, "is you living good? There ain't no man——"

"No, Mama."

"Thinking back to it, 'pears to me you was awful roused up over Snake."

"Yes, Mama. There ain't nothing wrong about the way I'm living."

"You be a good girl, Honey. I wants to hold to that. You was always the best of my children."

Honey hurried down the steps and toward the corner. Just before she turned, she looked back and waved. She loved Mama again. I reckon, she thought, being a mother is mostly wanting your children to be good. Even when you don't know what good is. Maybe to a mother being good looks the same as acting so as you'll stay safe.

14

It FELT STRANGE TO BE IN THE FLAT ALONE. HONEY EMPTIED ash trays and folded newspapers, seeing again that this was a fine place to live. The square front room and the long dining room with the table near the side window had grown together as the meetings more and more made it necessary for the two to be one. The chairs had been pushed back, the couch out of the way.

Beyond the kitchen and bathroom was the bedroom which Lamb and Glory would now occupy. Honey was determined not to make the front room into a bedroom. She was through with that kind of living. In this flat she had used all the domestic arts she had learned while at the Palmers'.

In the side hallway there was a nailed-up door. That must lead to an attic, and it was up there Honey planned to live. While she was struggling with the nails, she heard steps. Those who had not gone to the Regional Conference were coming. It had not occurred to Honey that they would come while Glory and Lamb were away.

Others besides CIO members had been joining the group in recent weeks. Liberals, writers, painters, newspaper men and women. The liberals said they came because it was only the CIO which could save "the social gains." The painters came to sketch a scene they called exciting; they talked of getting ready for exhibits. The newspaper people spoke of themselves as delegates from the Guild. Once Lamb asked, with cheerful impudence, "Delegates to what?" A man with a press pencil in his hand answered, "Delegates to the future."

Tonight someone brought a visitor. The girl would be upstairs in a moment. She was "here on assignment. Learning something few colleges try to teach. Looks like the Junior League on the way to church, but says she's interested in labor and race relations, so I brought her along."

It was Dorothy Jane.

For a while Dotty kept the talk a conversation between herself and Emery. The others sat silent, listening to his answers to her questions: making this survey on the colored woman in industry, ought she start with the war-work factories or ought she start, say, with the garment industry?

Emery said there was a curious situation she ought to know about. The Negro woman in the garment industry really belonged in the Cotton union because mostly they worked on cotton, but there was more resistance to them in Cotton than in Silk. Silk had let them come in. That had given rise to a strange situation. Now, a year later, Cotton wanted them—and their dues.

Although Emery had been in the city only a few days, he knew how things were and in detail. Sometimes his wife reminded him of bits he had told her and forgotten. Mollie Marshal was an exotic-looking young woman with slate-colored skin, gray eyes, and long hair bulked within a snood. Watching her, Honey saw that Mollie Marshal thought with Emery, worked with Emery, was his second hand and his second mind. She was a black white woman. Their identification with each other had spread even into the corners of their lives.

Emery handed Dorothy Jane a slip of paper. "There is a step-by-step procedure which might work here."

Dorothy Jane, looking it over, said it was swell, simply swell, but would it be hard to get into the meetings?

"Bob can get you into a lot. Honey Hoop can take you to the local at No. 24."

Dotty wanted to keep on asking questions. She was writing things down and then frowning at what she had written; clutching her pen in her teeth as she searched the pocket of her notebook for a clipping to show Emery. She kept after him for more help and more and more. When he said he knew the author of her textbook, she gasped with respect. Honey saw that, grieving for her father, Dotty had become more his daughter than when he was alive, more under his influence.

Emery put an end to it. He turned to the group, his steady eyes sizing up the writers and the artists and Ben and some white women dressed as if they were Mrs. Palmer's friends.

He said, "The CIO has set up the Political Action Committee. To re-elect Franklin Delano Roosevelt and a Congress to support his program. That's why I'm here. To see that the colored people vote PAC."

Ben stood up, his head thrust forward. "You're going to ask colored people not to vote Republican?"

"I'm going to show them where their advantage lies."

"Ever been down South?"

"We have to quit voting against the southern Democrats, who, God knows, deserve to be voted against! We have to learn to vote for the man who issued Executive Order 8802."

Ben sat down. "You'll never do it. Not in this city."

Most of the Negroes agreed with Ben. Had the Democrats even put a decent plank in their platforms? They hadn't even made their platform look nice!

Emery nodded. "Looks rotten. It's better than it looks."

Ben reached into his pocket and brought out a Dewey button. Other colored hands in the room did likewise.

Emery narrowed his eyes. "You'll all vote for Roosevelt

before this campaign is over," he predicted and got up to leave.

When the others followed, Ben lingered. "Honey, I'll be over in the morning to fix up your room. I'll fix it up as nice as I can. I'll make it real nice, but I'm still hoping you—you——"

Honey nodded.

"While you were gone I moved Mama and Loraine into my house on Enright. It's a pretty house. Big. I want you to come to see us in it. I want you to meet my mother."

Honey sighed. "So Loraine and Honey both got out of the Ville."

The day was neither fully summer nor fully fall, for the sun was warm to the skin, yet the air was cool and now and again twirled in wild, wintry motion. Coming out of the factory, Honey drew a deep breath. A girl walking near by said, "Seems wrong to stay indoors on a day like this."

Honey looked up at a plane droning low. "Reckon those boys laugh at us lots of times. Fly out over the hills where there's plenty of room, and out there they don't see nobody. Come along in here and everything's crowded up."

The other girl ran for a bus. Over her shoulder she called back, "They better not laugh! Who makes their old planes? The city makes them."

Honey laughed too. She had never seen the girl before. Another like her would be along soon. They too would talk. And laugh. Working in the plant made everybody belong to everybody.

The care Honey formerly turned upon Big Mama's babies she was now turning upon the girls who hurt a finger, or forgot to bring lunch, or came out on rainy days without umbrellas, or who were just frightened or new. When a girl was in difficulties, someone on the shift was likely to suggest that she talk it over with Honey.

177

The girls confided their loves and hates to her. The way they looked, through their own troubles and joys, into her eyes put an end to her brooding. She tried to be someone whose only problems were their problems. At first she played the part as an actress might, knowing she wasn't the unassailable person they assumed she was. After months of putting on a good performance, she no longer needed to pretend.

In the mornings she would drop into her pocket things the girls lacked: a couple of bobby pins for this one, safety pins for another's baby, gum for the new girl from Mississippi who wanted to stop chewing tobacco.

Sometimes the foreman would call Honey aside. "Them two girls at the end of the line had a hair-pulling yesterday. See can you teach 'em manners."

Later Honey would say, "It's going to be all right," but she didn't tell the white foreman what was wrong. She didn't carry tales.

Today, with the sun warming her neck, Honey's mood stretched happily. Ah, this was her world, Honey Hoop's!

Poor Mrs. Palmer, she thought, I'll bet she's right lonely. Then she remembered Dotty Jane had said her mother wanted Honey to come to see her.

She hurried home, changed to her best street clothes, and took the car in the direction of Mrs. Palmer's hotel. The white conductor was one of the old, grumbling ones whom the war had placed at the wheels of the city's transportation. Because she hesitated to ask him for directions, Honey remained on the wrong car. She didn't care much. It was a fine day for being outdoors.

Walking along the crosstown boulevard, Honey now and again saw a woman in war worker's slacks. She tried to imagine what it would be like to live in one of the handsome houses or big hotels and go to work among women who came from the crowded regions. Reckon they feel right strange, she decided.

She was in a wealthy white neighborhood. She tried to see it as she had months—or was it years?—ago when she felt ashamed of being black and of having been born.

Now she was a pretty brown woman whose work was needed by her country, and she was here to get nothing for herself, only to give a little comfort to a lonely old woman. She stepped lightly.

Within the wide lobby was a central path flanked on either side by chairs and davenports grouped into two vast, wall-less parlors. The rugs around which the furniture stood were orientals. In the parlor to the right sat plump old men with canes and cigars and newspapers. Their moist gaze followed Honey. In the parlor to the left sat old women with nibbling mouths. Their stabbing eyes pinned price tags on Honey's turban and matching dress.

Honey had never before been in a large hotel. Hesitantly she approached a Negro elevator girl and asked for Mrs. Palmer. There were two elevators, both empty, both glittering and pink, both with colored girls in uniform sitting on stools waiting for summons.

The first one answered Honey. "You asks yonder at the desk. I'm new here. I don't know nobody."

Honey smiled as comfortingly as if the girl were one of the frightened ones at the factory. "You'll soon know everybody," she assured her.

At the desk, no one came forward. A woman jabbered at a switchboard. A man sorted mail. He wore a dark suit and a little evening tie such as Honey had noticed on the men in the orchestra the night she danced with Snake.

As the man looked up, one of the swift-eyed old ladies came to the desk. Querulously she complained about the temperature of her room and about dust on the rug in the hallway outside her door. The man shook his head gravely. He apologized; he spoke of the war; he made promises; he was sorry,

179

very, very sorry; he would talk to the maids at once. The woman waddled off. Then Honey asked for Mrs. Palmer.

"Mrs. Andrew Palmer: Room 842," he answered. He called after Honey. "Take the freight elevator."

Honey looked at the two empty cubicles and wondered what he meant. He lifted a section of the counter, came through, and led her past a mirrored door into a hallway which smelled of laundry and cooking. Mops and buckets and brooms stood about. A colored man in a dirty striped coat was rolling the electric cord of a vacuum cleaner. Some colored maids were waiting near a half-open elevator shaft.

The bottom of the pan ain't so pretty, Honey thought as the man said, "This elevator for the help."

The tone of his voice brought Emery to her side, Emery the black white man. This man with the tie was a white black man, or why had he been so afraid of the quarreling old lady? Honey saw Emery's lips speaking quickly. She said, "I didn't come to work. I just come to call on Mrs. Palmer."

From among the Negro maids a faint cackle rose and suddenly sizzled out within a pool of silence.

The man said, "You'll take this elevator!" He waited to see that she did.

Honey's heart hurt her throat. All her years of service hurried her into the back elevator, waiting now, filling with her own people. But all the talk she had heard in her own flat from white and colored too held her immobile.

She turned slowly and walked out, past the mirrored door, through the lobby, into the brilliance of the late afternoon. The shadows were long and lay beautifully across the wide boulevard. At one place the sunlight from a gash between buildings flickered helplessly against the roofs of rushing cars, just as the white man's voice had flickered against her ears as she left. He had called, "Not through the lobby! Not through the lobby! The service door is back here!"

She had gone through the lobby anyhow, and now she was outdoors, walking in America again, where he had no right to give orders.

On her way to the car stop, she heard someone call her name. It was Dorothy Jane, a notebook under her arm, her eyes happy in a tired, smudged face.

"Had a swell day! Mr. Marshal gave me some marvelous steers. I sat in at a labor-management committee meeting and, oh boy!——" She stopped. "How was Mummy? I'll bet she was tickled to see you!"

"I never saw Mrs. Palmer. Dotty Jane, I don't know whether I done right, but I didn't ride that there freight elevator like that man said I should, not with two elevators as empty as——"

"The dirty louse!" Dorothy Jane made a face. "Come with me."

Together they entered the lobby, achatter now with what had happened. Together they walked toward the front elevator. The man with the tiny tie started after them, then became overbusy with the mail. Dotty Jane's chin was up. She walked as other women tried to walk when entering a ballroom. The old ladies ceased talking to stare indignantly. The old men looked above their glasses at Honey and Dorothy Jane, at the man behind the desk, at the demanding eyes of the old ladies. The men smiled, though not happily.

In the elevator the new girl closed the door, and they began the ascent; a faint shivering, and the sound of a deep breath inhaled. Honey said to her softly, "I hope this don't get you in no trouble."

The black jaws continued to chew gum. The brown eyes rolled. "Ain't no trouble come you do lose a job pays like this job do."

Walking through the long hall, Dotty Jane, smiling mischievously, said, "Tell me about it."

Honey told what had happened, mimicking the little man.

181

They laughed at him. They laughed at the old men. They roared at the old ladies. Repeating what the black elevator girl said, they laughed so hard they had to lean against the wall and hold their sides. They laughed softly in deference to the people back of the double row of doors.

Indicating them with her thumb, Dorothy Jane said, "The dead unburied. Poor things, they haven't anything to laugh at."

Mrs. Palmer hadn't dressed for the afternoon yet. She had been lying on the couch. She explained that on hot days she never dressed until it was time to go down to dinner.

Crisply Dorothy Jane answered, "It's not been hot, Mother. It's swell out. I'll bet you were in this place all day."

"And why not?" her mother demanded. "Your face is dirty. You'd better bathe and get ready. I'll dress while I talk to Honey."

Honey could see that Mrs. Palmer had some secret things to say about Dorothy Jane. The apartment was too small for them to be said until the bathroom door was closed and the water running. Then Mrs. Palmer leaned forward: "Miss Dorothy Jane is much sweeter than she used to be, Honey, much sweeter. Talks quite a lot when we go down to dinner. She brought me this talcum. She brings me nice presents. . . . But she doesn't tell much." She waited for Honey's answer.

"Tell what, Mrs. Palmer?"

"Why she's so different. Why she changed——"

"Just so she's better——"

"One of the professors at her college writes me nice letters about her work. . . ." Her head pushed back against several flabby chins. Mrs. Palmer had grown stouter, and she had more wrinkles than she used to have. "Nobody explains why a nice girl should want to do that kind of work, whatever it is. It would be all right in a smart shop. Or real estate even." She raised her eyebrows and looked guiltily toward the bathroom. "She's had some very nice offers. Proposals, you know."

"She's prettier than ever."

"Yes, she's pretty." Mrs. Palmer sighed as if there were some things she couldn't say even to Honey.

"Ain't she a lot like her papa?"

"She says some of the same things he used to say, but it's different for a man. A man says those things, and after that he goes on living, following his work—well, as he ought to. When a girl says them, they take hold of her life more." Mournfully she shook her head.

"I wouldn't fret, Mrs. Palmer. She's happy. And she's good. She don't do nobody evil."

"She won't go out dancing when she does get the chance. She's different, different, that's all."

"Everybody's different. I reckon I different too."

Mrs. Palmer looked up in surprise. It wasn't usual for Honey to talk about herself. "I guess it's all that money you're earning."

"I reckon maybe the world's different, Mrs. Palmer."

"You mean the war and all . . . I buy bonds and I save my waste paper. Stack it up as neat as I can."

"Yes'm."

"I had a Red Cross card from Mr. Junior. He says he's well."

"And Bruce?"

"Mr. Bruce is in the South Pacific. His letters never tell much."

They were sitting in silence when Dorothy Jane came out half dressed to join them.

"Mrs. Palmer," Honey said, "your furniture, it looks right nice here."

"It's good furniture."

"I reckon you've got lots of friends right in the building."

"Four of us play cards on Tuesdays. When Miss Dorothy Jane isn't here, I usually eat my dinner with one of the ladies. Different ones, whoever happens to be down."

"Yes'm."

"How's everything at your house?"

"Nicely, thank you. . . . Mrs. Palmer, I don't see Mr. Palmer's picture."

"It's in my bedroom."

Mrs. Palmer led the way. Standing in front of it, worshipfully, Honey said, "I reckon you wanted it where you could look at him first thing and last thing."

Mrs. Palmer hesitated. She twisted her handkerchief around a finger. "A decorator helped me arrange my things. She said it should go back here. She said it isn't really good."

There it was again! Good! What was good? A body was expected to be good, and nobody, not even high-up white folks, knew what was good. Not even when it was only a picture.

Honey sighed, "Come she knew Mr. Palmer, she could see it's him. It looks just like him when he was doing for others and forgetting to look to his own self."

Mrs. Palmer shook her head. "They never did find out whether that rope was cut or just pulled loose."

Dorothy Jane joined them. "I can't imagine anyone's wanting to hurt Dad."

"Come somebody did——"

Mrs. Palmer continued the sentence through furious teeth: "—he ought to be strung up. Dying's too good for him. He ought to—he ought to have his throat cut!"

Silently they walked back into the living room. The decorator had thinned out Mrs. Palmer's things. She had moved the sewing basket into the bedroom with the picture. She had made the room into a place for company, a place to sit and talk. It wasn't a room which invited people to do anything. Empty of company, it was a room for loneliness. Honey got up to leave. She looked at Mrs. Palmer pityingly. Mrs. Palmer had always seemed too small for her big house. Now she seemed too small for these few rooms.

"I'll be going. I didn't aim to stay so late," Honey said.

Dorothy Jane said, "I'll bet you haven't eaten since you came off the shift."

"I'll get something."

In Dorothy Jane's clear blue eyes mischief twinkled. "How about having dinner with us?"

Honey grimaced at her.

Mrs. Palmer said, "If Honey's hungry, I've got some cake——"

Dorothy Jane's mischief turned serious. She wet her lips, about to speak.

Softly Honey said to her, "How many ladies you want to die of heart failure? Some of them old men look right frail too."

They laughed together. In her eyes were memories of evenings at Honey's flat, amusement at the flimsiness of partitions aslant as war dynamite rocked the world.

Mrs. Palmer said she was ready to go down to dinner, but Dorothy Jane told her to wait. She closed the door firmly on her mother.

In the corridor Honey whispered, "I can take that there back elevator and not care, I reckon. Laughing at them, I——"

"You'll take the front elevator or I'll know why!"

When the pretty box opened, it was half filled with old ladies dressed up for the evening. One on a cane leaned forward and toward Honey. She whispered, "You don't know someone who would like to come in and cook my suppers, do you? I've got a nice little kitchenette."

Afterwards Dorothy Jane mumbled, "I was dying to tell her you'd come out to find someone to cook yours—so you could rest when you got home from the plant!"

"My! My! After all them years Honey put in trying to teach you pretty manners! . . . I didn't care, really. Dotty Jane, seems like nothing can't hurt your feelings come you can laugh at it. . . . The colored folks in this town are sure learning to laugh."

They were at the corner where the car would stop. "This survey I'm making is—well, I've gone far enough already to see that it's going to take the wind out of the sails of those who talk about factory absenteeism among Negro women."

"Your papa would be right proud."

Dorothy Jane's slipper kicked at some tufts of grass. "Do you remember that washout I nearly married? He married someone else the very next week."

"You ain't worrying none about Mr. Jim?"

"I got a card from Jim once from India. . . . I'm not worried about anybody. . . ." The girl's mood shifted. She winked at Honey and wriggled her trim shoulders. "I'm married to my work."

"For now you are," Honey answered. "You'll marry someone. This time you'll be sure he's the right man. You're more sensible now."

Dotty's eyes squinted at the tawny sunset. "Some of those husbands meant for us aren't coming back to make us brides. Lots of us aren't going to have the kind of chance we want. It's the price we're paying for democracy, so I figure I'd better be doing the sort of work which sees to it we really get the democracy our husbands are dying for. . . . Maybe I won't find the right man. Maybe I won't have a chance at my kind of marriage. I'm trying to live so I can take it or leave it. Take it or leave it."

The red-and-tan car was within sight, tossing toward them. Honey thought: That's what her mama wants to know. She told it to me instead.

"Honey, I always wondered about you and sex. You never married, or did you?"

"I reckon to me sex was always what give Mama too many babies and Eulatha too few husbands. Reckon I kind of drew back from it. Except once, and that time the man, he weren't no good."

"Did Bob let you know he had a wire from Lamb?"

"Bob Jensen?"

"Lamb and Glory are getting back tonight."

"Ain't it funny, Dotty, me getting news of Lamb from you?" Honey was still shaking her head as she got on the streetcar.

15

Lamb looked around at them, one by one. He was only pausing, ready to pace again. "This is the last evening you'll be welcome here."

Glory said, "Lamb sweet, quit prowling like a tiger. Sit down and tell them about it."

Lamb's mouth remained serious while his eyes flirted down at Glory, cross-legged on the floor. "No more sitting until after November seventh!"

There were perhaps thirty people in the room, as many whites as Negroes. The winds of a new day were coming over the horizon; the tiny whirl of advance motion, here visible, drew those who wanted greater winds to blow.

The reasons for coming were as various as the faces, and the faces were various with race and age and zeal and good and bad intentions. The trade unionists were the only ones whose eyes were sure and unembarrassed. In other eyes, shadows were enmeshed with compassion and hate and fervor and indignation and love and sometimes with scheming.

A few were bobby-soxers, young girls with sturdy, brown legs; girls resentful because their city denied them higher education. One wanted to study occupational therapy. Another wanted to study art at the great university. A third wanted to study medicine. The dizzy height of her target made them laugh. Women who were white had only recently been getting their chance. Men, if Negro, weren't accepted. Even Negro doctors working in the fine new City Hospital weren't members of the local medical society.

The bobby-soxer argued. "They put on campaigns to rid the Ville of t.b. and v.d. and then won't let our doctors learn along with the very white doctors doing all this for us! It's silly! Silly!"

Lamb answered her, "It's one of the silliest God-damned sorrows in the world!" He had been back and forth. He stopped. "We ought to give a race-relations show in this city."

"It would have to be a circus with lots of clowns."

The man who brought that forth was a white minister who had never before said anything. He came, and listened, and sighed. The Rev. Mr. Anton was a thin man who looked as if he habitually forgot to eat, or perhaps as if he couldn't eat because his stomach was made queasy by his feelings.

When he said that about the circus, Lamb's eyes gripped his. "A circus! A race-relations circus! Funniest show in the world!"

At once Lamb became a barker stalking across the sawdust of the side show. "Step right up, ladies and gentlemen! Step right up and buy your tickets! See the Streetcar Stander! Our Streetcar Stander's going to be famous," he assured his listeners. "She'll be a skinny white woman with an armful of bundles and mouth pickle-puckered. She'll hang to a strap with one hand and her bundles with another. The motorman will start and stop like a—like a motorman. We can rig up machinery under the floor. There'll be an empty seat with a Negro girl in it and bingo-bingo!" He showed how the Streetcar Stander would jerk and slide but keep on standing. Acting out the part, Lamb's gestures were witty. His listeners wiped tears of laughter from their eyes.

Then he cocked a hat far over one eye and became another barker: "Buy your seats, ladies and gentlemen, for the Tor-

189

mented Ticket Taker!" Now he was a hushed-voiced employee fumbling over theater tickets offered by a colored man: " 'Th-there's b-b-been s-s-some m-m-m-mistake. S-s-s-some m-m-mistake! The show's over—I mean the girl will refund your money.' " The Tormented Ticket Taker's voice was steady now. " 'Step over there quickly and get your money.' "

Lamb clapped his hands to announce the next show: "Right this way. Tickets for Go to Church—Somewhere. Go to Church—Somewhere!"

He became the deacon at the door. Glory jumped up and put a flower in his buttonhole. Lamb flipped the tails of his dress coat. Pompously he escorted a white woman to her pew and came cheerfully up the aisle. There he froze into horrified helplessness. He fluttered his fingers against one another and leaned forward to whisper in a deep voice which cracked with womanish high notes: " 'There is a splendid, perfectly splendid, splendid Negro congregation—ah, somewhere. I can't give you the address, but I understand strangers are always welcome. You look in a phone book—no, not here, down at the drugstore, and—and' "—calling loudly, as if down the steps—" 'be sure to Go to Church—Somewhere!' "

Next he was a department-store floorwalker keeping a Negro away from the tearoom. " 'Over there's the drinking fountain. You're quite welcome to use the bubbler. No, no one ever objected to that! Get right in line with the white folks!' "

He took one inconsistency after another, one social embarrassment after another, and created his circus side show, converting their humiliations into hilarity.

That was a month ago. Now Lamb said the fun and the talk had to stop.

"You got to get them registered: the war workers who've come up from the hills, from other cities, the ones who've never thought voting was important. You've got to get them to the polls! This has nothing to do with how they'll vote. Register everybody! Make it possible for everybody to cast a ballot in November. This has to be America really being American. You've got to go out and get corns. Go out every evening! Make them promise! Hilda here will assign you to districts. She's in charge of the chart. This has to be a house-to-house job."

It was Honey who said, "Lamb, come you want to invite the folks here to report, say, on Sunday nights, I'll have some cookies and a pitcher of something ready."

"Bribe us!" someone laughed. They wanted to come. The most insistent were several university students as resentful that their campus barred Negroes as were the barred bobby-soxers themselves.

"Only those will be welcome who can report having covered at least twenty houses each day after work. Talk to all you can contact. Leave dodgers for the others. Keep still about how to vote. This is registration only. . . . See you Sunday evenings."

The tact Honey had used with the Palmers, she now turned upon the Ville.

"May I see Big Mama?" she would say to the little girls who opened the doors.

When the Big Mama came, Honey would smile. "I'm not selling, begging, or prying—just stepped by after work to remind you to register. Maybe you is registered?"

She had fun doing it. The people would ask her in, and she would admire the way they kept their houses, or the baby's dress, or the framed diploma. Talking about why they should register, she'd say "we," meaning the CIO, and feel as if the best of this world were hers.

In one house a party was going on, brown women at bridge tables. They stopped and listened and joked among themselves.

191

The party was in honor of a bride-to-be. At one table the young women played; at another, their mothers.

One of the thin girls shook out her bracelets, arranging and rearranging them on her arms as she said to Honey, "I suppose we ought to be out doing what you are."

Quietly Honey answered, "I reckon you should."

One of the older women laughed heartily at Honey's frankness, a loud, bold, cackling laugh. She was tall and lean, more Indian in appearance than Negro. "I like a woman who knows her own mind and speaks it!"

The others joked about that. The tall woman was famous for "speaking her mind."

"Nobody ever accused you of being tactful," someone said.

"Tact is mostly lies," she countered. "I haven't had a life which left room for tact. I've gone my way, raised up my boys honest and smart. Four of them, four rich black men. My girl's educated too. I didn't do that on tact."

She stared at Honey's beauty with approval, listened to her with approval. She asked, "What do you think of tact, young woman?"

Amused, Honey answered, "I thinks highly of it when I can't tell what it is."

They laughed and made friends with Honey then, but they were suspicious and scornful of registering. Politics had a bad flavor for them. Votes sold at a dollar a vote. Promises made, and a break for every promise. Hopes raised up and thrown down again. They held themselves above all that.

Honey argued. Her answers were quick and good-humored, but gentle. "We got to live tomorrow on tomorrow. We done enough living it on yesterday. Living it on yesterday is what the boss-man wants."

The bridge players were women who either had never heard of a boss-man or were the daughters and granddaughters of women trying to forget boss-men. They turned back to their cards. They wanted Honey to leave. Only the Indianlike woman now looked at her with friendly eyes. She seemed fascinated by Honey's frank ways.

"What's your name?" she asked. "You talk sense."

When Honey told her name, the woman swung around in her chair, gathered up her cards, glanced at them briefly, and bid four spades.

She was Ben's mother.

That evening as Ben smoked his after-dinner cigarette, Mrs. Boston lingered at the table with him. She put down her knitting and reached for a cigarette too.

"She's pretty—Honey Hoop is pretty. I like her."

She wasn't inclined to explain where they had met or how it happened that she knew who Honey was while Honey didn't know who she was. Mrs. Boston wasn't given to explaining non-essentials. She had only one thing to tell Ben tonight. She told it without faltering: she'd be satisfied to have him marry Honey.

Ben let her say it and say it again. He frowned down in silence toward his cigarette.

"Well?" his mother snapped.

"I haven't been waiting for your consent."

Mrs. Boston turned the idea over in her mind. It could have many meanings. She didn't ask Ben to tell her more. He was probably like most men, not able to understand why the girl didn't want him. And Honey was probably like most women, not knowing why she didn't want the man who wanted her.

Mrs. Boston handed Ben a fresh ash tray and carried the soiled ones to the kitchen to wash them. With Mrs. Boston, scrubbing and washing and dusting was a way of fighting back at a hostile world. She kept Ben's house shining, not for his sake or for the sake of his fine friends or for Loraine's sake, but because all her life she had found pleasure only in grappling

193

with something. Grappling, a woman might win. For the same reason she kept a game of solitaire going. On a side table in the dining room the cards were usually spread, ready for her spare moments. Black cards on red, red on black, a woman fighting to prove her skill.

The house was large, with wide halls and a carved stair well; yet she cleaned every room every day. It made her feel younger than sixty-eight.

While she was in the living room folding the evening papers Ben had left unfolded, she heard him preparing to leave the house. She said over her shoulder, "Tell Honey Hoop if she'll bring me some of those leaflets, I'll give them out on this block. She said neighbors were the best to go to neighbors."

"How many do you want?"

Ben's face showed distrust of what his mother's tart tongue might say to Honey.

She answered, "Tell her to come."

All that summer Ben had watched Honey change. As a photographic plate gradually becomes more and more detailed, so Honey became a person he could know. He had always loved her. Now he loved her irrevocably.

He surmised that she was just becoming acquainted with herself. Talking about events, she would naïvely reveal her opinion. She would say to Ben, "I reckon lots of times killing is just getting ready to be born, like in this war." Once when Ben invited her to ride in his car, she said, "Let's go where it ain't all Negro. It's too comfortable to stay with your own all the time. I fancy a body ought to go out where he can feel more of the world even if he don't like what he feels. Most of us picks out just a little patch for our own. Most of us segregates ourself. Mr. Emery says——"

"Are you in love with Emery?"

She took a long time to answer that. She tried hard to tell

Ben the truth. They were in his car, and his unhappy hands were fiddling with his keys. Their tinkle hit lightly against the silence of the summer evening.

When she spoke she put her fingers on his. "I've been a maid a long time. I got feelings like a maid. I got away from being a maid for Mrs. Palmer. Now I'm working for the plant and for CIO, but I ain't working for CIO like Glory is. Glory works for it, sure she got something to do can make it better. Lamb, he is the CIO in his heart and in the CIO heart it's Lamb, but I can work for CIO only like a maid. That's the way it was at first. Then Mr. Emery comes along and makes me feel like as if I can make myself into somebody as much CIO as Lamb or Glory. I'm learning it the way some people learns in school. When I gets home and thinks back to how Mr. Emery looked when he talked to me like that, something stirs in my heart. It's an ecstasy like the kind Lamb used to get for his religions. I don't rightly know if that's love. It don't make me hate his wife none. I like Miss Mollie. It don't make me worry none what he got for breakfast, nor if he's eating right, the way I worries for you, Ben love———"

"When you call me 'Ben love,' are you thinking of———"

"I'm thinking of you. I'm thinking I never want to hurt you and I never want you should be sad. I'm thinking I like to look after you. Being with Mr. Emery's kind of like being with God. Right now I got a lot of religion for Mr. Emery. Being with you, Ben love, is like being with my own."

16

IN THE STUDY OF MR. DUPREE'S HOME THE SAME MEN WERE assembled who had met nearly a year ago to talk about the award for Andrew Palmer. This time they came together on a warm evening with the mumble of the air conditioner annoying their ears.

The wall which had been around them before was still around them; they no longer tried to scale it. Now that Andrew was dead, there was no one to shame them for not scaling it. Had he been alive, he very likely would have been behaving as the rest of the liberals in the country were behaving—truckling to the CIO and that man in the White House.

Like them he might claim to be acting in the cause of true Americanism even while advocating the un-Americanism of a fourth term. They saw that as treachery, as a threat to their future.

They were enraged men now. Their rage had brought them together from diverse political homes. Sam Smith was an incurable Democrat and would remain a Democrat. He met tonight in the cause of the Republican party as a way of expediting the return of his own party to its traditions. At an FEPC hearing, Mr. Smith's employment policies had been condemned; despite all Sterling DuPree's efforts, the company was commanded to comply with Executive Order 8802. To oppose the President's re-election was his best chance for revenge.

Sterling DuPree was not so much a Republican as a 1944 Republican because, believing in the past, he could only ally himself against the current governmental epidemic of innovations. Tom Rusk was a Republican because restrictive covenants had become imbedded in his thinking. He believed in America, but it had to be a blond, Protestant, English-speaking America. When he talked about the Melting Pot, as he frequently did, he assumed that the melting would intensify the blondness, the Protestantism, and the English accent. Seeing the minorities moving toward the fourth term, he automatically moved against it.

With Mr. Schneider the choice was simpler. The men he respected for their power and success denounced the goings on in Washington. They made clear where respectable men must stand. Gus merely fell in line.

Now Sterling DuPree's long aristocratic fingers turned off the radio. They had heard the President address the Teamsters' Union. They had heard laughter of the people, by the people, for the people, and against themselves. There was abandon in that laughter, and scorn.

Mr. DuPree held his pencil poised. "What support can we be sure of? Voting support?"

"The Negroes?"

Sterling dropped his pencil. "I hear there's some doubt——"

"They always vote for Lincoln's party."

Sterling shook his head. "I've been informed . . . All these war jobs . . ."

Sam Smith jumped to his feet. "I told you! I told you! They ought to be kept in their place!"

Sterling answered, "Our hope lies in a small vote. CIO is putting on a big registration campaign."

Mr. Schneider squirmed. Mrs. Schneider's dressing table had been littered for days with stacks of Get-Out-the-Vote dodgers. Her League of Women Voters had been talking Get-

Out-the-Vote for years. Never before had the results seemed sinister. The trouble with women was that, absolved from business responsibilities, they were always judging things on principles floating around in a vacuum. Like children.

Mr. DuPree, in a moment of marital blindness, had suggested that the wives accompany their husbands and visit with Mrs. DuPree while the political horizon was scanned. Since the evening with her book was destroyed, Mrs. DuPree tried to accept her visitors gracefully.

She led them into a sunroom, also air-conditioned by a unit nearly as large as a piano and as droning as a sewing machine. She explained its defects as part of the penalty paid for clinging to an old family home which couldn't be properly cooled from the basement up. There were fans at work too: a ceiling fan of the old saloon variety painted now a delicate green, a floor fan of a new noiseless type, and several table fans.

"My! How nice and cool!" Mrs. Schneider said. "Our fans aren't much, and of course you can't buy an air conditioner in wartime. My place has been like an oven all day."

Mrs. DuPree apologized for her wealth. "I smoke so much that in sheer decency I must have these."

She passed a box of cigarettes. Mrs. Smith hesitated among the brands but at length chose one, though decrying it as not her kind. Mrs. Schneider reached in without looking, but frowned and said, "I've smoked so much today, I really shouldn't." Mrs. Rusk said, "What fun! I love to smoke, but I'm afraid to when I paint. I spill so much turpentine around. I'm doing oils now."

Silently and slowly Mrs. DuPree affixed her cigarette into a long holder. Then they sat back and faced the evening of waiting for their husbands. Waiting, if possible, without offending anyone, without telling their husbands' business secrets.

They talked of the fans, of the lovely old house, of the handsome private place in which it stood, of poor Mrs. Palmer, of the wartime sacrifices, which they agreed weren't difficult at all, and so they came to the subject of maids, Negro maids. Then the evening livened up.

As one who had once spoken too much and learned her lesson, Mrs. Smith said little except by looking glum. It was Tippy Rusk tonight who led the way. She clowned, and her audience laughed at her enactment of the sharecropper girl with the vacuum cleaner. Then they divulged real and fancied grievances.

No one had full-time maids any more except Mrs. DuPree, who had a cook to whom she paid a salary "exactly triple what I paid before, and I always paid well." She also had an old man. With a twinkle she explained, "I keep him around, you know, to fall off ladders and lose the hammer and sprinkle the clothes on the wash line when I finally lure a laundress into putting them there."

Tippy Rusk giggled. "No wonder the war's going so well. Everyone with a grain of sense seems to be in the Army or Navy or making munitions."

Mrs. Schneider thought the maids were within their rights to want an eight-hour day, but why couldn't they work the eight hours when they were needed? Who wanted a maid who ran off without preparing dinner?

Mrs. Smith said no one could tell her anything about that impudent woman at the Negro agency who called herself Mrs. Somebody or other!

Mrs. Schneider, troubled, went on. "She said colored women want to be at home evenings with their families. To look after their children. She talked about prevention of juvenile delinquency. And, of course, she's dead right. . . . I told her I'd been chairman of a Juvenile Delinquency Committee for ten years and she'd have to send me someone to do my work in

199

the household if I was to go on being chairman. She sent an old wreck. I'll bet Lucy is seventy-five if she's a day. She's so deaf she doesn't hear the buzzer, and when she does wander into the dining room she's as likely to set things down on the table as to pass them."

Tippy Rusk giggled. "I've been having fun ever since I quit trying to get a cook. I have a good cleaning woman who comes in daily, and we go out for our meals. Tom adores to go to restaurants anyhow. Everyone stops eating to watch the handsome man, and I put on my best and boldest! We really are having a good time. We eat at a different place every evening, and the other night we danced! Poor Tommy began to puff, so we quit."

Again Mrs. Smith with considerable effort broke her silence. "Mine belongs to the Pushers and Shovers. She races out of my place like mad to be sure to be on time!"

Because Mrs. Rusk hadn't heard about the Pushers and Shovers, Mrs. Smith explained, "They have a club to push and shove on the streetcars. They get fined if they don't do it every evening between five and six. I'm not sure of the morning time."

Mrs. DuPree squinted quizzically. "Do you think that's so?"

Mrs. Schneider said she had heard about the Pushers and Shovers a long time ago, heard it from a woman who said they did it only on Thursdays and called themselves the Thursday Shovers. "She had put an ad in the paper, and a lovely-looking colored girl came to apply, not one of those fat, sloppy ones, but a nice-looking one. The girl had experience and references and everything. She was exactly what this woman wanted, but the girl wouldn't agree to take the place because she said she had to have Thursday off. Wednesday was better for the woman, and when she insisted, the girl said she had made a pledge to push and shove on the streetcar every Thursday." Mrs. Schneider raised her brows in unhappy bewilderment. "She's a nice woman, and she claimed the girl told her that herself."

Mrs. Smith said, "She should have had her arrested!"

Longingly Mrs. DuPree's pretty fingers toyed with the pages of her book, there half read on the side table. She mumbled, "I don't blame anyone for not wanting to do house-work——"

Mrs. Schneider broke in: "That's what I say! Out of loyalty to ourselves, a woman with any education just ought not succumb."

They agreed that nearly all their friends had succumbed, and some were actually claiming to enjoy it, bragging about their cooking and how shiny they kept the bottoms of their pans.

Mrs. Rusk's bright eyes had been fluttering around from one touch of DuPree elegance to another, her mind only half on what was being said. Now in her flightiest way she whispered across clasped hands, "Do you think maybe the colored girls feel that way about it too? Wouldn't it be funny if——"

Mrs. Schneider snatched her back into reality. "If they only stopped to figure it out with pencil and paper, by the time they get their board free and all that they are given out of a nice household, they're better off than with those big factory salaries."

No one had actually figured it out, but they agreed that the girls would be much better off, and if they weren't so unfor-tunately ignorant they would know it.

Mrs. Rusk mounted the broomstick of fancy again and zoomed, "Sometimes I think they kind of look down on us."

They ignored that as women polite in the presence of obvious insanity.

Mrs. Schneider cleared her throat. "I read an article the other day on race hatred."

Then they all talked at once, sparring for attention. Mrs. Smith said there was no such thing as race hatred. It was just that an inferior people couldn't be given too much leeway; they had to be kept under control.

Mrs. Schneider said she, of course, felt no race hatred for anyone. As a matter of fact, in her work in various organizations, she made it her business to be polite to everyone and to feel only respect for other peoples.

Mrs. DuPree peered through the smoke of her cigarette at her own feelings. "It isn't a question of hatred. I don't know anyone who hates Negroes, nearly no one," she added, careful not to look toward Mrs. Smith, "but when it comes to having them served in restaurants, our restaurants, and calling them Mr. and Mrs.—it's all so absurd." She smiled at her fancy. "I try to imagine them living exactly as we do, you know, and it always gets off into something comical."

Tippy Rusk clapped her hands. "It's like trying to do a literal portrait and a devil takes hold of your pencil and you find yourself making a caricature!"

Mrs. Schneider said, "I get along all right when I go to the League of Women Voters' luncheon and they are there and the chairman says, 'We'll now have a report from Mrs. Jones.' We get used to that at the League. . . ."

Mrs. DuPree smiled, "My daughter is used to it too. She works at a bookshop—this didn't seem the time for a debut— and she sells Negro books all the time, but then, Maideth, poor darling, thinks she wants to write plays. Of course, Anna Lucasta is a good-looking girl." She said the last with the air of a woman who recognizes feminine beauty as a skill and was willing to pay deference to skill wherever it occurred.

Mrs. Schneider continued with her own self-argument. "We have lovely colored members. A very active colored branch, and, of course, one vote is as good as another, but when you have the unattractive kind in your own home breaking things . . ."

Her voice died off, and then they were silent, each trying to think of colored people who were really like nice white people and who were deserving of the same treatment because they were educated and nice both. . . .

The fans droned. The women frowned down at the floor. Mrs. Smith sat apart from the others. She wasn't a lady in the same way they were ladies. She didn't try to be.

Disliking her, they began to like Negroes a little better. Mrs. Schneider, especially, secretly lamented her own inability to accept the Negro as a full citizen. She could see no logic in her position: "I agree with their struggle for equality, but . . ." Alone at night, wakeful at dawn, she had often tried to finish that sentence. Each effort brought her to the same conclusion. If the principle was right, no qualifying "but" could be right too. She would sigh and reach out her hand to touch the sleeping body of her husband. Loving him, she pitied him. Pitying him, she loved him. Living with him was helping him, being a helpmate for the load he had chosen to pull. She had to pull it in his way. Recently her mind had decided that the Negro deserved to be treated as a first-class citizen. But if she were to abide by that tenet, she would, in her husband's eyes and the eyes of the world, be pulling against him, slowing his journey. She couldn't urge Gus to think for himself, because by so doing he would be throwing away his key to success. He would lose the masterful ways she rather liked around the house. And he couldn't goose-step with the others and travel his own path too. Being part of a group meant to share its dislikes as heartily as its likes. More heartily. As a practical woman Mrs. Schneider saw that she must go along with him. It made her love Gus a little less and herself much less.

Tippy Rusk was more talented as a wife. Even as a flirtatious young girl she had sensed that to be a woman beloved was to agree. The slightest prick of disagreement could burst the bubble. Early she accepted her role of a mischievous and amusing child. Every age had its clown. Nor was it a dishonorable calling, since it claimed only smiles in reward. To be a clown required the heart of an artist, and to be an artist was a way of looking at life. Originality was all-important there. She knew her paintings were no good, but her performance as Tom Rusk's wife was excellent. She didn't grieve over wrongs to Negroes, but once in a while on a street corner she would impulsively open her purse into the hands of a Negro child. Once she had left herself without carfare while her automobile was in the shop. She took a taxi to Tom's office, and by her explanation of what had happened sent him into an uproar of laughter. He was sure she had spoken only to amuse him. He told everyone that his wife, who was a kid in lots of ways, had lost her purse—she had lost purses before—and what she had said to amuse him.

Mrs. DuPree was bored by women. Especially these women. She was interested in beauty: her own, Sterling's, her daughter's, and the beauty of houses and clothes and jewels. Indolence of movement was part of her beauty as a woman. It corresponded with an indolence of mind. The racial dilemma permitted her to remain quite calm. Her mind accepted the taboos as nonsense, but doing away with them meant struggle, and her own heart tabooed struggle. Swimming against the current was as silly as prejudice against the Negro. Why exchange one silliness for another?

But she understood that Mrs. Schneider felt it her duty to brave the current, and little Mrs. Rusk twittered in jest much she held as truth. Mrs. DuPree realized that she looked at them with the eyes of a courtesan, but she didn't scorn a courtesan. A courtesan could be more lovely than a crusader or a clown. A woman's first duty was to be lovely.

They could hear the men approaching. Mrs. DuPree stood up and said, "We'll have a drink together."

Mrs. Rusk whispered, "Make it powerful. They've been talking politics. Just look at their faces!"

The men tried to talk of the nothings they considered suitable for mixed company, but their talk kept reverting to the campaign.

Tom Rusk said, "We ought to get a liberal to use as a front."

They tried to think of one.

"I miss Andrew Palmer more every day," Mr. DuPree said. "A great spirit, an irreplaceable citizen."

They named men of his type. In the political campaign to come, many speeches would have to be made. Tom Rusk said, "We have men who can talk to business. Know the language. We have men who can talk to the small shopkeepers. We have men who can talk to the churches and synagogues. We need someone to talk to the masses, someone more respectable than Gerald L. K. Smith."

They struggled with their memories.

To pacify them, Mrs. DuPree said, "Does it do any good to talk to the masses?"

"Tom, who are the masses? Do you mean the unions?" Tippy asked.

"And the Negroes——"

Mrs. Smith blared, "You'll do better if you don't talk to them. Just tell them! Tell them how to vote! Down South we don't trust niggers, we tell them."

Mr. Smith grumbled, "That isn't working so well any more."

His wife flushed. "Then I'd ignore them!"

Mr. DuPree bowed from the waist. "My dear lady, we cannot afford to ignore a vote bloc large enough to decide the election. There stands the fact—regrettable, realistic, reprehensible—but for the present, at least, unalterable. Unalterable!"

17

FULLY DRESSED ABOVE THE KNEES, GLORY AND LAMB SAT AT either end of the bathtub, soaking their feet. The registration booths had closed an hour ago.

"Wonder where Honey is?" Lamb asked.

"Going around the Ville seeing that promises were kept."

"She's taking to this like a duck to water."

"Once she got into the pond. Getting her off the bank was the hard part. Lamb, what's going to happen if she marries Ben?"

"Honey's not the marrying kind. I got over expecting Honey to marry a long time ago."

"You don't understand Honey."

"I understand her. She's easy to understand. . . . Once I didn't. Once she surprised me. . . . Only once."

"It's as plain as the plain nose on your plain face. She's going to marry Ben."

"Nonsense."

"What have you against Ben?"

"Ben's a fine fellow."

"Why isn't Honey going to marry him?"

Lamb had been looking down at his feet. "I believe we got them registered." He wriggled his toes thoughtfully. "By golly, she might! You women know everything! . . . Hey, Honey!"

The outer door had slammed. Honey came up the steps

slowly. They called out, joking about their weariness and hers.

Lamb asked, "Is Glory talking sense? She says you're going to marry Ben."

They heard the hall chair creak as Honey sat down. "We're going to celebrate registration."

The bathroom was silent. Then Lamb roared, "When is this going to be?"

"Tomorrow evening after I come off the shift, if you and Glory can come."

"Look," Glory demanded, "you're not giving up your job?"

"I'm keeping my job. I've been to see his mother. I like her a lot. She's going to keep hers too. She'll keep right on tending the house. She's right pleased."

Lamb's voice warned, "Likely you're getting a Big Mama in your life!"

"You can't get one come you really got a life."

The water sound ceased. Lamb tossed a bath towel into the hall and stepped on it. "I'm going to throw you a swell wedding! There's a new night club—how about Emery and Mollie?"

"Nobody is going to be there but you and Glory and Loraine and Ben's mother and maybe Mama and Papa."

Glory in a housecoat stood on the towel too. "It works out fine," she said. "Lamb's going to be ordered East after the election."

Honey smiled down at their feet. "Reckon if I hadn't made up my own mind, CIO would have ordered me to do it. I've done so much like the CIO said, I kind of feel as if I ought to ask Hilda about this."

Lamb, imitating Hilda's nearsightedness, whined, "The national policy. . . ."

Honey got up to continue her climb to her room. "The woman downstairs asked me why we didn't have many meetings up here now. She used to like to hear us laugh. When I told her what we laughed at mostly, she got tears. She said she never could laugh at the slights. She used to cry about them when she got home."

Lamb's right arm, fist upraised, began to gesture as if he were before an audience. He shouted: "We are laughing today at the slights we used to cry about! We've got reason to laugh! We've got reason to laugh and to work—to work like hell!"

Glory nodded in approval.

Honey drawled, "Marrying Ben, I feel kinda like a bigamist. Marrying him when I'm already so married to the CIO that I got it running around my house barefoot making speeches. . . ."

The Boston household was as hushed and beflowered as if a funeral instead of a wedding were about to occur. Big Mama in a new blue dress and Papa in his country-club frock coat were sitting stiff and silent next to Mrs. Boston, who didn't bother to talk to them. She was at the end of the second row of chairs bearing on their backs the inscription: BOSTON DECEASEMENT HOME. She leaned against the highly polished inlaid table, bare today of cards. She leaned with the triumph of a winner who has unexpectedly scooped up all, for Ben was to be married and happy, yet she would not have to become either an outcast from his home or an intruder within it. She and Honey had talked it out. Honey was a girl who could talk straight and stay polite too.

A tinkle of laughter escaped from the kitchen. Mrs. Boston rose and tiptoed around the lace-trimmed dining-room table with its tiered cake topped by paper bride and groom. The door to the pantry squeaked; then the laughter ceased and was not resumed.

When she returned she saw that Honey's sisters had come. Carmen, as white as powder and net ruffles and cotton gloves could make her, sat stiffly alone on the davenport, which had been pushed back against the wall. From Eulatha's ears jangled long red earrings. Her costume was savagely expensive and her hands were bossy as she ushered eight uninvited small Hoops into the back row. Her own had wailed to come. Secretly, chuckling, Eulatha got all the children ready. She knew Honey wouldn't mind; she hoped Big Mama and those *dicktee* Bostons would.

The children struggled up into the chairs. One of Big Mama's wore pigtails, but the rest of the little girls wore straight, polished bobs topped by artificial flowers. The little boys' heads were shaved except for a sudden upstanding narrow fan of hair above their foreheads. Mrs. Boston approved the gleaming cleanliness. Her quick eye traveled the row of percale blues and reds and greens, observing all the Hoop economies: the dress trimmed from the left-overs of a shirt, the man-size neckties, the mended jumper. Satisfied, she nodded. These were respectable people. With a swoop of her arms she commanded the wrigglers to move into the front row where they could see.

Loraine, shapely in yellow chiffon, was keeping the door, opening it before the bell could be rung, whispering what she had to say. She was using her funeral-parlor habits. Following her example, all the household was hushed and reverent.

When at last Ben arrived, he walked between two men. The tan, plump one was the Methodist minister whose church the Bostons attended. The little man with the dark, pocked skin was the Baptist minister who had baptized Lamb. He was known as a shouter.

Lamb was looking at him as if at his own past. The minister dropped his eyes. Then he lifted them again, and he and Lamb nodded like old friends. Gloria's pop-eyed glance kept searching the wide staircase for Honey. Ben, a white boutonniere on his coat, had gone up two at a time.

209

When Honey appeared it was not down the handsome stair-way but as if from nowhere. Suddenly she was in the room facing the minister, her hands clasped lightly against each other.

Upstairs Ben had told her why there were two ministers: he couldn't slight either one. Both had performed many services for him, dozens and dozens of free ones for the poor.

"It's all right," Honey said. "Just so it ain't Episcopalian. I ain't high-up enough for that. And not Church of God. That's too new for Mama. She's Methodist, and Papa was Baptist, so I reckon it's about right to have both."

"You're a pretty bride, Honey, mighty pretty," Ben said thickly.

Honey's eyes rolled toward Mrs. Boston's long mirror. "I reckon so," she said appraisingly.

"You didn't want a white dress? Because if you did——"

"I didn't, Ben," Honey said hastily. "I done wore a heap of white in my day. Maid's uniforms, they was. I didn't want nothing like that. Colors was too bold. And black too sad. So I picked gray. It looks right nice with your orchid. I ain't never had an orchid before. I had one offered once, but that was all. . . . My dress, it's good, I reckon."

"It's pretty, mighty pretty."

"It's made plain, and it ain't long like some, but it don't make me look none like Mrs. Palmer's Honey. It looks like I'm my own."

"And mine."

"And yours, Ben. Yours. I'm mighty proud I'm yours too."

Rev. Topaz, Methodist, prayed before and after Rev. Higginton, Baptist. At first they prayed for show, in defense of their own craftsmanship; then they prayed in reply to Honey's wide-eyed searching for their meaning. Their prayers became admonition and well-wishing and social comment. The admonition and well-wishing wove lightly around and around, like

210

the circles of a spider's web. The social comment was the spread of sturdy spokes upon which they dared to rest their weight.

Closing his eyes and rippling out his full lips, Rev. Topaz spoke intimately to his God, reminding Him of black loyalty despite the unchristian behavior of white Christians, yet why, oh why was it that only dark Christians held to the doctrine of the brotherhood of man, held to it in deeds as well as words? Surely the All-Powerful had some divine motive for the sinfulness of white children. Rev. Topaz did not doubt the wisdom of the motive or that someday the white man would really catch religion and cease his sinning, but in the meantime colored men and women had to stagger forward, bearing terrific burdens on aching shoulders. He described the ache much as a union leader might have described it. It was college graduates working as porters—and slights everywhere. Honey, chin high, earnestly awaited his impending advice. To ease the ache—the ministerial bass scolded—colored men and colored women and colored children must practice Christian humility, must learn it and practice it!

Startled, Honey turned to look at Ben. How was he taking this unforeseen betrayal? She saw that Ben, masked by polite inattention, was adream with love of her. He had not heard.

The shouting of Rev. Higginton was louder and crisper, yet also self-righteous with condemnation of the ways of white folks. Remembering how he had stayed dry while his hired men immersed Lamb, Honey knew in advance all the talk would come to nothing.

Me and Ben, she thought, come we're going to be one, we got to make us one ourselves. All this here talk ain't going to do it. I reckon we got to do it every day. It can't be love and hate both, like it was with Snake. It's got to be love and taking care of each other. The sins of white folks got to be fought off so as we can be people, brave enough to know Honey and

211

Ben is as good as we is good inside, and that skin ain't where evil lives.

She began to be sorry she had let the salesgirl who sold her the gray dress talk her into having the short gray wedding veil too. It was becoming, yes, it was; but why must a brown girl copy white folks even when she was getting married?

Out yonder in the kitchen there was a cateress putting tiny sandwiches on platters. She had her chicken salad made and her coffee, the sherbet ready to be put into the tall blocks of ice. She had the white satin bow on the knife for cutting the wedding cake. She had champagne on ice. She had everything ready just as Honey would have had it ready for Dotty Jane.

I reckon we ain't got nobody to learn it from except white folks, Honey lamented. Only difference is that come Ben and me don't stick to each other and love each other and do for each other, the world, it's going to bear down harder on us than on white folks. I reckon I'm right lucky marrying Ben, because Ben, he's got nothing in him but goodness. Ben, he's for true.

She slipped her hand through his arm, the way she had been too shy to do at first. His elbow pressed it exultantly against his heart. Later, they agreed that was the moment which pronounced them man and wife. What the minister said was only a distant echo vaguely heard, vaguely remembered.

18

SEVERAL TIMES BOB SUGGESTED TO LAMB THAT THEY TAKE a few hours off some Saturday afternoon and go to the big park together. Lamb was too keyed up to want to do anything as unrelated to the CIO future as that, but when he realized that Bob had a purpose, he agreed to go.

They drove out in Bob's car, parked near the zoo, and following a wide macadam path soon found themselves in the midst of crowds.

"Where to?" Lamb asked.

"Just drift," Bob answered.

Lamb rattled the coins in his pocket. He began to kid Bob. " 'Fire in the east, fire in the west' . . . and you want to drift." He sang softly:

> "Dere's fire in the east, fire in the west.
> Send them angels down.
> Satan's mad and I'm so glad,
> Send them angels down!

"Fire in the east, fire in the west . . . That's the way things seem to me today. War, elections, riots, the world on fire with Mr. Willkie's idea. Fire on all sides of a guy! Satan on the run. Makes me want to hurry . . . and you want to drift!"

Bob was leaning an elbow against the low iron rail and stooping to hold the bowl of the pipe he was smoking. He motioned toward the bears. "The keeper will be here soon to feed them. These fellows always seem to know when he's coming. They begin to sit up and beg before he's in sight."

Lamb's eyes roved from one pit to the next and the next. "Lawd, Lawd," he mocked, "white bears begging same as black!"

Bob's lips twitched. "Craft unionism!"

A sudden quacking at the fowl ponds drew most of the crowd. A keeper was scattering food. The ducks made the greatest clatter and seemed to win the greatest gains. The keeper hurried away from them to carry food to the swans.

"Have to be served, the swans do?" Bob asked him.

"Swans are grand folk. Not much at waiting on themselves. We had one once who wouldn't come to the shore for her food. Waited until her mate brought it to her. Stayed out yonder squawking at him, but wouldn't come in herself."

"Just born a queen," Lamb said.

The keeper looked around at Lamb, looked from his black skin to Bob's blondness. Visibly, he wondered whether they were together.

Later they heard him say to someone, "Never can tell what you'll see out here. We see a lot. Folks look stranger to us than the animals sometimes." He laughed genially at his joke.

Lamb laughed too. "Just what I was thinking," he said to Bob. "Look at all this crowd! Look at their faces! Wonder how many of them know there's fire in the east, fire in the west. . . . Reckon the election will tell."

Bob said, "Let's sit." The sun was warm for September. He motioned toward a patch of benches.

Lamb said, "Now that I'm here, I'd like to see it."

"Never been here before?"

"Always meant to come. Used to feel too stared-at. Then I got too busy."

"The first week I was in this city, someone brought me to

214

the zoo. We live close to the outdoors up in Minnesota. Close to animals. I enjoy it here."

"So do a heap of others, seems like. Surprised to see so many of our folks." Lamb stood still and grinned. "A lot of black grownups may look like monkeys; I reckon they do. But the babies! I never yet saw a black baby wasn't cute!"

He went over to the refreshment stand and bought popcorn, peanuts, crackerjack, and gum. As he passed Negro children, he would hold out an open box. Some hung back at first. But soon they gathered around. Lamb pretended the children were taking it away from him. Then they did take it away. Only when the boxes were empty did he notice that white men and women and children were enjoying his performance too. Some of the white children rushed forward to get their share. One white mother thanked him.

He grinned and shrugged his shoulders. He said, "Won't let us feed the animals. Reckon it's as much fun feeding the kids."

After that, as they walked along, a child would now and then ask Lamb if he had any more, or just look up shyly and say, "Hello."

Bob saw that Lamb got along with people because he liked them so abundantly that some of the liking flowed back.

Raucous calls from the sea lions drew people to the pool. It was gracefully shaped, a level, glittering patch on a hillside. There were rocks for sunning and a semblance of a stack of rocks housing a shelter. The seals shot through the water and took up stations for feeding. They distributed themselves like a team, screamed at the keeper like men decrying the umpire.

"No begging here," Bob said.

"Demanding their rights," Lamb added.

The seals caught the tossed fish in their mouths and swallowed them at one gulp. They swayed and shifted as if glued to the rocks.

215

"Those flappers aren't much more use to a seal than an education to a black man," Lamb chuckled. He was completely fascinated and didn't want to leave the rail. "Graceful and awkward, graceful and awkward. Dancing with their feet nailed down!" He made it into a tune. Finally he turned away. "Nature must have done that trying to say something I don't get. . . ." He kept looking back over his shoulder.

Bob guided him to the top of an outdoor theater seating several thousand people. It was tightly filled with grownups and children, colored and white, stylishly dressed women and women in slack suits with cheap lace collars. People sat where they pleased, black and white next to each other.

"Wonder if they'd sit mixed up like that if the seats cost something."

Bob answered, "A dollar admission might ruin it."

Two trainers, white men, were putting chimpanzees, ponies, and dogs through a quickly paced show. The chimpanzees were the principal actors; they wore gay calico rompers, played musical instruments, rode the ponies, and responded to the trainer's witty and affectionate commands. It was a lively show. The loud-speaker enlarged the trainer's voice and the gay, circuslike music. The laughter smacked back quickly. The stage was trimmed in patriotic colors.

Bob said, "Might be a couple of seats on the side."

"None left," the man at the rope gate answered.

Lamb shook his head. "I couldn't sit down. This is too—too right. A free show to a free people! This is the way it ought to be!" He whispered to Bob, "This is America! Without any funny business."

Bob drew deeply on his pipe. "Whenever a municipality does a thing, it does it in a democratic spirit. That was an observation which led me from the pulpit to the labor movement. I came by way of faith in things by the people, for the people."

Lamb disagreed. "I've been in places down South where

216

there was a sign at the park entrance: No NEGROES OR BICYCLES ALLOWED. I got up before dawn once to throw one of those boards in a ditch."

"But by and large——"

"Yes, by and large. . . ." Lamb was chuckling. "This is wonderful and, by golly, we've got the chance to make it by-er and larger!"

He wouldn't leave until the amphitheater was emptied. He walked down to examine the sunken moat and the electrified wire. "Great! Great! Great stuff!" he kept repeating.

At 5 P.M. the houses of the zoo closed. "Too late to see the snakes and the elephants and the tigers," Bob lamented. "The birds are the best. I wanted you to see the birds."

Just before the attendant pulled down the side window of the refreshment stand, Bob bought some hot dogs and cokes. Seated on a bench, they ate facing the duckpond and a salmon-purple sunset beyond. They watched the crowds leave. Someone was calling a lost child.

The mother stopped near their bench. She was crying. "I wonder what happened to her," she said. "I've called and called."

Lamb started to go in search. Then he sat down again. It seemed a good way for a black man to get into trouble. Bob understood. "I'll go," he said.

The woman kept repeating, "I've got the others over there in my car."

To quiet her, Lamb drawled, "One in every flock always wanders away. Likely it's the one will turn out best."

She didn't answer. She ran to the right. She ran to the left. She stared down into the pond.

Lamb saw a little girl coming along a distant path. "That yours?"

"Doris!" the woman yelled. "You bad girl, where have you been? Where's your hat?" The child pulled it from her pocket.

As she came closer the mother said, "You look a sight." Through her pleasure and pride in the child she scolded even while kissing the youngster's cheeks and neck.

Lamb whistled for Bob.

When the little girl's coat had been buttoned and her hat put on, the woman rose to go. "Thanks for looking," she said to Bob. She hesitated for a moment. Then she said to Lamb, "My father used to say, 'The weak stay by the hearth. The strong venture over the hill.' "

They watched her hurry the little girl toward the car.

Lamb said, "That's the way it is. People are friendly a lot of the time. Then something happens——"

"They feel the taboo."

"It's an easy word to say."

"The restrictive laws, the segregation, a lot of things have been building it up for many, many years."

"Likely the laws are as much the cause as the result of prejudice. I've thought that for a long time. Then you look at that woman and you see that she's afraid. Not afraid of me. I don't think she was. Afraid she might be doing wrong. . . . It was that kind of look."

"A lot of it goes back to a bad conscience. . . . When I was beginning to feel I had to get out of the Church, I went East to talk it over with a bishop I had great respect for. The evening I arrived he hurried me in to a dinner party given in honor of a Londoner just over. The bishop said we could have our private talk the next day. Well, we had scarcely begun our soup when the bishop's wife asked the Londoner whether America was as he had imagined it would be. He said yes, in a way, no, in a way. The thing that surprised him most was that the Negroes weren't very black; he had assumed they would be as dark as Africans. The bishop's wife was from the South and spoke with a Virginia drawl. She seemed to think it was up to her to answer that. She said years ago a Negro slave who was unusually light-skinned married a slave girl who was also light-skinned, very, very light-skinned, very, and since then . . . She looked at the bishop for help. She saw her story wasn't any good. He kept a poker face and said to the Londoner, 'As it turned out, they were a remarkably prolific pair.' Nobody laughed. There were a lot of little smiles, and the bishop changed the subject. I never went back. . . . Somehow that settled it for me."

Lamb answered, "There used to be a lot of mixing. We all know it was mostly the white man's aggression that did it. Seems to me it has pretty well slowed down. Very nearly stopped—the mixing, I mean. I don't see any desire for mixing, not on the part of Negroes. We share a lot together. To go outside of that—well, I don't see why a man who has the choice of every shade of tan and brown would want white, but if he did, why doesn't anyone notice that nobody is forced to marry where he doesn't want to? All that intermarriage stuff is just a smoke screen."

Lamb's voice had been rising. Bob said quietly, "I think I know how you feel. Negroes don't want to marry white people. They just don't want to be told they're not good enough. Just as they don't want to be told they're not good enough to live where their pocketbooks can buy."

"That's it!" Lamb answered. For a time they were silent, listening to the evening noises: the twitter of the birds, the chatter of the ducks, the hum of home-going tires. Abruptly Lamb said, "Why did you want me to come out here today?"

Bob chewed at his pipe. "I think it's well for your city to see a white man and black man together. . . . It gets me sometimes—to think that in a city of a million, with more than a tenth of its people Negro, you never see a black man and a white going down the street together—in friendship."

Bob's teeth made little noises along the stem of his pipe.

"I suppose every man has to go at his job in his own way.

219

I like to study my men. As I see this thing we're doing, it's like weaving a rug. Warp and woof have to be solid union organization. After that you put in the pattern and colors, the stuff that shows and that makes people enjoy the rug or hate it. That part is sort of personal. Each man has different ideas and talents. Hilda understands the philosophy, and she's a good little executive. Handles that part O.K. We fight, but we couldn't get along without each other. My part is to understand how and where to use my men. I took a factory job after I got out of the ministry, but I wasn't born thinking of myself as a member of the working class. . . . I learn a lot from my organizers. The better I know them, the better job I can do."

Lamb was watching Bob's eyes. They were deep-set and sensitive, serious eyes, eyes used to looking objectively inside himself and beyond himself.

"We've each got to give this what we have to give."

Lamb said, "With you it's idealism. With me it's a struggle for rights. Reckon together we're 'singing with a sword. Singing with a sword in my hand.' "

"A swell phrase!"

"I use it sometimes in my talks. Depends on my audience. Where they don't know anything but spirituals, there's no use talking anything else. From that they'll step over to something farther. They're learning fast."

"That's what counts! This campaign isn't just for 1944. Not just for this election. This is part of something stirring in the blood of the world. . . . Let's go!"

"It's great to be in on it!" Lamb said.

Their car was parked a half mile away. They were ready to get into it before they spoke again.

Lamb said, "Sometimes I think I've got the easy part of this job. At least my people know the world's on fire. . . . 'Fire in the east, fire in the west.' Helps them to want a new world, one purified by all this here fire."

"CIO has a great responsibility to keep faith with your people. We know that. But . . . "

"But what?"

"Notice that great long alligator back there? Head 'way off from its tail. CIO head is O.K. on the color question. Tail is the rank and file. Too far behind. It concerns me——"

"The body——"

"Education and working shoulder to shoulder. Your people mustn't lose faith when the tail wiggles foolishly. It's bound to happen for a while."

"*You* telling *me?*" Lamb laughed. "The first thing the cracker does when he lands up here and gets the first decent job he ever had is to raise hell about separate toilets! Guys who all their lives have been using a little house in the back yard or even a back yard without a little house. . . . In this whole damn city of a million people the only war plant where we haven't any kind of discrimination, even that kind, is where an employer was sore about something else and said, 'Boys, this is the way your CIO contract reads and this is the way it's going to be!' The boss did that! For once he didn't tip the scale the other way. I have faith in what we're doing, Bob. And my men have faith! When they haven't any of their own left, they go on living on mine."

"It's the black man who has kept his dignity through these years. No doubt about that. In all this caste system——"

Lamb laughed. "Cast-off system, you mean. Let's get going. I'm scheduled for a talk. Ought to be there now. Thank God, I'm too busy to have time to get sore!"

19

THAT FALL TIME CEASED TO BE AN OLD MAN OF STEADY TREAD. He twirled and twisted as hysterically as a jitterbug. If he reached his goal no more rapidly than usual, at least he seemed to. He was not burdened with a scythe, nor did he march in funereal tempo. With one hand he fired devastating cannon. With the other he waved the banner of triumph and rebirth.

His dual ways created duality everywhere. Political tracts weighted the mails; children gathered precious wastepaper. Men punished their weariness earning overtime; and squandered what they earned profligately. Big industry shouted that government spending would raze the financial world to postwar ruins—and spent vast sums advertising their products to entice the postwar pocketbook. People aching for quiet turned on blasting radio oratory; people wanting to stay at home rushed out to political rallies. The hungry drank and the thirsty smoked.

The confusion caught up with Lamb when he decided that the Democratic ticket ought to be voted straight—since the people whose fate was being decided rarely bothered to split a ticket—but also became convinced that the Republican cigarette-dispensing, commission-appointing, cherubic-minded mayor deserved to be re-elected.

Bob and Emery considered the duality, Bob talking philosophy slowly, Emery talking reality in swift monosyllables.

Hilda, hearing them, suffered and interrupted and submitted letters for signing with prodding frequency designed to remind them that in her opinion action, not talking, was needed.

They decided to call a conference of the regional PAC. It would last one day, all day, with luncheon served while they talked.

Bob arranged everything. He selected a fine room on the eighteenth floor of a good downtown hotel: the Regal Room, used by the Chamber of Commerce for its luncheons. Its elegance seemed a symbol that labor was no longer a ragged vagrant. The summons sent out named the hotel but not the room, since its choice was made too late for inclusion.

On the morning of the conference the hotel lobby was crowded. People in a hurry were putting on their coats and going out the revolving door at the same time. Those coming in walked briskly. Their eyes were staring with haste. There was talk and motion and rush, yet the manager discerned a black man about to enter one of his elevators. He ran through the crowds and tapped Emery on his plastic arm. "Back elevator, please."

Bob tried to argue. The pallid man turned scarlet, but there was no change of mind. Emery said nothing, watching the scene as objectively as if neither he nor his color were involved. Actually, for Emery, they were not involved. The future of the world was involved.

Bob reverted to a farmer's brevity: "This man is one of us. This man cannot be separated from us. Where I come from we don't have to name the color of our guests." Then his ways reverted to the ministerial. He spoke of Christ and the brotherhood of man.

The manager replied, "It is impossible!"

Hilda tapped her foot. "You should have asked for a room downstairs," she said. "I thought you knew that!"

Forty PAC men waited. A crowd of outsiders listened. The congestion in the lobby became impenetrable.

"This is interfering with the war effort!" someone called out.

Bob ran his hand through his tawny pompadour. "Where is the elevator this man must take?"

"Around the corner. The freight elevator. I'm glad you are reasonable."

"We're all reasonable. We'll all go up the freight elevator."

They moved forward together. The manager barked at their heels: "It is impossible! The back elevator is overcrowded with freight!"

A young colored boy was unloading suitcases and boxes, sample cases and folded chairs, while the elevator buzzer hummed impatiently. He looked up the shaft. "They're sure wild up there this morning."

The manager pleaded. He whined of co-operation with the war effort. He pulled out all the stops. The tones vibrated with pathos and indignation and self-pity.

Bob said, "We travel together."

The manager shot through a narrow door. When he shot back, he said, "Come this way!"

As one of the front elevators emptied, he called out: "Private party going up. No one except this party on Elevator 3!"

The PACs stepped back to let Emery enter first. After capacity was reached, the others turned and hurried into the neighboring elevator.

They were in the midst of their opening discussion when Lamb slipped into the room and quietly hung up his overcoat.

Bob tried to go on. Then he sat back and asked, "Did you come up the freight elevator?"

"I don't ride freight elevators. Go on with the meeting."

"You didn't walk up those eighteen flights!" Hilda gasped incredulously.

"Go on with the meeting."

Bob said, "We won't be able to keep our minds on it. What's the deal?"

Lamb returned to his overcoat. From its pocket he drew a lavender-tinged turban. He put it on his head, letting a strand of straight hair stick out a trifle. He lowered his eyes in saintly aloofness and pulled down his Negroid lips into a pious pucker. He folded his hands into the opposite cuffs.

Then they understood. The hotel permitted Orientals to ride their elevators. Before entering, Lamb became an East Indian. His was a histrionic, not a sociological, triumph.

When they stopped laughing he said, "I haven't time to argue with such nonsense. When people get too silly, I just evade."

Throughout the rest of the day, Emery and Lamb and the three other Negro delegates who had arrived by freight elevator went up and down the front elevators freely, though only one at a time, since Lamb had brought but one turban.

"PAC headquarters better put in a stock of turbans," an official from the Chicago PAC said, "because, as I see it, you can't swing this town to victory without the Negro vote."

When Emery got up to summarize the conference, the faces around the table were attentive and solemn. As men who felt they were remaking the world, or ignominiously losing for the people their best chance in all history to remake it, they were frightened by the reports and their own deliberations. The reports revealed the swiftness and the duality. Choices were not clear-cut, yet a world hung in the balance.

"To summarize the mayoralty situation in the city," Emery said. "The incumbent has done a good job as such jobs go today. He is opposed by a labor man, AFL. The papers smear him as a gangster. Probably not that, but he is not an able man for the job. Negroes of the city want a Republican mayor, especially this Republican mayor. Race Relations Commission is a factor; lots of little courtesies to Negroes are factors too. Some AFL unions are working well with PAC. To oppose an AFL candidate wouldn't be so hot. To oppose a Race Relations mayor wouldn't be so hot. I recommend that we do not endorse a candidate for mayor. Plenty of these little independent voters' groups can endorse as they see fit. I recommend that PAC husband its strength for national candidates: President, senators, congressmen. It's what happens on Capitol Hill and in the White House that counts. Let the local boys fight their fights. We don't have to take on everything this year. There will be other years."

They accepted his recommendations.

Bob had promised they would vacate the room by five-fifteen. They had to hurry to make it. Emery in Lamb's turban was still consulting with Lamb when a white waiter began setting up tables for an evening dinner.

Still talking, Lamb picked up a napkin left from lunch. Deftly he twisted it into a turban. He and Emery didn't pause in their deliberations, but when Lamb reached the first floor and was nearly at the outer door, he pulled the napkin from his head and rushed back and shoved it into the manager's hands. "Nearly went off with your napkin," Lamb apologized.

Some white delegates waited on the sidewalk. One said, "Nothing like a good laugh after a day like this!"

They were tired, but they walked lightly, men eager to arrive at a wonderful destination.

In the midst of the campaign Lamb was assigned to an eastern city. He left on six hours' notice. Glory remained long enough to train someone for her job. She sold the furnishings of their flat to the new occupant waiting on the doorstep, and left in a flurry of smoke and coughing and jokes and last-minute asking of favors.

Honey at the station said yes, she'd attend to it all. "Yes,

226

Mrs. Palmer," she said, and Glory pinched her to get even.

Waiting for the gates to open, Honey and Ben rearranged Glory's things. They tied the pamphlets together and tied those to the bundle which couldn't be put into Glory's only suitcase. It was a large suitcase containing all her possessions, refusing only the last of them.

Glory had a berth and said she would eat in the diner. She was sleekly dressed, and her eyes were aflutter with excitement.

Honey looked with admiration at the green plush elegance of the Pullman. White people like the Palmers were on all sides getting settled for the journey.

"How times change!" Ben said. "I remember——" He shook his head. Then his face wreathed in smiles. He slipped his hand affectionately through Honey's arm. "The world's getting to be a grand place. Grand."

Honey smiled at him.

Glory said, "Oh yes, you two, the evening meetings will be coming to your house now. Very likely they'll be there tonight."

"To our house?"

"Isn't it all right? I told them yes when they asked. After all, they have to report. And even the talk isn't all wasted."

"It's more than all right," Ben answered, no longer a lonely man. "It's fine."

"I'll do my best," Honey said, "and you be sure to eat and say hello to Lamb."

With stern regularity plants poured forth planes and guns and bullets and bombs and landing barges. Crowds went to work on time and worked unremittingly.

After hours PAC worked with equal thoroughness. Block by block; house by house; person by person.

They complained of their feet. "This will go down in history as the Campaign of Corns."

227

The intellectuals also were tired. They belonged to the Independent Voters' League or the Liberal Voters' League. All had endorsed the President for the fourth term. Otherwise the platforms varied; yet none failed to coincide with the PAC slate as far as it went. Because PAC had funds and fervor and field workers, the fringe organizations had secretaries. Activity had reached a crescendo satisfactory even to Hilda.

One evening the Rev. Mr. Anton took out his faith to look at it publicly. "Why am I here? Why will my conscience refuse to let me stay away? Why are these writers here? These artists? These newspaper people? These ministers? These social workers? These students? Why are all these men and women of good faith here?"

Dorothy Jane closed her notebook and chewed on the end of her fountain pen. "I'd come even if I didn't have to make a survey—for college, I mean. I'd come because it's the only place I can meet people excited about the same things I'm excited about."

The Rev. Mr. Anton summarized that: "A meeting of the mind and the spirit."

Another minister said, "I come to watch Christianity in motion."

Everyone was there for PAC. They said so almost in chorus.

A Negro lawyer smiled. "I come to borrow books."

They laughed at that, Ben more heartily than anyone else. They called Ben's collection their Lending Library. When he first heard them discussing books he had not read, he would note the titles, buy them, and read them. When the group began coming to his house and saw his shelves, there would be squeals of discovery: "I've been trying to get *New World A-coming*." . . . "I'm dying to get at *An American Dilemma*." . . . "I'd like to borrow that anthropological pamphlet the USO banned."

Ben, beaming, would tell them to take what they wanted. He would buy extra copies for himself.

When he went to the Liberal Bookshop in mid-uptown, he met Dorothy Jane. She roved around the store, which looked like a parlor, bringing him volume after volume. The presses were rolling out great quantities of literary lenses for viewing the American Negro.

Ben laughed. "Everybody's so curious about us. You'd think we weren't right here to be seen."

She showed him Carey McWilliams's books and read a few sentences of his conclusion.

Ben asked in a whisper, "Is he a white man? Really?"

He bought more than he could carry. He was always made welcome at the shop, waited on in turn, never made to stand aside until all white customers had been served. Rumor said the shop was Communist-owned, but rumor didn't explain to Ben why society girls worked there as saleswomen.

When a handsome girl with a Junior League accent came to deliver Ben's books, she lingered to talk. She had somber eyes and a merry, mischievous smile.

She turned out to be Mr. and Mrs. DuPree's daughter, and she said she thought Dotty Palmer was "tops." As soon as she was gone, Honey sank down in a chair as if to save herself from fainting. She chuckled, "Ben love, this here city, it's as disorderly as Eulatha's dresser drawer. It's as mixed up as that."

"It's an improving world."

"Even Honey's improving. I try not to say 'ain't.' A few more years and maybe you won't have to be ashamed no more of the way I talk." Honey's eyes were timidly eager. She was a child unable to believe the Christmas tree was really hers.

Ben sat on the arm of her chair and took her fingers in his. "I'm not ashamed of anything about you. . . . Not of anything."

"Sometimes I think we Negroes are too easy on each other."

"A person can't know any better than he does know."

229

"Ben, I want to do for my people so the boys and girls coming up do know and they do find a chance to live so they can hold up their heads anywhere."

"Holding up your head has got to be a habit. It's hard to hold up your head in the Ville when you've got the habit of holding it down outside the Ville. . . . That's why I'm going to buy Loraine a house in a white neighborhood."

Loraine was about to marry a lawyer nearly twice her age, a tan man whose straight brown hair was streaked with gray. It was heavy hair worn in a pompadour. He was so proud of his white man's hair that he went around hatless winter and summer.

Lester had several unhappy marriages in his past. Struggling to get a professional foothold in a white world, he had become embittered. His hatred turned like the roving beam of a searchlight playing from the white world to the Negro world; from the handsome office buildings which wouldn't rent a Negro space to the Ville which had more confidence in white lawyers than in tan ones; to himself for being too good for a janitor's job and not good enough to earn a janitor's wage; to his first wife for being blacker than he was; to his second wife for being nearly white; to his third wife for no reason except that she wasn't his first wife whom he had loved.

For a few years he lived alone, dressing at times like a tramp, at other times like a rainbow. When war plants put money in Negro pockets and too much work on the desks of white lawyers, then divorce cases, property suits, assault cases, estate claims, all Negro, began to come into the People's Building. Another lawyer who understood what ailed Lester Loom aroused him to his New-Deal-born opportunities. Lester paid off his debts, bought a striped suit, and began to court Loraine, whom he had met at the funeral of his first wife.

For months they delayed their marriage because no place to live could be rented in the colored regions.

It was while walking away from the Liberal Bookshop that Ben met the red-haired real estate man from Rusk & Rusk.

Breezily, Ben asked, "Got a house you want to rent on Mount Vernon Street?"

Mr. Drowby squinted thoughtfully. He began to walk away. "You may be hearing from me," he said. He came back. "Give me your phone number."

A few hours later he faced Tom Rusk. He glanced cautiously at the partitions and whispered, "Want to sell your Mount Vernon Street houses for two thousand more—each—than you expected?"

"For what?"

"A thousand more than you're asking. Two more than you expect. Each."

Tom twiddled his pencil. "Darkies?"

"Sure."

"A man in business doesn't know what to think these days. . . . One of the richest men I know sent a colored fellow in to see me. Nicely set up fellow. Good suit. Educated. Professor or minister or something from a colored university. This friend of mine is sending him around the country. Studying the extent to which racial restrictive covenants cover each of a dozen big cities. To listen to that guy talk, you'd think the noblest thing a real estate man could do was junk every covenant he'd ever agreed to uphold. He talked about health and education and juvenile delinquency. . . . Sounded like a Rotary Club meeting."

"So why not?"

"So why not?" Tom scoffed. "You know as well as I do what the association would think! They'd take the title of 'realtor' away. I wouldn't have a friend in this city!" His fear of friendlessness gathered tiny bubbles in the corners of his mouth. He crouched down into his chair.

"It's done all the time."

"By that nigger real estate guy. Not by us!"

"If it was done quietly, the others very likely would be tickled to death. That property would go up a third in value overnight."

"Who owns in there?"

"A lot of realtors will own—as soon as the war jobs stop and the hillbillies go back to their hills. Realtors will get those places back on mortgages."

"It's the God's truth." Tom folded his arms and tried to think it through. "Neighborhood Association out there has been having some hot meetings."

"Largest church in the region sold to a colored congregation."

"Will it stay sold?"

Mr. Drowby shrugged.

Tom studied his newly manicured nails. "The Negro professor's got me so mixed up I don't know. . . . But, look, I can't go against the association! I can't do that!"

"It's a wonderful opportunity."

"I can't do it!"

"Why not sell to me? Then everything will be done quietly."

Tom glanced at the partitions. Their voices had been low. He lowered his even more. "If this comes out, you get fired."

Mr. Drowby figured on the back of an envelope. "That's O.K.," he said at last.

After Mr. Drowby had sauntered out, whistling, Tom paced the floor of his cubicle office. He wondered how it was possible for an act to be at the same time right and wrong. It wasn't fair to a man like himself who believed in doing the honest thing and keeping his friends.

He picked up the phone.

"Darling," he said to his wife, "come down to the office this afternoon. We'll have an early dinner and go to a movie. I need relaxation."

"Working too hard?"

"Tippy, I've had one whale of a morning!"

The next day Ben was given his pick of a half-dozen houses on Mount Vernon Avenue. He took ironic pleasure in selecting the one which had been refused less than a year ago to Honey's Big Mama.

20

COMING OFF THE SHIFT AT FOUR ONE AFTERNOON, HONEY got into an automobile waiting for her and the half-dozen girls she brought with her. The back of the car contained stacks of PAC literature to be distributed in the stores on the shopping boulevards outlining the Ville. The workers were instructed to ask permission to leave twenty copies and to say they would be back to replenish on the following day.

Honey assigned them to different districts, and they parted. Her shy, smiling ways made her task easy. In the fourth store she waited. The delicatessen proprietor was answering questions put to him by a man making a survey. Each time the proprietor answered only after excited sputtering in Yiddish into the face of his aged wife, who clutched her apron in distress. Mr. Chyaim also seemed nervous. His eyebrows would shoot up nearly to his skullcap; one fist pounded repetitiously against the other palm.

The survey man carried his question blanks clasped to a polished board and wrote with a gold pencil. He recorded the name of the store, the address, the name of the proprietor, the date, and to calm Mr. Chyaim, said the questions were very simple: "How long have you had the privilege of running this store?" . . . "From whom do you rent?" . . . His voice became mildly conversational. "That real estate company is white, isn't it?"

"Of course! Of course!" Mr. Chyaim agreed, and then, because the questions really were easy, he laughed. Belatedly, joylessly, his wife laughed too. She stood still, but now and then made a sale: a loaf of bread to a little Negro boy, a package of cigarettes to a Negro man carrying a lunchbox. She served them with one hand, without turning around.

"Do you plan to remain at this location?"

"But of course!" Mr. Chyaim scoffed. His wife muttered the foreign tongue. Mr. Chyaim amended. "Yes, sir, God being willing."

The survey man laughed. "God and the real estate company."

Both men laughed. Mrs. Chyaim frowned and wiped her dry hands on her apron.

The stranger drew a deep breath. "Only one more question, Mr. Chyaim." He glanced over his shoulders at the waiting customers: a few shawled white women, about twice as many colored women. He whispered, "Mr. Chyaim, we are asking this question of every merchant on the boulevard. Think carefully now: Do you like to sell to niggers, or wouldn't you just as soon sell only to . . . to white customers?"

The Chyaims turned to each other. Both talked at the same time. They looked angrily into each other's faces. Their voices wailed and rose and fell to a mumble.

"We want only *sholem*, peace, me and my wife. We want to make an honest living. We got children dead and grandchildren to keep in school. We have no reason to answer that question one way or another!"

The man drew back, astonished. He flipped through the pages already filled out. "Do you want to be the only merchant who refuses us that courtesy?"

Mr. Chyaim began to shout. He slapped a loaf of bread. "I have bread for sale! I want to sell it to people who have ten cents in their hands to pay for it!"

235

His wife yelled at him in the sputtering tongue. He shrugged and spread his ten fingers at the ceiling.

Then he folded his palms and shrank within his soiled white coat.

His wife, over his shoulder, suggested, "Ask again the question."

"It's a very simple question. Nobody else had to think twice: White or nigger—there it is!" His voice was low.

Mrs. Chyaim nudged her husband out of the way. She leaned forward. She waved her hand toward the stores across the boulevard. She smiled overamiably. Her head slanted against her shoulder. She said, "We do like the others."

"Fine! O.K." The stranger wrote on his paper, covered it with a fresh sheet, and left the store.

"What do you think was going on?" Honey asked the group that evening.

The Rev. Mr. Anton knew. "It's the school," he sighed, and then they all knew.

On a boulevard edging the Ville, though across the street from the Ville side, was a closed, boarded-up building. It had once been a school for white children, but had emptied as the region became industrialized. For the past six months the doors had been locked while Ville children were packed into huge classes in the Ville school. The Board of Education hoped to open it for colored children. Fearing the possible displeasure of the owners of the property still white-occupied or part white, as well as the opposition of the industries which had built themselves handsome, glass-walled plants, the board gave the community warning, and fortified its defenses, by making a survey of the racial distribution of the populace.

The neighborhood owners in collaboration with some realtors countered with another survey, the one whose taking

Honey had observed. Social agencies believed the change inevitable, yet desired to appease the tempers of those who were their large contributors; therefore professional social workers, speaking of community harmony, called a conference.

The Rev. Mr. Anton was to preside. He invited Honey to come. He wanted someone there who could give first-hand testimony as to how the second survey had been conducted.

Thus it happened that Honey and Mr. Rusk found themselves at the same conference table. Bob Jensen was there as a labor member of the Board of Social Agencies. The doctor who had treated Glory was there; he and Bob had first met as fellow members of the Agencies Board. Mr. Smith was present as owner of the largest and newest neighborhood plant, and Mr. DuPree as Mr. Smith's legal adviser. Dorothy Jane was there as a student observer. Mrs. Schneider was there. The leader of a neighborhood choir was there also, sitting next to the principal of the overcrowded Ville school. Loraine's Lester Loom was there, substituting for the overbusy attorney of a Negro protest organization.

Although the secretaries realized that Mr. Smith and a few others would not eat with Negroes, the meeting had been called as a luncheon meeting. Even those who came for luncheon came self-consciously, embarrassed by their divestment of the customary garments of prejudice and taboo, of fear and humiliation, still entangling their feet.

A few white faces wore amused my-wife-should-see-me-now expressions. The Negroes looked blank or solicitous or swaggered to show that they were thanking no one. A few with more experience at social negotiations seemed at ease, but everywhere within the room there was consciousness of race. A white executive from the Y.M.C.A. looked around the private dining room with its valley-lily and orange-blossom decorations and wondered how the women of the Y.W.C.A. could always get away with these interracial meetings when his own board of men would fire him for the mere suggestion.

"The others will come later," the secretary said, without explaining why. "We'd better start."

As newcomers entered they spoke only casually to the men and women they knew best. They saved their cordiality for use across the color line. Their manner said, "You see how friendly I am. If it turns out that I vote against you, you'll remember that I was friendly, very friendly."

The industrialists wore Dewey buttons and admired the Dewey buttons on some Negro lapels. Bob and Honey wore PAC ribbons. Those two won admiration, but in whispers. Mumbling, the paid secretaries said they wore theirs in the evenings. The Rev. Mr. Anton touched the tiny gold cross in his buttonhole and said he was voting right, he hoped, but that, too, he said in a whisper. The educators said nothing and wore neither buttons nor ribbons nor crosses. Most of the members of the Board of Education wore Dewey buttons and talked overmuch about the Republican commission-appointing mayor. Tom Rusk said he had come at the request of a fellow realtor, himself a member of the board, who had for that reason very honorably disqualified himself from testifying, though he was present and of course interested.

The talk at the table was mostly jokes. Tom kept it going as if he feared that silence for even a second might induce disaster. Looking down the narrow table at black faces, brown faces, tan faces, Semitic faces, Irish faces, pink English faces, dark Creole faces, his mind scrabbled for a subject which was suitable. Fantastically it offered him no topic but his wife. He told about Tippy's wonderful paintings, her funny OPA experiences, the way that little woman could bully a big policeman trying to give her a traffic ticket. A Negro woman in a mink coat had a few stories of her own about traffic tickets. A lawyer had a few about policemen. It was all very jolly until

238

after the coffee, when Mr. Smith entered. His eyes were blue marbles in a scarlet countenance. He walked with a bowlegged, side-to-side sway beneath a rounded gray vest with a bouncing watch chain. Following him were the others who had eaten elsewhere.

The negotiations began with praise of the schools already provided for the colored children of the city. They were fine schools, well built, many of them. The newest had buttons to do the work: one pressed button raised the stage curtain, another oiled the floors. The colored populace could view them with pride, and did, Mr. DuPree said, and with gratitude.

Lester Loom rose to convey a message from the lawyer who had sent him. He said Negroes were also taxpayers. Yes, colored children had some good schools, though not enough, and far too many bad ones, though not even enough of those. The colored children of the city usually got the left-overs and discards, nor would that situation be remedied until the state abolished its malicious practice of school segregation.

Mr. DuPree turned patient eyes upon the Rev. Mr. Anton. "As I understand it, Mr. Chairman, we were not summoned today to consider or to reconsider the pattern of living within this community. We were summoned to consider a specific situation within the existing way of life. In the interest of getting something accomplished, I respectfully suggest, sir, that we stick to the purpose of this conference."

While the superintendent of schools was showing the city map, with darkened areas for population centers, everyone was silent. The whites frowned as they learned the intensity of Ville overcrowding. When the superintendent pointed out the extreme overcrowding also existent in white areas, they leaned back, somewhat relieved. He described the district across the boulevard surrounding the school in question as a neighborhood half factory, half tenement.

At that the real estate men protested in unison, and the

239

superintendent agreed to call the tenements "multiple-dwelling units."

By the time the superintendent sat down he had, without voicing any plea, displayed the acute need for another school for Negro children in that region. In conclusion he said, "If we judge this situation by the educational requirements involved, I should say we need at least three new schools in this general area—in order, that is, to bring the Negro schools to the current level of overcrowding existing in the white schools."

The president of his board quickly rose to explain in apologetic tones that he knew from countless talks with the superintendent, an excellent man, that the superintendent was not unaware of the impossibility of building during the war or of the temporary character of the overcrowding. In the stress of explaining such a complex situation, the superintendent had failed to make himself entirely clear.

Tom Rusk rose, spread his fine shoulders, smiled, bowed, and said, "We in the real estate business also made a survey. I'll read the results. I do so with apology to our splendid colored citizens present." He nodded vaguely toward the mink coats. "A survey of the region discloses that in the territory back of the school across the boulevard from the Ville, the populace remains fifty-one per cent white. We found considerable tension there. Of those white citizens we found only two per cent who do not object to the presence of Negro residents in the region. Only four per cent are willing to have the school converted into a white school. Of the business houses on both sides of the boulevard, both on the Ville side and the white side, we found not one merchant who did not prefer selling to white customers. They resent the presence of colored customers. This may seem very narrow-minded to you." He again inclined his head toward the mink coats. "I believe it is a narrow view, but in my trade we recognize a fact when we come up against one. This preference for white residents, this high feeling against a Negro influx, is a fact!"

As he sat down he felt he had done a good job for the association. They'd better not raise a fuss about that little Mount Vernon Avenue deal!

Now the Rev. Mr. Anton, looking more frail and unassertive than ever, said in soft tones that he had taken the liberty to invite someone who had testimony, just as someone had invited Mr. Rusk. In fact, there seemed a number present not on the original list. This was a fine big meeting. His guest has been present at the taking of the survey in one store, and he would like her to tell what she had seen and heard. "May I present Mrs. Benjamin J. Boston?"

Honey rose and stood back of her chair with her folded hands resting on its back. A number at the table had wondered about the pretty brown woman whose grace implied that she might be one of those Negro stage successes so frequently photographed these days. Their eyes narrowed with curiosity. Honey was saying to herself: You learned how to get along with high-up whites at Mrs. Palmer's. Now you learned a new world is coming, and how colored and white got to get along together. Just use what you learned, and do your best.

As she began to tell what she had seen, she sensed that her words were falling into one of those iceboxes of good manners and stubborn judgment the white folks were so clever at building. She had often seen Negro problems come out frozen into the old mold of injustice.

She began to be Lamb. She acted out the scene between Mr. Chyaim and Mrs. Chyaim and the maker of the survey. She made it too vivid for anyone to doubt its validity. Bob Jensen applauded. The applause grew but did not circle the table. Honey remained standing.

She said, "Now I told you what I saw. What I heard. Likely the man Mr. Rusk hired, he didn't do like Mr. Rusk told him to. I only know what he did and, that way, no man can get any answer but the wrong answer. That man was raising up wrong ideas like we're doing here when we raise up talk about what those tenements—the ones we got to call by that other name—will sell for, and put that notion over against the notion of schooling children whose only chance to grow up their best is to have schools. I think we got to stop feeling so poor and find out this city, it's rich enough to do right by its children." She parted her lips as if to continue speaking. She stood very still. The room was quiet except for a slight murmur at the other end of the table where Mr. DuPree was explaining in whispers why both Tom Rusk and Sam Smith thought Honey looked familiar.

Mr. Smith jumped up and began to shout about social workers. "It all settles down to this: You people think you're running this city! You think a charity agency has the right to interfere with business. Who are you anyway? You're where you are because we keep you going! Without our money, there isn't any agency! We told you to see to it that the school board stopped this infernal nonsense. We didn't tell you to call a conference! We didn't tell you to invite a lot of—a lot of—— I know who that girl is and——"

The Rev. Mr. Anton banged for order. Honey stood up again. When they were silent, she said, "I'm not ashamed of who I am. I'm not ashamed I used to be a maid and served Mr. Smith and Mr. Rusk and Mr. DuPree their cocktails. But now I'm CIO. I belong to the same union works for Mr. Smith. Used to be I agreed with Mr. Smith that what happened to the schools wasn't any of my business. Now I see it is my business. Reckon I'm still a maid, only I don't carry in the cocktails. I just serves around what I believe in about the better world coming over the hill."

There was more talking, more shouting, more table thumping. Honey had stated the case unmistakably. Was the city really too poor to educate its children? Was being dark-skinned so unforgivable that Negro children should be denied the use of an empty school? Both sides referred again and again to what Honey had said.

At last the superintendent agreed to carry back the whole problem to the Board of Education. A new study might be made. Or it might not.

As he left he went around the table to shake hands with Honey. Dotty whispered, "You were swell!"

"But, Dotty, he never said they would give in."

"You showed them up, and they know it!"

21

Bob MOVED THROUGH THE PRE-ELECTION PERIOD, A THOUGHT-
ful giant among rushing pygmies. He worked constantly but
at a calm tempo. Irritated with Bob, Hilda scolded the pygmies
to ever swifter rushing. Emery's executive skill made their
rushing orderly and effective. Bob's philosophy, Hilda's energy,
and Emery's realism fused into intense activity which swept
the city.

When the election was only a week off, the usual group gathered to give Hilda their reports and to listen together to a political broadcast. The President's talks had been jocular; now they
were solemn. He had purposely infuriated; then stood aside
to let the nation observe the acrimonious nature of the fury.

Loraine and Lester came with funny stories to tell about
their white neighbors. Some were Jews, and those Lester
mimicked.

Later, referring to the school conference, he said, "What
beats me is how that Jew on the Board of Education doesn't
stand by us!"

The Jew was the real estate man who had surrendered his
talking rights to Tom Rusk. He had not spoken at the meeting.

Ben narrowed his eyes. "Lester, it seems to me you're talking
a lot of anti-Semitic twaddle these days."

"I'm not anti-Semitic! I just can't see why, with what they

went through in Europe, they want to turn around and do the same thing to us."

The Rev. Mr. Anton said the two most liberal men he knew on the color question were Jewish rabbis.

Lester looked down at his hands. "My son by my first marriage, he's overseas fighting the Jews' fight. So it seems to me the Jews here ought to stand by me in my fight on the home front."

A newspaperman said, "Jews are like everybody else: capitalists, workers, liberals, conservatives. A Jew founded the Rosenwald fund for Negro schools. Some Jews just drift with current, think it's their duty to drift with the current. I heard one say only yesterday that he thought it would be undemocratic to interfere with the will of the masses in a country. He thinks the Jews as a perpetual minority should be careful not to do that."

Bob spoke thoughtfully. "Jews have social vision. We have more than our share with us. They stand on both sides because their interests are on both sides. At that, their flair for social vision tips the scale a little in our favor. That's very likely the most we have the right to expect."

Lester argued and, arguing, quoted radio speeches delivered by the shirted supporters of whom the Republican candidate himself was ashamed.

Listening, Emery saw that Lester had lived too long in bitterness to be able to live without bitterness. It was his way of breathing. Emery scolded, "Our hating each other is swell for the enemy. Division in the ranks. CIO stands against all discrimination—racial, religious, national origin. That Jewish real estate man, like every other real estate man, thinks first like a real estate man; second, or not at all, like a Jew. How many men of conscience has any people got? How——"

"But look at the Jews!" Lester persisted.

"Look at yourself!" Emery snapped. "A man with a historic

245

opportunity whining it away! The shirt gangs will flatter you with their anti-Semitism. They'll pay you to take it up. And when they've got you divided from us, the chains will snap on your wrists."

Lester's laugh was bitter with hate. "They'll snap on theirs too, on the Jews."

"We'll all have chains! You're a slave right now—a slave to your shame of your black skin, to your pride in your white man's hair." Emery's eyes blazed. "This is a time to be for something—not against another people!"

Fury twisted Lester's features. "At least I've got my two hands! I didn't lose one fighting for those who deny me."

"You wouldn't risk your skin even for your own freedom."

The enmity between the two men remained in the room all evening. There was no group talk, no jesting about corns, no triumphant or angry announcement of interracial news. Lester Loom wove his way around the edge of the room, whispering.

Emery checked charts. He rarely stayed long, but tonight he was obviously lingering. He sat at the dining room table with Hilda. She summarized reports, and he checked.

When they finished, he came back to the front room. He stood and spoke for all to hear. "I have something to say about this anti-Semitic trend——"

Ben, frowning, interrupted. "I apologize for the rudeness you met in my house."

With a gesture Emery flipped the rudeness aside. "It's not just in this city. Lester Loom isn't its only spokesman. We'd better take a little time now to understand it." His voice was impassioned. "As early as 1866 there were white trade-union men who understood that labor couldn't gain a foothold while working men were divided into castes. The men of vision lost that fight 'way back there. So Negroes became a reservoir of strike-breaking labor. For the next three quarters of a century all workmen paid for that defeat with the necessity to climb a greased hill. . . . When Negroes were shipped into East St. Louis in cattle cars to break a white man's strike, we had the East St. Louis riots. That was in the wake of the last war. The last war promised the Negro a lot of gains he didn't get. The white workingman lost that war too. The world lost it.

"The Negro became a protest-organization man. The protest organization fulfilled its great historic destiny when the March-on-Washington group composed of black men only dickered successfully with the President of the United States. The President didn't want a mass demonstration as the country moved into a war for democracy. Nor did he want to put that demonstration down by force. In exchange for canceling the March, the Negro got Executive Order 8802. That order has given us our place in industry. It has forced management to accept the Negro and forced labor to accept him. It freed the feet of this nation from the mire of biracialism. It's given us a chance to make a run for victory. It has worked so well that it will inevitably become more than an executive order. It will become a part of the law of the nation.

"There will be other great opportunities for protest organizations to enforce gains. They will be able to use them effectively only if their leaders remain sane. Lester Loom is not as steady as those fellows. His principles are sick. As a man he is of no importance whatever. He can strut and whine and incite and mimic his neighbors and become a paid anti-Semite. That's a career open to a good many Negroes today——"

Someone tried to stop Emery. They saw Lester's livid face mumbling down at his hands. They saw the long, powerful fingers stretching into instruments for choking.

Emery's eyes defied them. "Lester Loom is important because he's fiddling with the only weapon which can stop the advance of Negro labor. Divided, we can't win. United, we can't lose."

Lester sprang to his feet. " 'We! We! We!' My God, who is 'We'? Not the black man, I'm sure of that!"

247

"You're sure of nothing," Emery shot back, "except that you're tired of being slapped down. You think it would be fun to slap down the other fellow for a while. The Jew is the most vulnerable other fellow. So what? You'll use negatively the energy which might be used positively."

He named men known to Negroes as enemies, strike-breaking agency men who in the past had made use of black labor for a while and then kicked it away when the strike was over, men with gangster minds.

"Those fellows are with you, Lester Loom, ready to be your pals. They're stooging for men who want you used but can't endure to be in the same room with you—Mr. Smith and his ilk!"

Lester shouted, "If I can't have my share of this country, I can at least fix it so the Jews can't have theirs!"

Emery scowled. "The Negro and the Jew are the goats. Minorities are always likely to be the goats. If they go to butting their heads together, they'll destroy each other."

"The Negro's being destroyed anyhow!" Lester insisted. His lips wavered as if about to sob. "Must the Negro always be the one to act with the wisdom of God and the patience of Job? Must the Negro always turn the other cheek?"

"Every man who wants to share the honor of building a new world must act with the wisdom of God and the patience of Job. He must quit turning the other cheek. He must learn to stop thinking about himself. He must learn to keep his eyes on the ball and go after it. He plays the game with a handicap, yes. You can't forgive the Jew for his relative invisibility in a hostile society. You figure that with that invisibility you, too, could get by. That's taking your eye off the ball. Maybe you're not big enough to play big-league ball."

Lester said to Loraine, "We're going home."

Hilda said, "I guess I'm a Jew. I was brought up a Methodist, but one of my grandfathers was a Jew. I guess I'm a Jew."

248

Lester answered, "One of my grandfathers was a white man, but I haven't the right to guess about what I am. Everybody agrees that I'm a Negro!"

Three days before the voting Honey had covered all the territory assigned to her and all the territory others who had caught the epidemic cold had failed to cover. She said to Ben, "I'm going to Mama's this afternoon to tend to the Hoops' voting. I reckon your own family is the hardest to win."

Mrs. Boston held a red queen in mid-air. "No need to kill yourself. The election's over."

Ben laughed. "Who won, Mama?"

"Miss Eleanor's husband won. Laugh, but I know! I was telling our white milkman that we were going to vote for a better world on the Democratic ticket, and he said, 'Down at the plant we never talk politics. All the fellows like the boss, and he's Republican, so why talk politics?' "

"And?"

"I hear that a lot. If the bosses vote Republican and the men vote Democratic—count it out for yourself!" The red queen went down, and other cards in rapid succession.

Honey shook her head. "Maybe I can't believe we'll win because I'm not used to being on the winning side."

Papa was home when Honey arrived. He said he was incurably Republican. The best men in the city were Republican. He heard them talk out at the club.

When Honey tried to argue with him, Papa said, "Daughter, the best I could do for you would be not to vote. My hand would cramp up trying to put a Democratic vote in the box. It would feel like as if I was betraying my slave-born parents. I've lived South, and I know how much better we've got it here. If the South is Democratic, that settles it for me. I'm on the other side."

249

Mama said she had overpromised Honey about registering. She'd been busy that day.

Eulatha, home from the factory, said she would vote Republican because the Republicans promised to bring the boys overseas home—"and fast! Cure this town of being manless!"

Mama said, "You got a letter."

Eulatha snatched up the V-mail. It was from Jo-Jo. "What's wrong with that black boy?" Eulatha laughed hoarsely. "He says to vote for Roosevelt. He says that's going to be good for getting the war over and done with. . . . Mama, was that the onliest letter?" To Honey she explained, "I'm taking an overseas vote of my own. I'll vote the way my boys want me."

Carmen said she had studied the matter thoroughly, watched the way the schools voted in their "pretend" voting. The public schools had been overwhelmingly for Roosevelt, but she, of course, would vote as the fine private schools at the edge of the city voted—Republican this time, though other years, when Negroes had voted Republican, she had voted Democratic. She spoke primly, her attitude an accusation.

She let Honey see that she had made up her own mind and that it was a white mind, nearly.

At the time Honey took Ben back, Carmen neither grieved nor showed anger. She behaved as if she had always known it would happen. Her eyes became more dream-filled, yet her face was that of a woman grown old.

Upon Honey's return home, she told her mother-in-law, "That election isn't won yet."

The danger of its loss was with her constantly. When she heard people were sick or invalided, she went to see them and promised to send one of Ben's cabs to carry them to the polls.

She made a special trip downtown to report her fears to Emery.

He answered, "We're having a pre-election rally. The audience will be mostly Negro women in industry, ex-maids."

"But the Hoops———"

"They can lick us."

"Maybe a meeting for Ville folks———"

"We've got to build this thing industrially! There isn't any other way to make it stick. Come to the rally. You're to sit on the platform." He answered the phone and swung around toward the window as he talked.

As the girls in khaki jumpers with photographic identification badges on their coats crowded into the meeting hall, they passed Honey, leaning lightly against a post. A number paused to talk. They spoke of letters come from husbands overseas, of letters long overdue, of babies, of sisters, parents, lovers, friends.

I reckon maybe I ain't never going to shake off the mother ways, Honey thought. First the Hoops. Now all these here CIO girls.

Union Hall was an old-fashioned building at an intersection. On one side the region was Slovakian, on the other, Russian. Strange tongues were heard everywhere.

Negro girls told one another, "It looks kind of like the Ville."

They were puzzled by the Russian Catholic Church, a round, domed building, said to be without pews.

Honey heard them as they came up the steps. One said, "Sometimes I feel like I never lived in this here city till I put on slacks." Honey smiled in swift agreement.

Dorothy Jane and her notebook went in too.

The meeting began with the "Star-Spangled Banner." Then Bob talked of what it meant to be a worker and have a vote. The girls applauded loudly.

Smiling, Emery said in an aside to Honey, "They'll rattle the balcony loose."

The hall was old and shabbily elegant.

Emery whispered to Honey, "You're next. I don't want a

prepared speech. Just get up there and tell the truth. Why they should vote PAC."

"Emery, I can't make a speech."

"Just say what you think."

Honey stood, trembling a little, at the side of the stage. She looked around slowly. "Today you're war workers. And I'm a war worker. We're proud of our badge. . . . But I want you to come with me in your thoughts back to when I was Honey without no last name and you were Ozala and Mildred and Mary and such. We got up at six and made it to our jobs by seven-thirty and we come home along about ten, when the last dish was washed and the company still in the parlor laughing. Sometimes we stayed to serve after the bridge game. Sometimes when the company was there for dinner we stayed to serve the late glass of water in the pretty glasses. Sometimes we just stood the pitcher and the glasses in the pantry and slipped on out the door. Then the next morning Madam likely said, 'I rang for water and was so embarrassed. You must never sneak off like that again!' "

She let the girls have time to chuckle. Then the laughter burst into great waves like the ocean pushing up on a shore, seeming to leave but pushing back again, again, again. They talked among themselves and laughed.

"We got into some mighty bad habits living that way. Mostly they sprung up because we were kind of afraid of losing that job. Afraid of losing that little old glass-of-water job. But we had ways of getting even. If Madam said things against our cleaning, we showed her next week how thorough we could clean. Pulled the rug crooked. Dragged every piece of furniture where it didn't belong. Slanted up every picture on the wall. Jerked out all the floor plugs. . . . That fixed that! No more 'Did you move this?' 'Did you clean behind that?' We made our cleaning right plain. . . . Then there were those times Madam would count things and look in the sack you brought your working clothes in. So you took another paper sack and stood it out next to the garbage can. Between the can and the porch railing. All day long you kept putting things in there. Things you wanted and things you didn't want. One time coming home on the streetcar I rode with a girl who had two bags full. Clear to the top.

"She told me why she did it. There wasn't a thing in them bags she wanted except a red plush flower for her hair. When we got to the place where-at we transferred, she dumped the whole mess except the flower in the weeds. And when we got on the next car she held the red plush flower out the window and let the wind have it. . . ."

The girls weren't laughing now.

"We were getting even. That's all we were doing—getting even. Trouble with that is that getting even we never get anywhere but even, and even ain't any place of our own. . . . There's been a lot of promises made here tonight about what a pretty world we're going to have if we vote PAC. I'm going to vote PAC. I hope you'll vote PAC too. PAC is planning things good. Still I see times ahead with tears in them. I ain't too much afraid of tears. But I am afraid of the kind of living made us lie and steal and cheat just to get even. I'm afraid of that. No matter how good the world gets to be I reckon you got to be ready to be good with it. We're getting the chance now to live so we don't have to be tricky to get by. That much we got to hold to! We got to do that.

"If we do got to go back to housework——"

A steady "No-o-o-o-o-o-o-o-o-o!" rose from the audience.

Honey waited. "Might be we won't all go back, but we got to go back sure in our hearts. Come we're sure in our hearts, we don't have to lie and steal and cheat and be sassy. We got to go back sure we got the right to speak up so long as we speak the truth. We got to know what is the truth. . . . CIO

253

has taught me a heap about that. PAC, it's going out on Tuesday and nail down the CIO tent. CIO has been making and putting up that there tent as shelter for all of us. PAC is going to nail it down so it can't blow away. . . .

"Hard times might come again. Hard times is what counts. I'm not afraid they're going to make a servant out of you. Nobody can't make a servant of nobody who ain't a servant in her own heart. I got the heart of a servant, but I ain't no more got the kind of heart uses it only on one family and that one better'n me. I got the kind of servant heart uses it for every growing-up child in the world! . . ."

For a second her eyes met Dorothy Jane's. Dotty was chewing on her pen.

"I always was so I could love a white child as much as a colored child. Some of those white children I pity more than our own. They ain't got nothing to struggle for. They ain't got nothing to believe in. Kind of caught between a new world and the old. Their mamas and papas got them living in a Ville. Ain't our kind of a Ville. It's worse, I reckon. A Ville's only bad because you ain't got the right to get out. Lots of white folks lives worse than we do in the Ville."

The heads nodded.

"Ville's not a bad place. Not as bad as where lots of white folks live. What's bad is not being allowed to get out. As if we're not fitten to be with other folks.

"I used to think the white folks ought to come and let us out of the Ville. Unlock the gates. I used to see them worrying about the wrongs they was doing, and I'd get to wondering why they didn't turn that there lock. They got a different worry about all this than we got. They got sin on their breasts. They say it. Say it loud to each other. Get mad and go back to hugging the sin—the way the Republican party is doing this year! My! My! Mr. Lincoln would be right ashamed!

254

Lucky he ain't here to live through the hurt. Having his own folks turn on him like that! . . .

"I was talking about the Ville and how we are going to get out of it. We're not going to get out by being let out. It ain't going to come that way. We're going to get out because the Ville bursts out like a big fat lady bursting out at her seams. And I don't mean just that we're too crowded up with people. I mean that our feeling and our thinking are going to burst out too. When that happens, nothing and nobody can hold us back in!"

They cheered her for that.

"Right now is the first chance I ever had to think my way past the Ville seams. The church never gave me the chance. It said, 'Go along and worship with your own! If you worship out here with the rest of the folks, the Lord will get all mixed up in His mind.' The school never said, 'Come along and study where-at the learning is.' It just said, 'You go back yonder where-at there ain't much learning but where-at your skin will match the skin of other folks.'

"That's the way it's been all down the line. Until CIO come along and said to me, 'Honey, you're a worker.' At first I drew back. I said, 'I'm just Honey, a brown-skinned girl.' CIO answered, 'You got a job in a factory. That counts more than the color of your skin.' First time in my whole life anything about me counted more than the color of my skin!"

They cheered and clapped.

"So I stood around and watched, not trusting sweet talk too much. I saw that they meant what they said. Not just because they were good men." She turned toward them for only a second. "I done listened to lots of good men talk before. White men. One in particular. He was the finest man this city ever had. I mean Mr. Palmer. Mr. Andrew Palmer, the best friend we ever had until CIO come along. Reckon just being a good man won't do it. Helps, but it won't do it. CIO has got itself at a place where it's trying to build a better world, and it can't build that world come it leaves us out.

"Used to be unions thought of us as enemies. We were just more folks fighting for jobs when there weren't enough to go around. That way they kept us down a good long spell, some of them union men just as ashamed about that as the high-up folks were. A conscience, I reckon, just grows here and there like trees in a park. Throw their shade a good long ways, I reckon, but when a drought sets in, there never seems enough trees to go around.

"When the war hit us, our own black men claiming jobs went to Mr. President. They went with a threat in their hearts and on their lips. He told them to sit down and talk out their troubles. He didn't need no threat to make him want to do right. He was with them on wanting to find a way. He had to find a way to be fair to us and keep a lot of white folks in law and order. He found that way, the man I'm going to vote for on Tuesday. He found it!

"He went right ahead and taught a lot of union folks that they can't keep us out no more. Some didn't want to learn that, some was right willing. Reason I trust them union men is that come they don't give us our place, they're going to lose theirs too. They know that. I been listening to them talk, and they know that. With some of them, it's kind of like an ecstasy. They want to do right by us because they don't want to live wrong. The rest, they know, come they poke a hole in the boat, we'll all be in the water. We sink and they sink too. That's the difference between the way things are with them and with men who are just good men. With the best man ever lived—like Mr. Palmer. Come there's a hole poked in the boat, the men like Mr. Palmer, they don't sink. Only their hearts sink with us, come they are good like Mr. Palmer was good. When a world is so that good men's hearts sink, it can't be a right world to live in. . . ."

256

The hall was silent.

"Tuesday I'm going to vote for a right world to live in. I'm going to vote for President Roosevelt because he's been giving us the chance to burst out the seams of the Ville, burst out with our thinking. Maybe he ain't going to bring Christmas all year round. Maybe he ain't Santa Claus. He's nothing grand like that. He's just kind of one of us. Wanting a better world. Lots of folks near to him gets to wanting it too. Miss Eleanor wants it. I reckon Mrs. Roosevelt would go to standing with PAC even if the man at the top wasn't her husband. Mr. and Mrs. Roosevelt ain't just looking for a nice place to live. The White House, it's been something more to them. It's been a place to be fair. I want it should go on being like that, now that this here has come to be my country. And yours. It's yours too. . . . I'm right proud of what it's trying to be. What PAC wants to make it. . . . You and I, we can vote for them old glass-of-water days or . . . for a new world. . . . I want that there new world, and"—she smiled at them—"I reckon you do too!"

She walked back slowly to her chair. The silence shredded into applause, and then the clapping rose to peak, pounding incessantly at the walls.

22

BEN SAID TO HONEY, "IT'S PART OF BEING IN LOVE WITH YOU.
I like to give you presents. You wouldn't let me give you a big
ring. You keep right on earning. You buy your own slack
pants——"

"I got some right nice dresses, Ben."

"I'm a rich man. Money's flowing in like water. Why can't
I give you something?"

"Taking it feels kind of like stealing. . . . " She smiled a
teasing smile. "Anyhow, Ben, I thought men gave things when
they were courting. I thought they quit after they won the
girl."

He took her face between his hands. "You're the kind of girl
a man wants to keep on winning. Again and again."

Honey opened the box once more. She shook her head.
"Ben love, bring me some flowers for my urns. They look
right pretty on your mama's mantel. Bring something for
them every week. . . . I can't go around wearing a diamond
bracelet. . . . Ben, don't look like that. It's got nothing to do
with love. . . ."

"Seems to me a man in love has to give presents. Seems to
me a woman in love ought to want to take them."

Honey shook her head. "These ain't days for loving, except
loving private. Wearing that bracelet, I'd be loving public."

"I'm going to buy you a car."

"A car hitched to an A card won't do much good. Ben, you

258

gave me lots of cars when you gave me that taxi pass. I call your cabs a lot. Your taxis have been plowing for PAC all through the campaign."

Ben chuckled. "My drivers report you fill them up with white folks most of the time."

"The folks they haul aren't white folks or colored folks. They're just folks in a hurry to win the election."

"You don't ride them to work."

"I got to go to work like the others. . . . Ben, you wouldn't want to—to——" She looked down at the box.

"Give the bracelet to PAC?"

"The money."

"I've been giving Bob something every once in a while." He picked up the box and closed it. "I'll take this back. I suppose a man ought to give a lady what she wants, but I never heard of . . ."

He went off shaking his head.

The quarrel between Lester and Emery was a lump in Ben's chest. He had bought a house for that fellow, a nice house, and instead of getting thanks in return, he got only impudence and strife and angry words in his parlor.

All the next day his annoyance revolved like a turning gear. After a time it enmeshed with Honey's refusal of the bracelet. What pleasure was there in being a rich man if he couldn't get decent gratitude from his brother-in-law? If he couldn't adorn Honey?

Lamb and Glory were coming back with no home to go to except his, and he didn't want them. He wanted the paradise of his present to remain undisturbed. Since Honey came into his household, it had been a home comfortable for all his feelings. His mother was happy. She no longer spoke tartly to save Ben from himself. Proud now of all her four sons and Loraine, she ascribed their success to herself.

She would say across the game of solitaire, "I never licked boots. I never bent a knee. I worked and I made my children work. I kept them away from white folks. Now white folks come to us!"

When the group was there she was always present, shuffling her deck of cards, silently planning her next campaign of cleaning. When she spoke of Honey to Ben, she would say, "Turned out she was the only girl in the world! Honey's all right. We get along."

The gears turned and turned. Enmeshing, they ground out a decision. He would buy another house on Mount Vernon Street. This one would be a present to Honey, who could in turn give it or rent it to Lamb as a place to live.

When he told her, she said, "Likely Lamb will fill it up with CIO. Ben, you take his rent money and save it for Lamb. He hasn't got a cent, and Glory writes he's coughing. . . . Oh, Ben love, that house looks like about forty diamond bracelets! To me, it looks——"

"I'm going to have it painted on the outside——"

"A necklace to match, I do declare!"

"I'm going to paper every room."

"Earrings too! . . . Ben love, you're wonderful! Wonderful!"

Her eyes glowed with the sort of happiness he wanted to see there.

Loraine and Lester's house had been unoccupied, but the other, Mr. Drowby said, contained tenants. The OPA would let you move people out only if you bought the place for a home. He wondered how the white tenants would take it if he showed Ben through. Shrewd lights flickered back and forth in Mr. Drowby's eyes. He advised Ben to buy the house "sight unseen."

All Ben's business experience cautioned him against it. He kept saying, "I don't like to do sneaky things."

Mr. Drowby laughed. "A man has a right to buy a house. Nothing sneaky about that."

"He ought to have," Ben agreed.

They walked up and down looking at it from across the street.

"It's not as far gone as the other one."

"Couldn't be."

The houses were similar. Ben, looking at the roof lacking only a few slates, saw Honey's smile. Looking at the rock foundation, he saw Honey's eyes flash with pride. Looking at the soiled curtains sagging at the windows, he admonished himself: When you picked out that bracelet, did they journey you down into the diamond mine?

"I'll take it," he said. "I'll take a chance. It's a bad way of doing business, but I don't want any trouble."

Tippy Rusk awakened slowly, feeling the lateness of the hour and that against all precedents Tom was awake and still in bed. He usually got up with a rush and roar, puffed through setting-up exercises, sang loudly in his shower, scattered towels everywhere, and then, pink and tall and handsome above a well-tailored suit, shouted for his breakfast and his paper.

She raised her head to make sure.

"Hi, beloved!" she said.

"Hi!"

"You didn't call me 'Honeybunch.' "

"I'm thinking."

She waited and watched while he smoked one, two, three cigarettes. "You're usually so bouncy," she said. "Do you feel all right?"

He stretched, shook crossly at the empty cigarette package, and said, "I've got a hell of a problem on my hands."

He left the room, and she could hear him in the bathroom. All the noises were the same except that there was no song.

She eased her worry with the faith that Tom liked to act mysterious and grieved. Just wanted a little petting, probably.

In the bathroom Tom argued with his reflection in the mirror. Sergeant Rusk, he said to the fellow who had waded in wet trenches during the last war, there's something dead wrong about all this! They've got no right to put you on the spot!

The frowns of the three representatives from the association who had called yesterday about the Mount Vernon Avenue deal deepened into scowls. So did the look on the face of that colored chap who talked in Harvard accents about restrictive racial covenants.

With his razor in his hand he walked to the window and looked across the roofs of neighbors farther down the hill. For his own home Tom had picked a fine hilltop. He called to Tippy, "A guy has to live in his own city. That's where he has to fit in."

"Of course, darling."

He opened the door to the bedroom so he could look at her. "A man doesn't want to go around making enemies. . . . All this talk about the war . . . I know what those boys over there are going through. I don't like to double-cross those kids. A lot of those guys mean all this talk about democracy. When they get back, we want things to seem—well, to seem nice to them."

"I don't see how it can seem nice to all of them, Tom, part wanting one thing, part another."

"You've got something there, baby! You've got something there! . . . Two thousand times six, that's twelve thousand. . . . Not to be sniffed at, twelve thousand."

"Darling, I don't know what you mean."

"Don't need to know. It's a help to talk to you without knowing. More of a help than if you knew." He was back in the bathroom under the shower.

While he was drying himself, he opened the door and shouted out, "No one realtor can buck the association, that's a cinch!"

"You can, sweet. Tom, I'll bet you could make them do the way you want about anything. Anything!"

He laughed at that and shoved the door closed.

When he came back to get dressed, he said, "I wish I wasn't so damned sincere. . . . I wish I didn't have any imagination about the foxholes. . . . Maybe we were fools to let the colored boys go into the Army at all. This way we owe them something."

Mrs. Rusk got up and searched at the foot of her bed for her robe. She was tying the side bow when Tom suddenly leaned his palms against the dresser as if he were in pain.

"That colored fellow who came to see me about the restrictive covenants, he was the sort of guy a man could enjoy a talk with—that is, if he hadn't been colored. He was intelligent. But, by God, he can't be right and the association right too. . . . If a man isn't in this real estate game to earn money, what the hell is he chained to a desk for? A man wants to stick by his own. . . . Those veterans coming home might come— with a hell—of a disappointed look in their God-damned eyes. . . ."

Suddenly he began to pull his clothes from his body. He got back into bed. "Baby, you run along," he muttered. "Close the door."

"Aren't you getting up, Tom? Are you sick?"

"Close that door!" he bellowed.

In midafternoon when he heard Tippy phoning for a doctor, he called, "Hang up that phone!" In a calmer voice he added, "Sterling DuPree's the only one can help me. Ask him to come in on his way home."

Sterling listened. With an adroit word here and there designed to make each revelation seem the expected next step, he got all the details.

He said, "You're not the only one. It's the same story all over the city. Smith's having trouble with his newest plant. Put up a beautiful building there, hoping after the war to convert it into something where he could have a nice white, walk-to-work pay roll living right in the neighborhood. Now they're threatening to open a Negro school at his very gate. You were at the meeting. We thought we had the thing settled. . . . Now we're not so sure. . . . Not so sure!"

"Thing is, Sterling, I'm the kind of a God-damned fool can see there's some right on both sides."

"That's the trouble with the whole business." Sterling rose.

"Don't go! I've got to get this settled."

"These racial restrictive covenants have been opposed in court in a good many places. Some places have declared for them, some against. . . . As I see it, you've got to go along with the association. Question is whether you want to challenge the whole program from inside the association——"

"Be a little Boy Scout, huh?"

"I have other real estate clients. There's a good deal of disquietude. Some of the men are disconcerted because they're losing out on profits they believe to be rightly their own. They refrain from selling to Negroes, then that Negro real estate man gets hold of things and takes the profits——"

"He's no Papa Bountiful to his own people either!"

"What would you think of serving an eviction process out there, just to fortify your position with the association? Give you time?"

Tom wondered how much Mr. Drowby would squeal. If that guy got talkative . . . "I wish we could just get those darkies to withdraw. Quietly. Ask them to do the sensible thing. Tell them how aroused the Neighborhood Self-Benefit Group is."

264

"I presume it is aroused?"

"Plenty! Even the ministers of the district are kicking. The white ministers. The hell of it is we haven't any other property to offer as bait. There aren't any vacancies."

"Who bought the houses?"

"A guy by the name of Boston bought both. Benjamin J. Boston."

Mr. DuPree remembered the name. And then Tom remembered too. "Probably her husband! I remember Honey at the meeting. Sure I do."

"She used to work for the Andrew Palmers. I've kept in touch with Mrs. Palmer. I see to her holdings——"

"If you can give me the chance to talk to those darkies privately, it might settle everything! I'd forget this democracy deal and go back to where I was a few weeks ago. A damned sight happier too."

"I'll see what I can do," Sterling said. "An eviction notice—not an eviction, just a notice—might loosen things up for negotiations."

Mrs. Rusk had scarcely closed the front door after Mr. Du-Pree when she heard Tom running around upstairs barefoot. He called over the banister. "We're going out for a good steak dinner. I'm starved."

"But, darling, you've been saying all day you had gall-stones!"

"To hell with them! Maybe all they need is food. Put on your new outfit and let's get going."

The morning the eviction notice was served on Loraine and Lester, they hurried into the Boston household. Their eyes were red; their faces angry. Loraine kept talking about the curtains she had made.

Lester sobbed, "And who brought that notice? Who brought it?" He threw the piece of paper on the table before Ben and Honey and Mrs. Boston. "A little Jew brought it!"

Honey said, "Reckon he was a man couldn't earn a living doing nothing else. Reckon all the Jews ain't as rich as you make out, Lester."

Lester paced the floor and threatened the ceiling with his fist and finally sat down and wouldn't answer when Ben asked him questions.

Loraine said accusingly to Honey, "You said CIO was building a new world. A fine new world it is!"

The phone rang. It was for Honey. Mr. DuPree's voice was very polite. He said he and Mr. Rusk didn't want good folks like herself to be caught between two fires in this thing. It might be that they could be of help. Would she come to his office?

"Yes," Honey said, "but not like you said, this afternoon. I won't have no time till after the election. The day after the election I could come at nine."

She was still telling the others about it when the phone rang again. Mr. Rusk, Mr. DuPree said, didn't want the thing hanging around so long. He'd like to have the conference today. But Honey answered no, the election was taking all her time. There was talking back and forth at the other end of the line. Then they agreed to Honey's hour.

Lester and Loraine were infuriated by her delay. "You care more about that God-damned election," Lester raged, "than about our home!"

"Get out!" Ben shouted. "Get out fast!"

Honey said, "Hush, Ben, it's all right."

His eyes were moist as he answered, "Lamb's house is in your name. You may do as you please. It's yours for selling or keeping. . . . I don't like trouble."

She could see that his joy in his gift had died.

The day for voting rode nearer on a chariot of fine weather. Handsome sunshine shouted of abundance and good cheer.

Yet anxiety came too. Would the people go to the polls? If they went, would they vote against something or for something?

On election Tuesday people were too tired to talk about it any more. Once in a while someone would say, "They're voting. It's O.K. There's a big vote." Eyes would glisten momentarily and then frown.

"There's a lot at stake," strangers said to one another.

When Honey came home from work near midnight, the Boston living room was filled with listeners. People sat on the floor and on the stairs as high as the second landing.

The radio gave reports from everywhere in the nation, but the returns, though encouraging, were partial and not decisive. Emery at a small table recorded each item on a score sheet. The only certainty was that the Ville had voted, and Enright Avenue too.

Bob paced the floor restlessly. "At least the people weren't apathetic," he said over and over again. "At least they know that what happens at the polls is important to their daily lives! That's new!"

"It's as exciting as hell," someone said in a fatigued voice.

Honey whispered to Ben, "Coming out of the plant, I saw some PAC dodgers lying in the gutter. I wanted to pick them up. It's hard to believe they don't count no more."

Bob kept examining what had happened.

"Where was the Democratic party?" he demanded. "Anybody see it? The Democratic party simply wasn't around! What votes they get, we got for them. It was a tussle between PAC and the other side. Those who believe in the rights of the people against those who believe in the rights of THE people. That's the way it was. Not even defeat can change the good in that! For once everybody knew what it was all about!"

As midnight became one o'clock and one o'clock became two, the victory for PAC became more and more certain.

Emery looked up once to say, "They cared enough to split the ticket. To split it right."

Some were elated. Some were merely relieved. All were thoughtful. For months their lives had swirled around the necessity to win this election. Now it was won. Now what? They looked at each other and looked away. They drank coffee and stared down into their cups.

Honey thought, They're afraid it's just a glory wagon after all.

She held up a piece of cake and said, "Ben's mother, she baked this. First she had to have a cake in her head before she could put a cake in the pan."

"Which we got?" someone asked.

Honey smiled. "Without no cake in the head, there ain't none in the pan. . . . A cake in the head's better'n no cake. . . . The one in the pan—that one we got to go on making! We can, come we try hard enough. We got it started!"

As the crowd prepared to leave, some kept saying, "It's wonderful! Wonderful!"

Bob asserted, "Now the test comes! There's plenty of raw anti-Negroism stalking this country. This might even give it strength for a while. What we do with our victory is what counts. We've learned we can be victorious. We have a big responsibility."

Emery folded his score sheet. "That's the next job on my list. I leave for Chicago in the morning. It's been swell knowing you. Keep the faith!"

His wife had tears in her eyes. "We've been like one big family," she said. She kissed Honey good-by and thanked Ben. She shook hands with Dorothy Jane and said, "I'll watch for you. You'll amount to something. I feel it here in my heart."

Dorothy Jane looked past her to Honey.

Honey said, "Dotty's like her papa, only she's getting an earlier start, and these times is different. These times might let her do a lot of things her papa wanted to do, but maybe his times weren't ready."

When the door was closed, a tap on the glass brought Emery into the hall once more. "I want to say good-by again. When I think back to this city I'm going to take comfort in what Honey's doing, making the daughters of the Ville into women the labor movement can count on."

Tears stood in his eyes and in Honey's. She moved toward him. Firmly, he kissed her. It was a kiss of sorrow and of faith.

He shook hands with Ben. "I know we can count on you too."

Ben answered, "I take that to be a compliment."

"The best there is!"

23

Mr. DuPree explained that something had come up everyone was sorry about; Mr. Rusk was sorry, everybody concerned was sorry, but the fact was the Neighborhood Self-Benefit Group was unfriendly to the idea of having colored residents on Mount Vernon Avenue. Describing the restrictive covenants, he used long words Honey couldn't understand. She asked him to say it so she could.

He repeated it more simply and looked at Tom, who nodded. Then he took a deep breath and said Mr. Rusk wanted to be fair, to be very fair, and in the name of peace——

"We don't want any violence around here!" Tom put in.

—in the name of peace, Mr. Rusk was making a generous offer, a very generous offer.

Tom took it up. "I'm willing to buy back those houses at exactly what your husband paid for them."

Mr. DuPree said, "I couldn't let my client be penalized too much, but Mr. Rusk is a generous man and very likely he will make good the moving expenses if you submit a paid, receipted bill."

Honey shook her head. "Nobody ain't going to move, Mr. DuPree. Mr. Loom is getting some papers ready to take into court. CIO lawyer told me we got right on our side. Course I know you can put us out. You can do that one way or another. You can ruin Mr. Loom's pleasure in his home. You done that already. But we got a right to go to law to prove this is our country too. . . . That's what Mr. Loom is fixing to do."

Mr. DuPree drew a long paper from a leather folder on his desk. His finger tapped at Lester's signature and at Loraine's.

"He and his wife just left my office," Mr. DuPree drawled. "They've been very sensible. Sold us their home. Giving occupancy in ten days. . . . We'll offer you the same advance we gave them. It was a handsome, sizable sum."

Honey breathed rapidly. "Might be Mr. Loom would sell, but Lamb Hoop, he won't sell. Lamb don't even know we bought for him, but when he do find out, he ain't going to sell! He ain't that kind."

Mr. DuPree leaned forward, far forward. "Who is to occupy the other house? Who is——"

"Lamb Hoop."

After Honey left, the men sat in silence for a while.

Then Tom said, "Sterling, you have interests both ways——"

"That isn't it. It isn't only that CIO is a power right now and that Lamb Hoop has been a straightforward man to deal with. What worries me is where this thing is going. I mean the whole thing. My family were pioneers in this city. They and a few other families have been in large measure responsible for its growth and direction. . . . Go out to the Historical Society Museum and see for yourself. I've always taken pride in it. I've felt responsible for what happened here. There's never been a drive for funds or for any other detail of civic expansion in which I didn't take personal pride or for which I didn't feel personal shame. Now this thing's come along. . . . Tom, I have faith in the past and the ways of the past. As your attorney I can only advise my client to stick to the ways of the past. But as your friend, I can also see what you're worrying about. This is everybody's worry."

"It's one whale of a worry! I sometimes wish to hell I'd

never been in that God-damned war. Then I wouldn't know what disappointment would mean to these fellows. I've taken pride in being a veteran. I'm proud of Sergeant Rusk. Damned proud of him! The other night lying there awake for hours I tried to think of something else I was as proud of."

"You're a successful man, Tom. Lots of the rest of us see many things you can be proud of."

"Ye-ah-yeah. It's what I'm proud of that counts, I guess. . . . And all this other stuff you guys admire—Sterling, don't you see, this tangle I'm in could ruin all that—bust it higher than a——" He clapped his hands. "Like this!" He seemed about to cry.

"We haven't exhausted our resources." Sterling stared down at his knees. "We have other approaches to that girl. She's Mrs. Palmer's Honey, you know. Mrs. Palmer and Dorothy Jane are coming to our house for dinner tonight. It seems our daughter and the Palmer girl have been going around together a bit. Both lonely. No men around. Suppose you and your wife come in, say, at eight promptly. I'll try to arrange to have that girl come a little later, when we're all there. Very likely Mrs. Palmer can appeal to her. I hear Honey was very loyal to Mr. Palmer, and as Andrew's old friends we can put it up to her to settle this thing in a ladylike way. . . . Make her see she'd be repaying him for kindnesses. . . . We can bring pressure."

Tom's spirits revived, but before he left the room he turned and faced Sterling. "This whole interracial thing is one hell of a mess. In principle we got to agree the Negroes have the entire democratic philosophy squarely on their side, the brotherhood of man and all that stuff, but in practice—— My God!"

Sterling answered, "See you about eight."

When the Palmers arrived, Mrs. DuPree, very handsome in a gray wool dress with a salmon silky scarf around her shoulders, greeted them with a warning. "The house is an igloo.

Sterling lets us freeze rather than speak up to the ration board. Dotty darling, Maideth will give you a sweater. She's upstairs in her room, and she wants to show you some new pictures she brought home from the bookshop. Done by a genius, but look for all the world like the ones she used to do in kindergarten."

While the aged butler took the last of Mrs. Palmer's wrappings, Mrs. DuPree said, "We'll go in by the grate fire. I have a shawl for you."

Sterling rose as the ladies entered. He greeted Nancy with elegant cordiality. He pulled the petit-point chair closer to the hearth, placed its matching footstool at a convenient distance, and from his own nearby armchair explained his and Tom Rusk's dilemma. Tom was a fine man and, like the rest of the city's big men, carrying more than his share of the load. "What do you think about talking to Honey?"

Mrs. Palmer looked up from the fire. "Honey was never a girl to give trouble."

"I've plugged in the phone right there. It's next to your elbow."

He dialed the number and handed the instrument to Mrs. Palmer.

"Honey," Mrs. Palmer said, "I haven't heard nor seen anything of you for a long time now. . . . I'm out at Mr. and Mrs. DuPree's. . . . Yes, I heard from Mr. Bruce last week. He's in the Pacific. . . . Mr. DuPree would like to talk to you, Honey. . . . Yes, tonight. Mr. Rusk will be here too. After dinner. . . . What time?" she asked, looking up at Sterling.

He whispered, "About eight-thirty."

"Yes. Yes, she is. . . . It's very important, Honey."

When the phone was in its cradle again, she said, "Aren't they funny? She asked if Dotty Jane was here. Miss Dotty Jane, I think she said. . . . I think so. . . . She was always very devoted to my children."

273

During dinner Mrs. Palmer sank into silence. Mrs. DuPree joked about the wartime menu and their butler's eccentric inefficiency. She twitted the girls about the way they "let themselves go."

Drooping her lashes in mock sorrow, she said, "The shock those poor soldiers will get when they come home!"

Maideth winked at Dorothy Jane. "Mother thinks mascara is more important than the masses."

"But certainly! When I was a girl growing up, my mother used to say to me as a good-by phrase, 'Be charming!' She never said, 'Be good!', only 'Be charming!' I think it was very perceptive of her, really. *Ma mère* understood what the world wanted of a woman."

"Mother's major grudge against the war is that I'm working in a bookshop instead of making my debut."

Mrs. Palmer stirred. "At least you know what your daughter's doing. I can't even understand what that college and Dotty are up to. They're giving her credit for her visit at home."

Dotty laughed. "Not for visiting at home, darling. For the survey I'm making and for the term theme I'm going to write."

Then Mr. DuPree launched a long discussion of education and its obligation to abide by well-established traditions. The colleges should never have abandoned Greek and Latin.

That reminded Mrs. DuPree of an amusing story. This morning while at market flirting with the butcher in order to get a decent cut of meat for their dinner, she had overheard something funny, very funny. A woman standing at the counter too was talking to a friend about some school the Negroes were making a fuss about wanting. Well, the other woman told about Lily, a Negro girl who had been sent by her employers to high school. One day another colored girl from the same high school came to call for her. "She asked Lily, 'Is you did your Greek?' "

Before they had finished laughing, Sterling said, "That tells the whole story about the limitations of the Negro and the limitations which should rightfully be put upon his training!"

Mrs. DuPree lifted her eyebrows prettily and smiled at him. "How dull I am! I just thought it was an amusing story. The funniest sentence in the English language! I didn't see another thing in it, but then I was never an intellectual. Couldn't bear to look like one." She sank back against her chair and imbedded herself within the ritual of adjusting her cigarette into the long red holder and then her enjoyment of a languid smoke.

They were in the living room around the fire when the Rusks came. Mrs. DuPree had extra little gold-and-green cups on the coffee table ready for them. In the confusion of pouring and greetings and talk, Dorothy Jane heard Honey's name mentioned. Mr. DuPree and Mr. Rusk had called Nancy Palmer aside for a moment. When she returned to her chair, Dotty asked softly, "What is this, Mother?"

Maideth, who had heard nothing, suggested to Dotty, "Shall we go up?"

Dotty answered, "Not yet."

In the distance the doorbell sounded.

Mrs. DuPree, though unused to hurrying, rose quickly and said as she walked briskly toward the hall, "I'll go. After all, with a white butler——"

Mrs. Palmer said, "I don't believe Honey would come to the front door. Unless maybe in the dark, she couldn't find——"

Then Dotty asked very clearly what was going on.

Mr. DuPree answered, "Mr. Rusk and your mother and I wish to advise a little with Honey. . . . Very likely you girls will want to go upstairs."

Dotty stood up slowly. "I don't want to really, Mr. DuPree. This keys right in with what I'm doing, and besides—I'm fond of Honey."

Mrs. Palmer said, "You may stay to say hello to her." She raised her brows in rebuke. "You don't want to be rude, dear."

275

Mr. DuPree smiled wryly. "The girl was at my office today. I don't think she needs your help."

Sterling led Tom, Mrs. Palmer, and Honey to the far end of the room. The others remained by the fire. Dotty looked and listened.

In low tones Mr. DuPree said to Honey, "Since we met this afternoon, the entire situation has changed. Mr. Rusk has found a fine little cottage in the Ville. He is in a position to offer it at a special price. A very low price. It would cost you about half what you paid for the Mount Vernon Avenue house, and I'm sure a sensible person like you can see that the whole situation would be considerably pleasanter . . . more advisable."

Honey stirred. She fingered her gloves. "Lamb and Glory would have liked a smaller place at first, but then we had no choice. This is just a chance you made for them."

"Mr. Rusk is being admirably generous in this matter."

"My brother is one to think about how a thing like this is for other people. How it is for the people who get put out to let him in——"

"You needn't worry about that! It's all taken care of."

"How it is for the thousands and thousands of other people sardine-packed into the Ville."

"Your brother is doubtless a good man, but even your brother can't change the whole world overnight." Mr. Du-Pree's voice was stern.

"It's what he's trying to do," Honey answered calmly. "And I don't see I've got no right to interfere."

Mr. Rusk sat up straight and banged his fists against his knees. "Why isn't your brother in the Army?" he demanded.

"It's his lungs, Mr. Rusk. They got to be bad when he was a little boy from living too packed up, I reckon."

"He looks like a good strong healthy man to me," Tom muttered. "I'm a veteran of the last war and——"

Honey said, "Likely the draft board knows what it's doing,

but I don't want you to think Lamb is living easy. Lamb's been living a kind of foxhole life for a long time. He's right sorry not to be in the Army, because he believes the veterans this time is going to come back toting democracy along with them."

Tom wiped his moist brow.

"I figure Lamb, believing that, wouldn't want to choose no easy way out of this. Lamb, he's scarcely got time for at-home living, much less fussing around where-at he's going to live. He knows about neighbors throwing rocks through windows and all that. He'll likely think it's his duty not to be afraid of rocks."

Mr. DuPree leaned forward. "Do you realize this is a serious business——"

"Yes, sir, I do. It's more serious, I reckon, for Mr. Rusk than for Lamb, because no matter which way it comes out for Mr. Rusk I reckon he ain't going to feel right about it."

Under his breath, Tom said, "I'll be damned!"

Mrs. Palmer took that to mean that he was angry.

"Honey," she said firmly, "you know Mr. Palmer and I were very fond of you. Proud of you. I feel as if when you do wrong——"

"Mrs. Palmer, when I come in, Mrs. DuPree, she was right polite to me, but she said, 'You're Mrs. Palmer's Honey, aren't you?' I used to be Mrs. Palmer's Honey. I took a heap of pride in it, but now I'm CIO Honey. . . . That changes a whole lot!"

Mr. DuPree said, "We don't want to bring on any trouble in this splendid city. Detroit had riots. Thank goodness, we don't behave like Detroit."

Honey sat up straighter. She began to button her coat. "Mr. DuPree," she said, "you're a big lawyer. Mr. Palmer always used to say you was the best lawyer in the city. I reckon if the law ain't on Lamb's side in this, you'd go to the law and get your will that way. If the law is with us, then I don't think it's right to talk about using riots against us. I just been getting to know America this last year, and from what I learned, I'd say that ain't rightly American."

Mrs. Palmer shook her head. "Honey, you mustn't tell Mr. DuPree what is right and what is wrong. Mr. DuPree knows——"

"Yes, Mrs. Palmer, I reckon he does. I feel right sorry for Mr. DuPree and for Mr. Rusk too because they do know what is right—and they don't want to do it."

Mr. Rusk said to Mr. DuPree, "I got a pack of wolves at my heels! The association——"

Mr. DuPree said to Mrs. Palmer, "We have the good will of our fellow citizens to consider."

Honey looked from one to the other. "I feel sorry——" Sudden tears came to her eyes. "I feel right sorry for anybody who has to think, 'This is right, but I'm not going to do it.' Once I got to thinking, 'This is wrong, but I got to do it!' That kind of thinking ain't easy on a body. I'm sorry for you. I'm sorry for all white folks today. Come they got a conscience, it ain't letting them rest easy. I know that, and I'm sorry. When I was Mrs. Palmer's Honey, I never knew which side I wanted to stand by, the Palmers' or the Hoops'. Now I got so I know. I'm standing by Lamb because Lamb, he's standing by what's right for both sides. . . . I know this ain't going to be easy on Lamb, and for me it's going to be like watching Lamb leading one of them there invasions—an invasion out of the Ville. . . . Lamb, he's already thought his way past Ville walls. Now his body, it's got to go past too. This is the best chance Ville folks is likely to have, because Lamb, he knows how to get along with white workers. But if Mount Vernon Street do get to acting up, Lamb ain't going to like it. . . . And Glory, either way Glory's going to be right lonely, she being the onliest one, I reckon, on the whole street ever been to college. . . ."

"You mustn't feel hard toward Mrs. Palmer," Mr. DuPree said.

278

"I don't feel hard toward any Palmer. I feel right sorry for all the Palmers—except maybe Dotty Jane—and for all their friends, all the white folks who got to live with a bad conscience, knowing what's right and not knowing how to live by it."

"Honey, what ever has got into you!" Mrs. Palmer's voice squeaked. "Mr. Palmer would be very much surprised."

"I reckon Mr. Palmer, he would say I'm doing right."

"Indeed he wouldn't!" Tom muttered. Tom had tears in his eyes, and his hands shook. He made a last effort. "I got word today my nephew's been killed over there. In wartime there's got to be harmony on the home front."

"Yes, sir," Honey said. "I took a no-strike pledge for harmony. I know we got to stick together, but sticking can't be except from both sides. Come only one side sticks, there's hate growing, and with hate, there can't be no harmony at all."

"This is a difficult problem." Mr. DuPree rubbed his long chin.

"Yes, sir. Not knowing what is good to do and what ain't is something I've puzzled over a lot. I reckon it's the biggest puzzle there is. . . . You folks can't be sure which way is good, because no matter which house Lamb lives in you done already confessed to your sin, and now you ain't able to figure out no way of stopping. It ain't sinning what's so bad. It's not putting down your sin come you got the chance. I feel right sorry . . . I feel right sorry for what you must be feeling . . . but we can't go to giving in to your sin. That wouldn't help, only hinder."

She got up and turned to leave. No one moved except Dorothy Jane, who hastened after her into the hall. Neither Dotty nor Honey spoke. Looking into each other's eyes, they saw there was no need for speech.

Dorothy Jane stood in the open doorway looking down the long flight of terraced steps. She watched Honey walk briskly from darkness to lamplight to darkness to lamplight, her slacks flickering palely among the shadows of the sidewalk. When she was out of sight, Dotty lingered, loneliness and sorrow pounding in her throat. Her eyes blurred with tears as she stared at the tall, night-blackened trees whose bare branches frayed into the starlit, azure sky.

Maideth came into the hall. "Where is she?"

"Gone. Has to make the eleven-o'clock shift."

"Aircraft plant?"

"Yep. . . . Planes for our husbands to defend themselves with . . . at the front . . . against the fascists. . . ."

Maideth put her arm around Dotty's shoulder. Back of them excited voices in the living room rose and ricocheted wildly against the walls of the old house.